AN ASSISTED-SUICIDE FAMILY THRILLER

WHEN I KILLED MY FATHER

JOHN BYRNE BARRY

For my mom and my siblings—
Anne, Patrick, Brian, and Michael.

PART ONE

Cheeks as Smooth as Ice

1

Stop That Man. He Took My Teeth.

Edgewater Cares Retirement Community
Sixth Floor Memory Care Unit
Chicago, Illinois
January 7, 2016
11:05 pm

Lamar Rose slipped a folded postcard between the strike plate and latch bolt of the sixth-floor stairwell door. He descended seventeen steps and—with two large paper clips—picked the lock of the janitor's closet. Took him two minutes, way faster than on his dry run.

No one would suspect that was something he would do, but it was easy, even for an amateur like him. He hated feeling so hard and cold, but that was how he had to be.

In the corner of the closet, a rolling cart bulged with folding chairs. He unfolded one and sat. In the dark. In November, when he'd done his first reconnaissance, the closet had been crammed with Christmas decorations—stockings, wreaths, strings of lights. Now they were on display, at the nurses' stations, in the bingo room, by the elevators, even on the fifth and sixth floors, where the residents might never notice.

The small room had a pleasant lemon verbena smell, from a plastic tub of cleanser. Under that, the moldy odor of damp rug.

The wind growled outside, whipping across Lake Michigan, rattling the window. Lamar zipped his coat to his chin. Everyone was talking about the "polar vortex," this rush of Arctic air sweeping over the Great Lakes. On TV, he'd seen a clip of brave souls walking on the frozen Chicago River—brave not because they were in danger of falling through the ice, but because of the subzero temperatures.

Dread and duty duked it out in the pit of his stomach. He had never felt so alone in the world.

But he had promised.

After shivering in the closet for two hours, he walked up the seventeen steps, his legs creaky. He nudged the door open with his shoulder, slid the postcard into his pocket, peeked into the corridor.

It was so quiet in the middle of the night. No wailing or cackling or crazy ranting. So quiet he heard his father snoring, two doors down.

He had charted out half an hour to take care of business, but it was not going to take that long. Once inside the room, he tiptoed past Clay Trapp, his father's roommate, who was also snoring, and hid behind the gray plastic curtain between the beds, feeling the weight of the nitrogen tank in his shoulder bag.

Robert Rose lay on his back, his hands crossing his chest. Peaceful. Deep in sleep. Lamar used to be able to sleep like that—"You could probably nod off on a fire engine with sirens blaring," Janis once said, not hiding her resentment.

He couldn't sleep like that now.

Robert Rose would be eighty-four in two weeks. He wanted to be gone before his birthday.

And he expected his dutiful son Lamar to make it happen.

The talk was that people like Lamar's father, who were occasionally lucid, had it worse because they *understood* their condition. Some days were better than others, but there was no recovering from dementia. He had bile duct cancer too, but it was taking its sweet time killing him—he had recently been kicked out of hospice for living longer than six months. The cancer was painful even with strong meds, but he didn't complain about it. He had always been stoic in the face of physical pain.

Lamar stroked his father's freshly shaven face. His cheeks were as smooth as ice.

When he first moved into the memory care unit, his father had shaved himself, until he started forgetting what he was doing.

One humid night, the previous summer, Lamar flew in on the red-eye from Albuquerque to find his father in the bathroom, the faucet running, his face half-shaved, his eyes vacant. On one cheek was a dollop of shaving cream, the other a speck of blood.

When he saw Lamar in the mirror, approaching from behind, his eyes jumped to life, but they were filled with fear. He dropped the razor and it clattered on the floor. Then he cringed as if he were bracing for a beating.

Lamar turned away.

He couldn't bear it, so how could his father?

Still standing at the sink, his father unleashed a torrent of profanity the likes of which Lamar had never heard, certainly never from him. Fuck, shit, damn, and more—first in an anguished mumble and building to a furious rant.

"You fucking parasites. We paid our premiums, and now

you greedy bastards want to stick a fucking hose up my ass and suck out my insides. You're hiding Celeste from me."

"Dad, it's me. Lamar. Your son. I love you." His words sounded hollow.

"You're bleeding me dry," his father said, even louder, "Locking me up in this fucking shithole. Why can't I go home? Where's Celeste?"

Lamar came closer, but not too close. "Dad, it's going to be OK. Let's get you back to your bed. Mom died, Dad. Six years ago. Remember? She had leukemia."

His father blinked his eyes as if registering what Lamar said. Lamar felt a stab of sadness himself, for the loss of his mother.

"She died? Well, I wish someone would have told me."

Lamar waited until his father ran out of steam, and took another step toward him. Then, as gently as if he were holding a soap bubble, he caressed his father's arm with his fingertips. "I'd like to help you," he said.

He retrieved the razor, rinsed it, and turned the faucet off. From behind, he reached around and clutched his father's chest with his left forearm, his palm flat on his sternum. With his right hand, he shaved the cheek where the cream had dried. His father wrapped his fingers tight around the foam grips of his walker, locked his elbows, and held his head high.

When Lamar finished wiping his father's face with a warm washcloth, their eyes met again in the mirror, and then his father started crying. Lamar had never seen him shed a tear before.

Lamar needed a walker too—his legs were about to buckle under him. He grabbed the edge of the sink.

Then he guided his father back to his bed, and sat with him, holding his hand, long after he fell asleep.

That had been such a solemn and heartbreaking moment in front of the mirror, their bodies close, their eyes locked in a rare embrace. Lamar hadn't treasured it until later—he had been too distressed at the time. Looking back—it had been six months now—he realized it had been his most heartfelt connection *ever* with his father. *Ever.*

Was that sad or what? But it would have been far sadder if he had backed away. He ached from the memory, but it was the good kind of ache.

Now the Edgewater staff shaved his father twice a week, after his shower. That was why Lamar picked Thursday— so he would be clean and smooth. Also, the mask would seal better on a freshly shaved face.

Lamar could see in the dark now. Shapes but no colors. Light drifted in from the streetlights on Lakeshore Drive, far below. Lamar could see his faint shadow on the wall.

His father had always *managed* everything, whatever life threw at him, even his wife's death.

But the dementia broke him.

Now he *needed* Lamar. His father, who had never played favorites, *chose* Lamar, who shuddered at the responsibility and yet...and yet, here he was, with an opportunity to give his father what he wanted.

It wasn't that Lamar was uncomfortable with his father dying, or death in general. As a volunteer for the New Mexico Hospice Center, he had been present three times when someone died, and it had been more profound than tragic. But he had witnessed those deaths, not caused them. He wished his father would just die, and he wouldn't have to do anything except let it happen.

Drawing another deep breath, Lamar reached into his shoulder bag for the ten-pound tank of nitrogen, but it slipped out of his hands, and clanked on the floor.

He froze. Held his breath.

His father continued to snore, but Clay Trapp bolted up and yelled. "Stop that man. He stole my teeth. He broke my arm. He took my money."

His father's roommate had advanced Alzheimer's and Lamar had *never* heard him speak a complete sentence before.

Rocking in his bed, the springs squeaking, Clay whimpered again. "Why is this man taking my teeth?"

Lamar heard footsteps in the corridor. He dropped to the floor and slid under his father's bed, grabbing the nitrogen tank and nestling it to his side.

He recognized Pierre's languorous gait and the clack of his boots as he came down the corridor. A dreadlocked nurse from Haiti, Pierre was one of the most grounded men Lamar had ever met—he never let the urgency of others create urgency in him. He had always been kind to Lamar's father.

"Mr. Trapp, my man," he said as he entered the room. "Did you have a bad dream? You're going to wake Mr. Rose."

That was not likely. His father continued his raspy snoring.

"That man came back," said Clay. "He took my teeth."

"Hasn't been no one here but Robert's son, and he went home. No one is going to take your teeth, Mr. Trapp."

Pierre walked between the beds, the heels of his boots a foot from Lamar's face. He hadn't turned the light on when he came in, but even in the darkness, all he would have to do was look down to see Lamar sticking out from under the bed.

"Take my hand, Mr. Trapp. We're safe and warm inside. Put your finger here. See, your teeth are where they've always been. So damn cold only fools outside tonight."

"He came back," said Clay. "He left, but he came back for my teeth."

Pierre's boots were so close Lamar could pick out the smells—leather, foot odor, mildew, and—was that dog poop in the mix?

His elbow was jammed under his torso, his funny bone like a sharp stick between his ribs, but he held still, taking silent breaths through his mouth. What would he say if he were caught?

His practice run two weeks earlier had gone smoothly—Lamar had wrung himself dry, squeezed out his doubts and his fears, and he was as ready as he was ever going to be.

But how dare his father put him in this intolerable position? He should have said no. He still could say no.

Clay stopped rocking as Pierre soothed him.

"Time to sleep, Mr. Trapp." Pierre sang a lullaby in a soft falsetto, and then stopped at the end of a verse and slipped out with barely a sound.

2

Good Cop, Bad Cop, Savior

Edgewater Cares Retirement Community
Apartment 1603
Chicago, Illinois
October 6, 2012

Lamar knocked on the door of his father's apartment. Nothing. He knocked again.

Andrea groaned in her wheezy, overwrought manner, fished out her key, unlocked the door. They found their father standing in the kitchen in his boxer shorts and one black sock.

"What the hell are you doing here?" he barked.

Three times Lamar had told him they were coming, at noon. He remembered *at least* three.

He steered his father to his bedroom, helped him dress, led him back to the kitchen. By then Brigid had arrived, according to plan.

Andrea positioned herself in front of the sink, folding her arms across her chest. She looked less haggard than the last time Lamar had come to town, but it wouldn't have hurt if she smiled instead of scowled. He knew how conflicted she was—resolute that their father shouldn't drive anymore, but reluctant to confront him. He felt sorry for her. She didn't have it easy, and she always made everything harder than it had to be. She wasn't depressed the way Janis had been, but she had this free-floating anxiety that touched down on anything and everything.

"Dad, we have to talk," she said.

Their father retreated into the corner, raising his hands to ward off the attack.

I can take care of myself," he said. "You're ganging up on me."

The kitchen smelled of ammonia. Brigid treated this apartment as if it were her own—cleaning, decorating, hanging large oil paintings on the walls, even in the kitchen.

Andrea was always complaining about the undue burden of having power of attorney for their father's health. But when Lamar offered to take more responsibility, on his last visit, she bristled. "I live in town. You don't. I did it for Mom. I know what to do."

Lamar beckoned Brigid to sit next to him. Then he spoke in a whisper, in the hope that his father would come closer. "Dad, of course you can take care of yourself. Of course you value your independence. We do too."

Brigid slid into the chair, pushed aside cartons of prunes and oatmeal on the table.

She lived in the same wing of Edgewater, four stories below, and slept with Lamar and Andrea's father in his apartment several nights a week. He was adamant she keep her own place. Brigid had lived at Edgewater since before her husband died, and had encouraged Lamar's parents to buy this spacious apartment in 2006. His mother had been entranced by the glamorous Art Deco lobby and the spectacular views of downtown and the lakefront.

For a century, this sixteen-story orange-brick apartment building, with five elbow-shaped wings, had been called Edgewater Towers, then it was retrofitted into the Edgewater Cares Retirement Community. The apartments on the top eight floors—for people who lived independently—were spare but elegant. So much nicer than the lower floors, which were more like a nursing home.

"Look, Dad," Lamar said, "we're being selfish because we want you around. We want to keep you safe."

His father hissed. "You act as if I have a foot in the grave."

Brigid jumped up. "I'm going to make coffee. Any takers?"

Lamar raised his hand.

"Andrea?" asked Brigid.

She shook her head no. "Is it too early for a drink?"

"Your vodka's in the freezer," his father said. "I borrowed some last week when a friend came over."

"If you're trying to make me jealous," Brigid said, "you're going to have to work harder." Lamar knew more than he wanted to know about his father's wandering eye.

Andrea poured a healthy shot of vodka in a glass, then a splash of orange juice. "We only want to discuss options, Dad. You can't keep avoiding this conversation."

"Want to put money on that?" he said. "Fifty bucks you can't make me talk."

Andrea pounded the cutting board on the kitchen counter, rattling everyone. "*Dad,* tell them what happened with the car?"

"I forgot where I parked it." He stared them down. "Don't say this never happened to you. They towed it. Once. This is not a symptom of decline."

"No, it's *not* once." Andrea turned to Lamar and Brigid,

repeating what she had told them several times already. "He sideswiped a van in the parking lot. He left his front door wide open a week ago. He didn't pay his Edgewater dues. Until they called *me*. I have a truckload of my own problems, thank you very much. I can't always be around to catch him when he falls."

"Why not?" Robert said.

"Why not?" snapped Andrea. "Why—"

"I'm joking," said Robert. "Jeez, you're all so serious. The last thing I want to do is be a burden."

"You're not a burden," Brigid said, then more gently, "Tell you what, Robbie. Next time you need to go any-where—*anywhere*—let me know. I'll drive you."

Andrea drained her glass, then slammed it on the counter. She loved to make loud noises. "Brigid, you're not dealing with the situation. What if he wants to woo one of his lady friends? He's not going to call *you* to be his driver. You know that."

They had scripted their opening gambit in the lobby before getting in the elevator—Lamar was the good cop, Andrea the bad, and Brigid the savior who would sweep onto the scene, chase away the cops, and talk sense to Robert. But Andrea loved her drama. And Brigid had her own agenda.

"Let's stop pretending," Andrea said. "We have to take away his car or he's going to kill someone—"

Brigid stood again. "I said I'd drive him anytime, any-where, and I mean it."

Lamar jumped in before his sister went too far. "Andrea, imagine it was *you* backed into that corner."

"He can take a cab," she said, "and then there's no prob-lem with parking."

Robert cleared his throat. "You're talking about me as if

I'm not in the room."

"Not true, Dad," Andrea said. "We are addressing you. You don't want to listen."

"I'm hungry," said Brigid. "How about we head to Broadway and find some spot we haven't been to before? Take a chance. Leave this discussion for another time."

"I like that Vietnamese place on Argyle," Lamar said. "Oh, right, we're living dangerously. Trying somewhere new."

"I have my phone with me all the time," Robert said. "If by some—"

Andrea grumbled. "I'm not at your beck and call, Dad. I have a life, excuse me—"

"And *Brigid* is at the top of my favorites list," he said.

"You put her before me?" said Andrea. Lamar hoped she was joking.

Brigid approached Robert and placed her hand on his shoulder. "Maybe it's time for me to move in here," she said, "like we've talked about."

Robert backed himself into the corner again, his fingers twitching by his side, a blank look in his eyes.

No one said anything. Lamar caught Andrea's eyes, then Brigid's. Time stopped.

Then Robert snapped back into focus and strode toward the front door. Lamar followed behind and spoke quietly so Brigid and Andrea couldn't hear. "It means a lot to you to drive, I understand, so let's postpone this car question, but you know—"

"Are we going to eat or not?" Robert pulled open the front door and marched to the elevator.

3

Don't Have the Balls?

Edgewater Cares Retirement Community
Sixth Floor Memory Care Unit
Chicago, Illinois
January 8, 2016
1:20 am

Lamar relaxed a little, as much as was possible for some-one lying on a linoleum floor, next to the nitrogen tank he was going to use to kill his father. He moved his elbow, then raised his knees so he could press his back to the floor. What a luxury to flatten his back.

He meditated, knowing he had to wait until Clay was deep in sleep. What could be better practice than this? Whenever a thought settled in, he pushed it away, taking long inhalations and exhalations and counting to ten for each. He managed to clear his mind for at least two, three, maybe even four minutes. Not bad, all things considered.

After ten minutes or so, Clay was snoring. For a short stretch, his snores and Robert's were synced, and they were snoring in harmony. And then they weren't.

He waited another ten minutes, then stood, wiggled his fingers, and pulled on the thin latex gloves he had taken from the nurse's station on his dry run. He carefully lifted the nitrogen tank from the floor and wedged it in his shoulder bag so it wouldn't fall again. He waited until his heart was as still as the night.

Then he leaned in close to his father and whispered. "Hi Dad, this is it. The moment you've been waiting for and I've been dreading."

He paused to listen to Clay snoring. "I'm giving your roomie another minute to sink into a deeper slumber," he whispered, "then I'm going to turn on the nitrogen. Like we talked about. You're going to keep on sleeping, but you're not going to wake up. Then I fly home and well—I'll get a call from Edgewater or Andrea or Brigid, I don't know—and I'll repack my suitcase, with my black wool suit, and head back. Then we celebrate you, your life. That's our plan and I'm here to get it done."

Lamar sounded bolder than he felt. He wasn't sure if he was courageous because he was taking action or meek because he was obeying his father.

Even though his father was asleep, Lamar found it calming to tell him what he was going to do.

He had shared the plan several times with his father when he was awake and he had seemed comforted. Also acutely curious about the details, like how Lamar was going to slide the postcard between the strike plate and the bolt of the stairwell door. He wanted to know what the picture on the postcard was. So Lamar bought one he knew his father would like—a picture of the two snow-dusted bronze green lions standing guard in front of the Art Institute on Michigan Avenue, red holiday wreaths around their necks.

His father had also approved of the nitrogen, which

Lamar had learned about from the web page of a man known as the Australian Dr. Death. The nitrogen was allegedly painless. Allegedly. And left no trace.

He had purchased the nitrogen tank earlier in the day from a brewing supply store in Evanston. He had paid cash.

It seemed as if his father marshalled every functioning brain cell he had left to focus on this final project. He and his father were plotting a caper together, like a bank heist in the movies. With the gauzy camaraderie of thieves. Lamar felt so connected to his father in these clandestine moments. Maybe because there was not going to be another caper.

Lamar cringed from the sharp pang that ripped through him. For the brief conspiratorial connection with his father as much as for the loss of it.

"One more quick story, Dad," said Lamar. "You'll enjoy this. I heard this on a podcast, from Ram Dass. There was this old Chinese farmer who was too worn out to work in the fields, so he sits on the porch all day long while his children toil on the land.

"One day, his eldest son lugs a wooden box to the porch and tells his father to get in. Too many mouths to feed, the son says.

"The farmer gets in. The son puts a lid on the box and drags it toward the cliff at the edge of the farm.

"He hears a knocking from inside the box. Takes off the lid.

"His father sits up and says, 'Son, I understand what you're doing and why, but I have a suggestion. Why don't you lift me out of the box and throw me over the cliff? That way the box is there for your children when they need it.'"

His father continued to snore. It was time.

With sweat trickling down his back, Lamar placed the mask over his father's mouth and turned the nozzle on the tank. The rush of gas whooshed into the quiet night. Noisier than he expected, though it quickly became part of the night sounds. The heating vents, the fierce wind, the pulse of medical machinery.

Then, with no warning, his father jerked awake, his hands open like claws, yanking the mask from his face.

Lamar jumped back, dropped the mask, which bounced against his leg, dangling on rubber tubing from the valve of the tank.

Relief washed over Lamar, like a hot shower. He didn't have to go through with this. He turned off the valve. The sudden silence startled him.

His father opened his eyes, blinked them. He looked bewildered, tense. Then he relaxed. "Oh, *you're* here. Get on with it."

If his father was lucid, as he appeared to be, it would be no mystery what Lamar was doing there, with latex gloves on his hands and a nitrogen tank sticking out of his shoulder bag.

"No, Dad, you just pushed me away. When I put the mask on. You don't *want* to die."

"What, are you chickening out? I'm as ready as ever."

Lamar leaned in close to his father, whispered, "Dad, *quiet.* We already woke Clay up once, and he made a fuss. *You* slept through it. But you didn't sleep through me putting the mask on your face."

"Don't have the balls, is that it?"

"What the fuck, Dad, you could like...*not be an asshole?* Clearly there's *part* of you that does not want to die. Why wouldn't I listen to *that* part of you?"

Lamar bit his tongue. He was too loud. Too heated. But Clay continued his rhythmic snoring.

"You know, it wouldn't hurt if you were a *bit* more

solicitous. I don't think you grasp how *huge* this is. For me."

His father had always been a man of few words, but he had become more loquacious and blunt in his later years, like a leash had been cut.

Lamar suspected it was the dementia. But maybe his father knew exactly what he was saying.

"I was waking up," his father said, loudly. Not whispering. "You startled me. It took me a second to get my bearings."

Lamar wondered if this was a test—his father measuring how far he could push his son, how much filial duty he could wring from him. A test from hell.

He started again, in a soft, plaintive tone. "Dad, I haven't been able to talk to Andrea about this. I bring it up, what you want, and she puts her hands over her ears. She's going to be *so* distraught."

"She'll get over it," his father said.

Meaning, she *should* get over it.

Lamar was shocked by how lucid his father was. That was what made this whole experience so wrenching—his father, an engineer, a thinker, was losing his mind, but he was capable of sharp and focused thinking, and all he talked about, during those increasingly rare moments, was how much he wanted to die.

"It's natural to have second thoughts," Lamar said. "I mean, there's no do-over."

And then, his father changed his tone. Softer, calmer. "I don't have second thoughts. *None*."

His father did not sound like an angry man losing his mind.

"Yeah, well, I'm going to need a moment myself," Lamar said. "I'm certainly not going to do this while you're awake.

We talked about that, remember?"

"Remember? I don't even know who you are." Now he was practically smiling.

So inappropriate, his father. To joke at a time like this.

"I'm not going anywhere," his father said. "I'll be asleep in five minutes. This is your chance to be my knight in shining armor."

"You make it sound like you're doing me a favor," Lamar said.

His skin itched, as if ants were marching down his arms. He felt like he was going to cry, but he held back his tears. He would not let his father see him cry. His father would call him weak.

He was here to help, so why was his father making what was already excruciating even harder. Even a hint of gratefulness would make a huge difference.

But his father was harsh *because* he was in pain. How could he expect him to be generous on his deathbed? Lamar felt like a rabbit, caught unaware, the coyote a leap away.

But *he* was the coyote, and his father the rabbit. How could *he* be the one to do the deed, and still feel like he was the victim?

"I'm closing my eyes," his father said. "It's your turn, son. Just do it."

4

Tales of Lubrication

Coal Avenue
Albuquerque, New Mexico
June 3, 2012

When his father called, on a hot summer morning, Lamar was sitting on the living room floor, his back against the sofa, listening to a Beethoven piano concerto, and reading, again, from his wife's journal.

Dust motes swam in a shaft of sunlight and tears streamed down his face, one dripping onto the page, smudging Janis' tight handwriting.

He did not want to talk with anyone, least of all his father.

It had been a year since Lamar's mother and his wife had died, within four months of each other, and he was stunned by how immobilized he continued to be—every day a climb through blackberry thickets with open sores.

He was grateful for his therapy practice and his uncanny ability to care about other people's problems when his own were so daunting. It was a blessing to be good at something.

He packed his schedule as tight as he could, and volunteered at the local mental health clinic. The nights and weekends challenged him the most.

But Lamar's demons were nowhere near as ferocious as Janis' had been. Her journal entries were repetitive, her writing overwrought, but the rawness of her emotions was powerful. He had read some passages five or six times. She had been in so much misery.

She used to say he didn't understand how deep and debilitating her depression was.

She was right. He didn't. Couldn't.

He would never forgive himself for what he did to Janis.

The phone would not stop ringing. He answered it by mistake. Not used to his new phone.

"It's your father."

"Hi Dad, let me turn down the music."

He and his father had been talking more since they both lost their wives.

"I called to see how you're doing," his father said.

"One foot in front of the other," said Lamar.

"It's going to take time to get over this."

"Yeah," he said, under his breath.

"You don't feel like talking."

"Not so much."

"Look, we're widowers together," he said. "We're both alone, and I'd like it if we kept in touch more."

"Andrea says you're not so alone," Lamar said.

"Yes, I do have the good fortune of being surrounded, and I'm only exaggerating a bit, by women interested in me. I'm in a pickle actually."

"What do you mean?"

That was all the encouragement he needed to regale Lamar with the tale of how Celeste's best friend Brigid had moved quickly to "claim" him, but he had taken up with Fae, a younger African American nurse he had met when Celeste was undergoing treatment.

"Your mother's friends are outraged. Not because Fae is black, they are quick to assert, not even because she's younger, though I'm certain that has a lot to do with it. But apparently, there was this *expectation* that someone in your mother's circle would get first dibs on me. Who knew?

"It's not that I'm such a hot ticket," he added. "There just aren't a lot of tickets to be had."

His father's modesty came from his breeding, his DNA. But he was more than a bit disingenuous. He was only seventy-eight. There were plenty of men his age still kicking.

He was a thoughtful man, active physically and socially, and more gregarious than when he had been younger. He even had more hair than Lamar. It was no surprise Celeste and her friends were after him.

"So anyway," Robert continued, "I got greedy."

"What do you mean, greedy?" He knew his father wanted him to ask.

"I was a faithful husband to your mother for fifty-five years," Robert said, "despite some rough patches and temptations. I know how to keep promises. But I have not made any promises, to anyone. That hasn't stopped Fae, or Brigid, from expecting me to keep them."

Lamar didn't say anything, just hummed, "mm-hm." He was standing now, pacing across his living room. He had engaged in plenty of frank discussions about sex with his clients, and, as a client, with his own therapists. He'd talked sex with friends and lovers, sometimes explicitly. Never with his father.

"Brigid has been relentless," his father said, "and it's not like I don't care for her. It's just that I thought I might explore the world before settling down."

Lamar went back to packing Janis' clothes into boxes for the St. Vincent de Paul store on Menaul. He folded a sweater that smelled of mothballs and detergent.

"Andy says this is too soon," his father said. "That I haven't allowed myself to fully grieve. It's been over a year."

Lamar folded a fleece bathrobe with one hand and placed it in an empty box. Lamar had called his sister Andy when they were little, but now their father was the only one she allowed to call her that.

"I'll spare you the gory details," Robert said, "but let's just say I've become intimate with each of them, separately, of course, and I have been discreet, but *they* have not."

Lamar tried to *not* listen.

The problem, his father said, was that Brigid was too dry, even with lubricant. "We wanted to have sex, but it was painful for her, and I didn't want to hurt her, and then she started talking with her friends about the best lubrication."

"Dad!"

"Well, you asked."

"No. I didn't."

Lamar and his father could never have talked this way if they were in the same room. Waist deep in his own depression and self-loathing, and not having any sex or anticipating any, Lamar could barely stay on the line.

And yet, part of him cheered.

Underneath his pain, he was still capable of rational thought, and the conversation with his father reminded him of what he had lost sight of. That *his* life was far from over.

If his father, going on eighty, could get himself into trouble, so could he.

5

As Still as the Night

Edgewater Cares Retirement Community
Sixth Floor Memory Care Unit
Chicago, Illinois
January 8, 2016
2:05 am

Lamar stood by his father's bedside, leaning against the wall, waiting for him to fall asleep. Whether he kept his promise or he left, he wasn't going to do anything while his father was awake. Except breathe.

Breathe as if his life depended on it.

Breathe as deeply as was humanly possible and stop the tiniest suggestion of a thought from taking hold.

Every minute felt like an hour, and still his father wouldn't fall asleep. He kept rolling from his back to his side. His legs twitched. Was he doing this on purpose, to poke deeper into Lamar's doubt, to make it harder than it already was? Or was it the drugs they were giving him?

Lamar was determined not to let his emotions get the better of him. He'd evaluated all the pros and cons already, upside down and inside out. Now was not the time to revisit any of that. It was time to take care of business.

His father's breath smelled sour. Even from a few feet away. Lamar hated the smells on the sixth floor. Body odor, disinfectant, liniments. The smell of decay.

An unexpected thing had happened on Robert's descent into dementia. He had dropped his guard. He had become more vulnerable. That may have been what tortured him most—being so exposed.

Sure his father pushed away the mask, but it was like he said. He was startled.

Before Lamar agreed to help his father and before he decided on the nitrogen tank, he had asked around at Edgewater about other ways to accommodate his father's wishes.

He met with the social worker when Andrea was out of town, saying he wanted to better understand the protocol at Edgewater Cares. "You honor the DNR, but you ask questions first as a matter of course, do I have that right?"

"We always ask," she said.

"What if someone were to stop eating? I understand that's how some people die."

"We're going to make them eat, one way or another. Feed them IV if needed. And we would be talking to you, the adult children."

Lamar nodded. "My grandmother, Robert's mother, she died with family surrounding her and a morphine drip. I don't know if buttons for more morphine were pushed, but I understand those things happen."

"Not here they don't," she said, not angry, but with a chill. She drummed her fingers on the desk. "That was most certainly in a hospital, not a place like Edgewater Cares, and just so you know, those morphine IVs where the patient pushes a button, they have set limits. Those drugs are to make a patient's exit more peaceful, not to hasten it."

Lamar felt chastised, but in such a clean and cutting way, he hardly noticed it.

"I get what you're asking," she added, her voice no longer scolding. "We don't do that here."

He thought he had asked his question in an oblique way, but apparently not.

Finally, his father started snoring, with a regular rhythm, in opposition with Clay's choppy snorts. Lamar approached the bed and held the mask over his face, but not touching. Then he opened the nozzle. Once the nitrogen was flowing, and his father continued to breathe in an even, natural rhythm, he placed the mask as gently as possible over his father's mouth and nose.

Lamar breathed along with him, paying attention to his inhalation, then his exhalation.

Until his father stopped breathing.

Lamar held the mask in place for a few more minutes.

He had done what he came to do. He thought he would feel sad and relieved, but he didn't feel anything.

When he tucked the tank and mask back in his bag and touched his father's hand, it was cold. He kissed his father on his forehead. Which was still warm.

Then he left.

At the bottom of the stairwell, he bundled up for the cold. He had been wearing the same navy parka to Edgewater all winter, but he had bought a new green coat that was extra large and covered all his other layers. He zipped all his zippers, wrapped his face with two scarves, and pulled tight the strings on his hood.

He pushed the metal bar of the exit door, but it wouldn't budge. He leaned into it with his body. Still nothing. It must have frozen shut. He waited. Tried again. And again. Nothing.

He couldn't go back through the main corridor. There was a doorman, even at this time of the morning, and cameras were everywhere. Though not on this landing. He had checked meticulously.

The loading dock would be empty, but there was a camera there. He would huddle inside his hood. What else could he do?

The loading dock, down a leg in the corridor, was still and quiet, and as he pushed the door open with his hip, he pulled his head down into his body. Still, the wind off the lake whipped into his face. He gripped the railing as he stepped down the icy stairs.

He was determined not to let his emotions get the better of him. There was still business to take care of.

The next step was to discard the tank and mask in the dumpster behind Mariano's. Two blocks away. The plan was to wrap the tank in a heavy black contractor bag—it would go from dumpster to garbage truck to landfill, and *no one* would ever see it.

But Lamar walked past it. Kept walking. In a daze.

He was walking down Winthrop when a car honked from behind. He was in the middle of the street. A police car. He stepped aside. The car pulled up next to him, and the window rolled down.

"You alright? You have a place to go?"

He blinked. Felt the cold. Saw the badge on the officer's jacket. The man's face was pale and fleshy. Now he was awake. Now he was alert. Now he felt his shoulder bag heavy with the weight of the nitrogen tank. Were they after him? Had he set off an alarm? Could the officer see enough of Lamar's face to identify him?

"I do have a place to go. One block ahead. I'm so bundled up I feel like I would bounce on the street if I fell."

"You want to walk on the sidewalk," the officer said. "Morning's coming and there's going to be more cars."

He made his way to the sidewalk, then continued in the same direction he had been walking until the police car was no longer visible. Then he turned around. He was at least six blocks from his rental apartment. He found a garbage can in the alley to dump the nitrogen tank.

He had to hustle to make his flight.

6

Orphan Andy

Schaumburg, Illinois
January 8, 2016
7:15 am

"No, I do *not* know when I will be home for dinner," Andrea said. "Excuse me if my father's illness is interfering with your rigid schedule."

Andrea had a splitting headache, so what else was new? Her back was stiff and sore, the story of her life.

She had bolted awake in the middle of the night, her heart pounding wildly. *That was new.* She hadn't been able to fall back asleep.

Now her worthless husband Drew was interrogating her before she poured her coffee. He was usually sleeping at this hour, but he had a blood test and he wasn't supposed to eat anything, so he was up early. He had to have everything mapped out. So anal. Wore a watch on both wrists. Well, one was some sort of smartwatch prototype he was testing.

"I will be home by six," he said. "I'll make chicken pesto for dinner, and if you're here, we can eat together."

"I'm tired of pesto."

"Then we won't eat together. You win."

Not only was Andrea sleep-deprived, anxious as all get out, and under incredible pressure at work, but now her self-centered brother had gone back to New Mexico, leaving her to deal with her father, who was so agitated these days.

Lamar seemed to think he deserved a medal for waltzing in once a month to take their father out to dinner. As if that balanced out all her visits and insurance forms and staying on top of the staff at Edgewater, who were well-meaning, but if you turned your back, they dropped the ball.

And when they took away their father's driver's license, Lamar was so invested in being *compassionate* and *validating his feelings* she had to play the heavy. Her father held that against her even though she did it for his own good.

Drew offered to accompany her on her visits, but he only made things worse. If her father said anything at all, it was about how he wanted to end his life, and Drew refused to dissuade him. Her brother and her husband seemed to be fine with whatever her father wanted—if he asked to be thrown out of his sixth-floor window, they would ask if now was a good time. Fortunately, the windows only opened six inches.

Her phone rang. Edgewater.

"Andrea. This is Pierre." He hesitated too long. Something was wrong. "I'm sorry to have to call you so early, but your father passed. The shift nurse found him this morning."

Andrea slumped, but didn't say anything. She motioned to Drew to wait.

"The doctor was here a few minutes ago," said Pierre. "Pronounced him. I'm so sorry. I know how close you were."

She bit her lip, placed the phone on the kitchen table, face down, as if to shield it. "Dad died," she said to Drew. "I hope that won't inconvenience your plans."

"Oh, honey. Come here."

First she resisted, but then she went to Drew, who wrapped her with his big bear arms and spongy torso.

She wasn't ready for her dad to be gone.

She had been missing him for a long time, her whole life really, and she was *just starting* to break through. He had shut her out for so many years, and, sad as it was to see him losing his mind, one side effect was that he didn't pull away like he used to.

She talked to him about everything, not like with her mom, but the crap at work, how Sully was turning from a goofball into a scholar, how her vegetables were doing. Getting *him* to talk was the hard part. She would ask him about Mom, ask him to tell the story of how they met in the lunchroom at the Argonne Lab, or how they found the house in Los Alamos where she had grown up.

She knew her mother's version of these stories. Her father's version changed from day to day. She asked the same questions, and sometimes he gave the same answers, verbatim, as if he had memorized a script. Other times, he was off in some dream world. He talked more than he ever used to, but he didn't make sense half the time. More than half the time.

She pulled away from Drew. "Lamar just flew home this morning. He's going to have to turn himself around and fly right back. Oh God, I'm going to have to call in sick at work and I'm so far behind and they are going to totally crucify me."

"I don't think so," Drew said.

"You don't know anything." She walked to the

coffeemaker to fill her cup.

She knew this day would come, so why did she feel so crushed? Why did she feel such a gaping hole? Death was part of life. Everyone had to deal with death sooner or later.

"Lamar did it," she said.

"What are you talking about?" said Drew.

"My brother. He killed my father."

"Really? You really think that?" Drew had taken off his jacket and put down his briefcase.

"Think it? I know it. Like Tuesday follows Monday. You heard Dad talking about wanting to die. So has everyone at Edgewater. And Lamar had that conversation with the social worker, remember? We were getting closer, Dad and me. He was opening up. There must be some mistake. This can't be happening. We need more time."

She had tried to tell her father how happy she was they were getting to know each other better, but he wouldn't listen. He would sit there stony-faced and blink his eyes.

She felt light in the head. She had to grab the counter. It was alright to cry. Why couldn't she? She'd been inconsolable when her mother died. Soaking one handkerchief after another with her tears. Dad had checked out, walked away, and Lamar had already flown home. She had been alone with her tears.

"Dad never wanted a daughter," she said. "He disapproved of how emotional I was. Like it was a sign of weakness. What did he know about feelings, anyway? He never understood women. He didn't even try. Mom said that too."

"Look, you're upset," Drew said. "Let's go to Edgewater and figure out what we need to do next. I'll cancel my appointment. We'll go together."

"You really know how to melt a girl's heart." She took a

big gulp of coffee. Scalded her tongue.

"Just yesterday, or maybe Tuesday, when I showed up at Edgewater, I found Lamar and Dad in the chapel. They were whispering to each other. They stopped the moment they saw me."

She knew. She just did.

"Lamar listens to your dad," said Drew. "You won't let him talk when he starts—"

"Now is not the time to remind me of my flaws," she said. "You're always so quick to judge."

She was so not ready to face what she had to face.

"Goddammit, Drew, who does Lamar think he is, playing God?"

"No one is playing God," Drew said.

7

The End of Honesty

Flying Star Cafe
Albuquerque, New Mexico
January 8, 2016
9:15 am

When Lamar arrived, Sierra was sitting, in their usual booth, steam rising from two tall glasses on the table.

Sierra. His amazing, wonderful daughter. God, was he glad to see her.

He had called her from the airport to tell her about her grandfather, and to see if she was free for coffee.

The Flying Star Cafe was bustling on a Friday morning. Years earlier, this had been a haunt of sorts, where he met his internet dates, back when he first left Janis, back when he treated it like a sprint, not a marathon.

The high cantilevered ceiling was the same bright yellow-green, like cyclists wore, and long legged pendants, red, gold, and blue swooped down low.

"Got you a latte." Sierra stood. "Still hot. How are you?"

She gave him a hug, and he wrapped his arms around

her tightly and leaned his forehead on her shoulder. It felt so comforting to be holding her, the pride of his life. He didn't want to cry in public, even though he had ample reason to.

She pulled away. Lamar wanted to hold on to her forever, but she had always been like this, squirming away from her parents' embrace.

It was natural to feel emotional. He had lost his father and that was primal enough. But the finality of it, the hubris of it, even the Greek tragedy banality of it—he was still wrapping his head, and his heart, around that.

Sierra was his only child, low maintenance and high achieving, and she had an easy relationship with her grandfather, but he had not been a big part of her life.

Lamar remembered once when his father had asked a young Sierra what was her favorite color—she was four or five—and she gave him this long to-do about why did she have to like just one color, and how some colors were good for shirts but not for drawing. Later, his father told Lamar he felt like she had been chastising him for asking the wrong question.

He also remembered the night after his mother's memorial, when he hadn't been able to sleep and he had padded into the kitchen with his slippers on and found his father standing at the sink staring out the window. He wasn't crying—he didn't do that—but there was a weariness to his posture that made Lamar ache for him. Lamar had lost his mother, but his father had lost his wife, his soulmate. Lamar stood by his side, looking out into the night, and his father turned and opened his arms, and instead of Lamar comforting him, which was what he had been about to do, it was his father comforting Lamar.

Lamar leaned his forehead on his father's shoulder and

wrapped his arms around his back and the tears that had merely drizzled down his face during the memorial gushed from his eyes. His father didn't comment on the tears.

Then his father pushed him away—Lamar must have squeezed him too tightly. He stepped back and looked into his father's eyes. His cheeks were wet. As if he were tearing up for Lamar's loss more than his own.

That was why he hadn't been able to say no when his father asked for help. Though he had said no many times.

Lamar was determined not to have a meltdown in front of his daughter. He blinked back his tears.

He cupped the warm glass in his hands and looked Sierra in the eyes. "You know I believe in that Buddhist thing about pain being inevitable, and suffering optional. But that's aspirational, not the way it happens. Your grandfather was in pain, *and* he was suffering."

"Andrea said he asked you to help him die."

"Did she?" he said. "Why does that not surprise me?"

"When I was there at Christmas. I wish I would have seen him more often. I—"

"I told him no."

Sierra had to answer a text, and Lamar watched her, as she fidgeted with her phone, for any sign that she doubted his denial. He didn't see one.

He recalled Sierra's transparent attempts at lying when she was young, how frustrated she was that he could see through her. Until he no longer could. He had been reading the Scottish psychiatrist R.D. Laing back then and had been struck by his observation that when children successfully tell their first lie, they learn how alone they are in the universe. Sierra seemed to relish it. Not that she lied with any regularity, but she seemed more comfortable in her existential aloneness than he did.

If it were Lamar lying in bed on the sixth floor of Edgewater, asking for his daughter's help, he knew how she would respond. "Not a problem, Dad. We should put this in writing. I've got to run."

He wasn't sure what future frightened him more, losing his mind or knowing that his daughter would take care of things, wouldn't even push back.

No matter. He was never going to ask.

She put her phone away. "How about you? How are you holding up? You don't look like you've been up all night."

"I slept on the plane, believe it or not. Amazing how the body works."

"We've had a lot of deaths," said Sierra, "haven't we?"

"We have," he said. "Doesn't make it easier, does it?"

Sierra looked weary. Her long, thick black hair, the envy of her friends, was dirty and disheveled. She had barely started her campaign for city council and already she was skimping on sleep. He knew better than to say anything. She made her own decisions.

But even tired, she was a beautiful and inspiring young woman, and sitting across from her made him happy. He had done at least one thing right, though he was the first to say that she raised herself.

"So is there a memorial soon?" she asked. "I'm pretty booked, but of course, I'll be there. Will be great to see Sully."

Her cousin Sully, a.k.a. Sullivan, was Andrea's son, six years younger than Sierra, and brash as a turkey. He had always looked up to Sierra, even though he was taller than her by the time he was thirteen.

Like Sierra, Sully was an activist-intellectual, who could match her quickness, and he had that arrogant edge she seemed to like. He was also more handsome than one might expect from parents like Andrea and Drew.

Lamar asked Sierra about her campaign, and she talked for fifteen minutes before he had to leave.

■ ■ ■

He called Julia from the airport. He still wasn't sure about calling her his "girlfriend," though they had been seeing each other for five months. When she invited him to Christmas Eve with her family, she said, "Tonight I'm going to call you my boyfriend, and you can call me your girlfriend." She was more cautious than he was.

It was an easy and friendly relationship, and sometimes Lamar worried there wasn't enough intensity. Lately, he'd decided things were just fine.

He was nervous calling her. He hoped she wouldn't ask him any questions.

She picked up on the first ring. "Oh my God," she said. "I'm so glad you called. I've been biting my tongue so hard it's bleeding. Jesse brought home a new girl. I mean, I'm glad he's not hiding her, and I've been working so hard at being welcoming and not making judgments, but this girl shows up in this teeny t-shirt, bra straps showing, belly button showing, a ratty leather jacket around her shoulders. Jesse's a good kid and he says he uses condoms—that one time we had 'the conversation,' he claimed he did. Why can't he find a girl who doesn't look like a hooker? You saw him—"

"Maybe another time we can talk about that," said Lamar. "I wanted to let you know my father died."

"Oh, I'm *so* sorry. So sorry about your father, I mean, and of course about my oblivious blathering on. *What a horrible person I am.* Oh, do we need to reschedule our dinner?"

Julia owned her stuff—he liked that about her. A few

days earlier, she had invited him to dinner and he had said yes, though he knew he wouldn't be available. But what could he have said, *Sorry, I won't be able to make it because I'll be smothering my father to death?*

"You're not a horrible person," he said. "I'd like you to come to the memorial with me."

"I'd be honored," she said.

Later, on the flight back to Chicago, Lamar replayed his conversation with his daughter. His first big lie. The first, he feared, of many.

He had held it together, no histrionics, no waterworks, but squelching all that grief inside, not to mention the anxiety and ambivalence about what he had done *to* his father, *for* his father, that was not a healthy strategy. He knew that.

At least he had been honest with his father. And did what he promised.

But now his father was gone, *and* his mother, *and* his estranged wife, and he was lying to his daughter. Soon enough he would be lying to his sister and everyone else, and this was not the life he wanted for himself. His father's suffering was over, but Lamar's was only beginning.

He never believed that suffering-is-optional bullshit anyway.

8

To Determine the Cause of Death

Edgewater Cares Retirement Community
Chicago, Illinois
January 8, 2016
9:20 am

Andrea met Brigid in the Edgewater lobby after Drew dropped her off. They rode up the elevator together, had the car to themselves. Brigid was so comforting, but she kept saying it was a blessing Robert died in his sleep, that his suffering was over.

Andrea blurted out, "He didn't die in his sleep. Lamar killed him."

"You know what I'd like to do," Brigid said, as if Andrea had been talking about the frigid weather. "Skip this whole funeral home thing and take care of his body ourselves. We could do it together. Wash him, wrap him in a shroud, keep him in my apartment for a few days. The way people used to."

Brigid could not be serious. She was just avoiding the question.

"Did you hear what I said? Lamar killed Dad." The

elevator door opened. "And it's not your apartment, it's Dad's. I mean, it *will* be yours, but not yet."

Brigid tilted her head and waved her hand at Andrea. Was she dismissing her accusation of Lamar or her reminder that she didn't own the apartment? "Robert said he was fine with leaving out the funeral home. Whatever you and the kids want, he said."

"Won't the body start, you know, decomposing? Get stinky?"

Brigid walked into the sixth-floor lobby, but Andrea stayed in the elevator. She had pushed Drew to drive as fast as possible to get to Edgewater—she *had* to see her father—but now that she was here, she hesitated. The staff had moved her father's body to an empty room.

The elevator door started closing. She had to push the button to open it again.

She got off, but stopped at the nurse's station. On the wall where the activities and menus were posted was a dark rectangle she'd seen hundreds of times. The story was that some bright soul had put up a plaque commemorating the residents who had died, and it fell off one day and they never put it back, leaving a shadow that was not as faded as the rest of the wall.

Brigid waited until Andrea caught up with her. "I saw this video," she said. "You use dry ice to keep the body cool. Hell, we could leave him out on the fire escape, it's so damn cold out there."

"But where? What, you're going to lay him on the couch?"

"I'll put him on my bed," said Brigid. "I'll sleep somewhere else for a few days."

"That's too creepy. No way. You don't think Lamar did it?"

"I don't see how he could have," Brigid said. "Pierre said Robert was alive at two in the morning."

"Really?"

"Apparently, Clay had some outburst and Pierre sang lullabies to calm him down while Robert sawed away."

Andrea knew in her gut it had been Lamar, but it was *possible* she was wrong.

She stopped again. Brigid was waiting in the doorway of the room at the end of the hall. "Are you coming? He looks like he's sleeping."

Andrea lifted her shoulders, swallowed, and strode down the hallway and into the room.

He did look like he was sleeping. A white sheet came up to his chin, but there was no up and down of his breathing.

She leaned over her father and kissed his forehead. When she stood back up, she wobbled. Brigid hugged her, then sat her down in the chair by the bed. By then, Drew had arrived. He said he couldn't find a parking space and then he had to eat something because his blood sugar was low.

The room faced the lake. There were icicles melting just outside the window. The sun was shining. She thought she was going to cry, but she didn't.

She asked Brigid and Drew to give her some time alone with her father. For one more goodbye.

She had spent countless hours sitting with her father the past several years. He had never been much of a gabber, not like her mother, so she often brought videos or audio books with her from the library. That had been Lamar's idea, though she had chided him at first, said they should be talking with their father, not watching videos.

Andrea brought popcorn and those chocolate mints she used to buy at the movies. Her father didn't always follow the story, but when they watched *Terms of Endearment,* they were both tearing up toward the end. If he didn't understand it, he felt it.

She kept waiting for her father to take a breath and sputter back to life. She couldn't do this. She couldn't.

But.

She *had* wished, more than once, that he would die. When he went off about how he couldn't stand it. She hadn't meant it. It had only been a couple times. It hadn't been a wish, more of a what if.

Now he was gone. Now the tears flowed. She didn't sob, though she wanted to. The door was closed, but who knew if Brigid or Drew were listening in the hallway.

Why would it matter if they heard? Wasn't a girl allowed to cry for her father? And why was Brigid so calm? Maybe she didn't love him as much as she said.

Oh God, her heart felt like it was going to explode.

"Dad, thank you for everything." She touched his cold cheek. "I wish we had more time."

After lunch with Drew, she sat in the first floor lobby of Edgewater, making a list of what else she had to do. She was a project manager. She made lists. Who knew there were so many bureaucratic and logistical details that came with death?

Drew kept following her everywhere she went, which was sweet, but she told him he should go to work, that she'd let him know when she needed him.

She was on the second page of her list when Alicia, one of the food service workers, approached and asked if she had a minute. No, she didn't, but she nodded yes.

"I heard you say your brother killed Robert," she said. At least she dispensed with small talk. "I know someone who can help you. From my church."

Her church. Of course. Alicia, never without the black

cross around her neck. Alicia, whose English was excellent, but somehow Andrea had never talked to her before. Barely noticed her.

"Her name is Paula and she's fighting to stop euthanasia, like what happened to your father. I can ask her to call you. You know you have to demand an autopsy. To determine the cause of death."

"I've been going through the day in a daze," Andrea said, "signing papers, doing what people tell me. You mean they won't do an autopsy if I don't say anything?"

"People die here all the time. They stop breathing. Their heart stops. They're sick. They're old."

Paula called two hours later while Andrea was at the Mariano's on Golf Road. She was in the produce section, sorting through potatoes and onions. All the potatoes had bruises or blemishes. The garlic bulbs were huge and pungent. Drew was driving to O'Hare to pick up Lamar, and he had just texted her that the flight was delayed.

Once Lamar arrived, they would all head to Edgewater for a gathering at Brigid's, and then tomorrow would be another full day. She asked Paula if they could meet right away, at Starbucks by the Woodfield Mall.

When Andrea arrived, Paula was sitting up straight sipping black coffee, her heavy coat on the back of the chair. Young and fit, with short black hair and glasses. Her face, though, not exactly pretty. Thin lips. Pockmarked cheeks. Not that Andrea was some beauty, but she had decent skin. When they shook hands, Paula flashed a tight smile.

Straight to business. "You said on the phone you wanted to meet now because your brother is arriving this evening, and there won't be a good time tomorrow. You said you don't want him to know. But if you're convinced your brother killed your father, you have to be comfortable saying so out loud."

"But what about Lamar? Won't he cover his tracks?"

Paula pulled a stack of colored index cards from her purse, bound by a thick blue rubber band, like the ones that came with broccoli.

"Either your brother killed your father deliberately, trying to make it look like natural causes, in which case, we have to do some digging, or he was careless, in which case, it might be open and shut. Of course, this is about evidence and the law, but it's much more about appearance and narrative. I have to warn you, however, that you cannot make accusations like this, no matter how well founded, without backlash. If you're not comfortable with unwanted attention, you're best off letting this go."

"I'm convinced. I'm committed," Andrea said, with more confidence than she felt.

Paula followed with a barrage of questions, taking notes in tiny block letters on her color-coded cards. How do you know your brother committed this crime? Where did he stay when he visited Chicago? Did he rent a car? Did he bring a computer with him? What browser did he use?

Andrea was tempted to defend Lamar at one point, and say she suspected him, but wasn't positive. But she was positive. There was no doubt in her mind. If she had any doubt, it was about herself. Was she up for a public fight? Yes, she decided. She could feel herself getting incensed, and it felt right. Her father still had life in him until Lamar took it away. Took *him* away. From her.

Now she was an orphan.

But she was doing this for her father, not for herself.

When she said Lamar would be staying with her in Schaumburg, Paula pulled a thumb drive from her pocket and handed it to her.

"You say he has a Mac laptop. I want you to stick this into the USB port and copy everything you can onto this drive. You said you're an IT manager, so I assume you know how to do that."

"Yes, but what if he has a password? What if he sees what I'm doing?"

"Do you want to do this or not? Accusing your brother is not for the faint-hearted."

Andrea bit her upper lip, the thumb drive still in the palm of her open hand. What was Paula's story? What was *her* agenda? Was this really for her church? What was in this for her?

"I do." She closed her fingers over the thumb drive. Lamar probably didn't even have a password. If he did, it would be easy to guess.

"The first thing you're going to do now is call the police." Paula handed her two index cards, one green, one blue. "Here's what you say."

"Now?"

"Now."

9

The Power of Curiosity

Saint Sebastian Church
Chicago, Illinois
January 13, 2016
11:20 am

Lamar climbed the circular staircase to the pulpit, grabbing the polished wood railing with his right hand, and counting the stairs. His dress shoes echoed off the worn white marble steps. He hadn't been able to pay attention to Father Slater's sermon. Too many emotions and worries swirling around in his head. In his stomach even more.

When he got to the lectern, on the fourteenth step, he took a deep breath and made the sign of the cross. Not something he had done since he was a child. He could smell the candles, the incense, the musty odor of winter coats.

Wow. His father had a sea of mourners. Seemed like half the residents of Edgewater had wound their way to the church. Was there going to be enough food? Brigid had organized the reception, so he had to trust that she knew what she was doing.

He saw Sierra make the sign of the cross, too. She hadn't learned that from him. Her boyfriend looked a lot more like a good catch in his sharp gray suit than when Lamar first met him, sweaty and manic after soccer.

Julia sat on the other side of Sierra. She had been late and he was worried about how she would handle his family, not knowing anyone. And being the new girlfriend more than anything. He had never seen her in a dress before, and she looked striking—in a modest understated, middle-aged kind of way. She didn't like to stand out, but even in a black dress, in a sea of black, she did.

As he took one last breath, Lamar thought about how much his father would enjoy hearing this eulogy. All about him. Of course, he would pretend he didn't like it. All that attention.

Lamar couldn't stop second-guessing what he had done. He had given his father what he wanted. That much was certain. For years, all he had done was take things from him—his car keys, his apartment, his independence, his dignity.

"Good morning. It's great to see you all here." His heart thumped in his temples and he felt dizzy. And not because of the steps he had just climbed. He took another slow, deep breath, studied his notes, adjusted the microphone.

"I'm heartened that so many of you care enough about Robert to be here. I hear we have a delicious spread waiting for us in the gymnasium, so perhaps a few of you are here for that as well. I welcome all of you to join us."

There were a few chuckles, but not from Andrea, in the first row, her bulky black camel hair coat still on, her hands clenched in her lap. Lamar paused, they locked eyes, then she looked down. Brigid sat on one side of her, Drew and Sully on the other.

"When I was growing up in Los Alamos, there were some big, tough kids who made my life hard. One lived on our block. I know I'm not the only person who was bullied as a kid, but at the time, I thought I was."

"My father was sympathetic, to a point, but he did not allow me to play the victim. He told me to ignore the bully's taunts, to ignore even physical torment. But I couldn't do it."

The truth was he told Lamar to toughen up, said he was too soft. Now was not the time to bring *that* up.

"He wasn't quick to dish out advice, but he shared one idea that I was open to, and, surprise, surprise, it worked.

"He suggested I engage the bully. Ask him about himself, where he lives, does he have siblings. To be curious instead of timid. I thought that was ridiculous, but one day I tried it, with a kid who I hadn't encountered before, and he instantly went from tough to friendly. He didn't know how to reach out except in that tough kid way of posturing. He became a friend of sorts, almost a protector, because being seen with him, sitting at a table next to him at lunch, gave me new stature.

"All this is to say that one of Robert Rose's great gifts to the world, to the rest of us, was his curiosity and his engagement. He was a tall and lanky man, and he leaned into the world, his eyes open, his ears open, his arms open. Interested in what was going to happen next and how he could be part of it. I learned the power of curiosity from him, as did my sister and my daughter. It's one way of many that Robert Rose lives on."

It was actually his mother who suggested being curious. She claimed it was his father's idea, and probably it was, but he had asked *her* to deliver *his* advice.

Lamar returned to his pew, and Brigid and three other

friends of the family spoke briefly. Then Andrea stood up, and walked to the pulpit with an exaggeratedly slow gait. As if she wanted everyone in the church to watch her climb the stairs.

Oh shit, Lamar thought, and then, wait, I'm in a church, I'm not supposed to swear.

Andrea had been adamant that she didn't want to say anything. She hated public speaking.

At their mother's memorial, she had been a sobbing mess. Lamar had been moved, had hurt for Andrea more than for himself.

She paused before the final step. The church was as quiet as if it were empty.

"I don't have anything prepared, like my brother," she said, "but I can't sit by—" She stopped, and then pointed her finger at Lamar. "He *killed* my father. That's the truth. My brother killed *my* father."

Oh shit! What was Andrea doing? Lamar held his breath, determined to treat this as a hysterical outburst by his drama-queen sister. Nothing to get defensive about.

But the crowd erupted in a sea of murmurs and whispers. Julia nudged him with her elbow and gave him a look.

"While we're on the subject of curiosity," Andrea continued. "I find it *curious* that my brother is not telling the *true* story of Robert's death, which is that Robert was indeed curious about what was going to come next, but the dementia made him crazy and in a weak moment, he asked Lamar to help him die."

Lamar couldn't sit anymore. He wiggled his way out of the pew. Sierra grabbed his sleeve as he passed, but he shook her off. The murmurs got louder. *Oh God, this was not part of the plan. He and his father had not anticipated anything like this.* But why should he have? Andrea was acting crazy.

"Lamar was the dutiful son and he killed his father. He didn't think about my father's children, his grandchildren, his friends. Robert Rose had a strong support system. Look at all of you. But Lamar poisoned him with this idea that he could check out early."

Lamar bounded up the steps and wrapped his sister in his arms. One part hug, one part wrestling hold.

"He killed my father," Andrea whimpered. "He told him he didn't have to suffer anymore, and then he killed him."

"Calm down, you're upset," he whispered. "We're all upset."

That was an understatement. This was his sister, his flesh and blood. What had come over her?

"Take your hands off me," she said, wiggling away from him.

Drew had climbed to the pulpit too, and Lamar stepped back and pressed himself against the marble wall to give him space. The murmurs had stopped, as if someone had pressed the mute button.

"We have evidence," Andrea said, reaching for the microphone as Drew led her by the arm down the steps.

Sierra and Sully were climbing the stairs, Sierra in the lead, and they backed down to make room for Drew and Andrea. Sully took his mother's other arm and he and Drew led Andrea to the back of the church. Sierra led Lamar back to his pew.

One part of Lamar's brain was shouting, "*What evidence could Andrea possibly have? My life is over. How could this be happening?*"

But another part was heartened by seeing Sierra and Sully together, knowing that Sierra, an only child, whose mother was gone, was so close to her cousin.

Father Slater took his place in the pulpit and, with his

hands, urged everyone to sit back down. "Our father, who art in heaven. Hallowed be thy name. Thy kingdom come, thy will be done. On earth, as it is in heaven. Rest in peace, Robert Rose. We will miss your generous spirit."

Lamar couldn't squeeze what Andrea had said back into the bottle, but her accusation would have no weight without evidence and he had been so careful to erase any trail. She had nothing. Lamar had successfully lied to his daughter, who had a strong bullshit detector. He would just have to keep on lying.

Somehow, the priest finished the service and Lamar sat through it, his stomach roiling, his head exploding. He held Julia's hand, until he squeezed too tightly, and she pulled away. Father Slater said the "Our Father" a second time and there was a moment of silence before the church erupted in murmurs again.

When he left through the side door to the gym for the reception, he saw a white TV van with an antenna on the roof parked at the curb.

He wrapped his scarf tighter around his neck. The wind bit through his coat. Only ten feet more to the gym. God, it was freezing.

He heard Andrea shouting behind him. "That's Lamar," she said. "My brother. In the blue coat. The one who killed my father."

55

PART TWO

You Must Be Present to Win

10

Leave Me Alone

Coal Avenue
Albuquerque, New Mexico
June 24, 2008

Today was the day. Lamar was going to tell Janis he was leaving.

He had taken Caro for a walk, done his yoga poses, eaten his breakfast, read the paper. It was after nine and Janis was still in her bedroom.

He knocked on her door. Pushed it open.

"You awake?"

Her curly gray hair, the back of her head, was buried in her pillow. She turned and pulled the sheet to her ear.

He would have liked to ease into the conversation, good morning, how are you and all that. But Janis could take a simple "how are you" as a reproach. As if he were saying, *hey I'm going out into the world today like a healthy, functioning person and why don't you?*

"We need to talk," he said, his toes on the threshold.

Shortly after the new year, he had begun sleeping in the

guest room. Janis had complained that his snoring kept her awake. He volunteered to sleep elsewhere, and was relieved when she agreed. He had stayed in the master bedroom out of duty for years.

"Who is this *'we'* you speak of?" She shifted again so now she was looking up at the ceiling. But not at him. "*I* don't need to talk. *I* need to sleep. *I* was awake all night."

She had *not* been awake all night. Lamar had heard her snoring when he went to the bathroom around dawn. But yes, of course, she struggled with sleep. If she could get a few nights—or days—of quality sleep, things *might* be better.

He had promised himself, before he fell asleep, before a fitful night of grinding teeth and twitching legs, that tomorrow he would tell Janis he was leaving. Tomorrow.

Which was now today.

"How about we talk at breakfast?" he said.

"I'm not hungry in the morning."

"OK, well, *you* may not need to talk, but *I* do. And you need to *listen*."

"You think talking fixes anything?" she said, covering her face with the sheet. He only saw her forehead.

That was a new one, talking never fixes anything. She didn't believe that. She was even more of a talk therapist than he was. Or had been. Before she lost all her clients.

He waited. Already, the morning was hot. Soon enough, it would be too stuffy for Janis to hide under her shroud.

Maybe later would be better for their talk. When he got home from work, Janis would be up and about. He could also make himself a stiff drink.

He had imagined the conversation in the kitchen or living room with them facing each other.

"Will we be eating dinner together tonight?" he asked.

What a tortured way to ask a question.

"I don't know," she said.

"You know what you have to promise me," he said, his fingers curled around the oak molding on the door jamb. He wasn't sure what he was going to say. "Not to turn on the TV. And do your stretches."

"At least TV gives me some company."

"Why don't you get dressed? Take a walk. Get out of the house."

He waited. Nothing.

"I know you have no energy, and you think I'm insensitive to your situation. But I've been depressed too, though never as bottomless as yours. It saps you, I get that." He wasn't sure why he was saying this. She had heard it all before. In fact, to his credit, he had stopped giving her advice—it was clearly counterproductive. But sometimes he couldn't help himself.

"It's a gorgeous day. Why not walk to campus? Watch the kids play soccer. Breathe in our wonderful mountain air. Get your heart pumping. Exercise is no panacea, but it can help. And this isn't me saying this. It's the surgeon general, the American Psychological Association and—"

She pulled the sheet off her face. "You take your walk with the surgeon general and leave me alone." Then she covered her face again.

How many times had she uttered those words? *Leave me alone. Leave me. Alone.* She couldn't get more direct than that. If she were to say to him, *you shithead, you haven't been there for me, you've cut me off, you've retreated into your yoga and books and cactus garden,* if she said anything like that, he would have cheered.

But a plaintive "leave me alone" was all. Her mantra, as it were.

He leaned his forehead against the door jamb. Outside

the open window, jasmine crawled up the trellis Janis had built from plumbing pipes years ago, and a thin branch with two delicate white flowers nestled on the windowsill. A bee hovered above the flowers.

Janis had taken a welding class, which she said she enjoyed, and she was proud of how the trellis turned out. But she never welded again.

Lamar had stayed up late the previous night, browsing dating sites in his basement office, and editing, *again*, the ten emails he had composed to women he was interested in. He didn't believe in cheating, so he wasn't going to *send* the emails until he talked to Janis, told her he was leaving. This evening. He would tell her this evening.

Once he left, he would have to tell his daughter, his sister, his parents. Not conversations he was looking forward to.

Sierra would handle it, like she handled everything. She would be angry at him, but surely not shocked.

Andrea would change the subject, complain about her sad-sack life. He would call her first. She wasn't going to challenge his decision, like Sierra might.

His mother would disapprove, but would be sympathetic. He hoped.

His father, well, he wasn't a talker.

Lamar spoke gently to Janis. "We'll talk tonight."

11

Lamar Lawyers Up

Chicago, Illinois
January 13, 2016
2:55 pm

The first thing Lamar did, after escaping the church and bulling his way through the excruciating reception in the stuffy gymnasium, was race to Andrea's house, grab his things, and vacate her guest room before she got home. He called Edgewater and rented one of their family apartments.

He could not believe Andrea had gone after him like this.

As he was hanging up his suit in the tiny closet, he got a call from Todd, a lawyer who also volunteered at Dying By Choice. He and Todd had worked together for years, but lived eight hundred miles apart and had met in person only four times. A lawyer, but also a friend.

"I was going to call you," said Lamar. It was getting dark in Chicago, but it was two hours earlier in L.A., where Todd lived.

"So sorry to hear about your dad," said Todd. "How are you?"

"I've been better."

"I assume you've seen the video," Todd said.

"Video? You mean Andrea?" Lamar had not seen any video, but had spotted the TV van on his way to the reception, heard Andrea shout his name.

"Three people sent it to me within the last hour," said Todd. "It's all over the DBC twitter feed."

Lamar dug his laptop out of his suitcase and flipped it open. "I suppose you're calling because I need a lawyer."

"Here's the deal," said Todd, "I can represent you in my capacity as legal counsel for DBC. I'd have to talk this through with our board, but it seems likely, and we would do it pro bono, again likely. I can't promise without checking. Two, I represent you as a lawyer with Ledger Knight Calabria. You'd pay through the nose, but there would be advantages. Three, we get you someone else. I propose option one, for now. You retain DBC to represent you for the next week. Legally binding. Temporary. Easily dissolved. Then you can talk to me and be protected."

"Won't being represented by a DBC lawyer make me look guilty?"

"Any time you get a lawyer, any lawyer, someone's going to say that means you're guilty. You can't worry about that."

"A week seems like a good idea."

"I'll be there in the morning. We'll talk. In the meantime, do not say a word to anyone. No one."

Before Lamar could protest, Todd said he had to run. "Who are you going to speak to?" he asked.

"No one."

"That's right. No one. No emails. No texts. Nothing."

Lamar found a clip of Andrea's impromptu press conference outside the church and watched it five times, as if it might disappear or mutate into something different upon repeated viewings. Andrea told the reporter she had Lamar's web browsing history, which showed visits to euthanasia websites, where he could buy nitrogen.

How did she get that? When he was taking a shower? No wonder Todd had called.

Obviously, Andrea was unhappy their father was gone. But she knew he was suffering. Surely he had asked *her* for help, too. But to accuse Lamar, to make a scene at the memorial, that was so over the top, even for Andrea. And then to go on TV and start trumpeting evidence. *Unbelievable.*

If she were so upset, why did she put her hands over her ears and babble whenever he tried to talk to her about what their father wanted? She refused to discuss it. He had tried to engage her, but clearly he hadn't tried hard enough.

He had no idea how many people had seen this video, but he was already getting calls and emails from reporters. He didn't answer the phone, but he listened to the voicemails.

He forced himself to stop watching the video and reading the internet. He closed his laptop and put his hands to his head and pressed hard, as if that would hold it all in. Somewhere in the crazy brew of feelings there was guilt too, not for what he did, but for not feeling more grief. Not missing his father more.

His father had been suffering. He had asked for help. *Begged* for help. *Demanded* help.

At least *he* was at peace.

Lamar had no idea what was going on inside Andrea anymore, only that she was not happy and it was *always* someone else's fault.

Over the past few years, starting around the time they took away their father's car keys, Andrea had been giving him grief for not taking enough responsibility. Maybe he hadn't.

But Andrea wanted it both ways. She was upset that she had to shoulder so much of the burden of taking care of their father, but when Lamar flew into town and took his father out to dinner, she criticized him for doing too much, for tiring him out. When Lamar offered to take on the power of attorney for health care or finances, so she wouldn't have to do both, she said no.

Once their father moved into the memory care unit, Lamar scaled down his practice to three days one week, four the next, so he could visit his father more often. Andrea said he should have done more—even suggested he move to Illinois. "Other adult children do that," she said. "You remember Greg Bird, who Dad knew from work. He moved to Florida to be closer to his parents. You could too."

He could have. But even if he had camped out in a sleeping bag on the floor of their father's room, she would have found something else to complain about. Maybe he could have taken more responsibility along the way, but he had certainly stepped up in the end.

One of the first times Robert asked Lamar to help him, Lamar answered with a firm "no" and reminded his father how hard Andrea would take it when he died.

"She takes *everything* hard and doesn't let *anything* go," his father said, surprising Lamar with how well he knew his daughter, the daughter who complained that he didn't understand her. The problem wasn't that he didn't understand her, but that he didn't *accommodate* her.

Lamar's relationship with Andrea had been deteriorating for years, but they were still talking, still acting like a family. They would never again share that wonderful and silly play world they had as children. That had been special.

They connected more in their college years and early twenties, but by then Lamar was in New Mexico with Janis and Andrea was in Illinois with Drew.

Their kids brought them closer. Sierra was born first, Sully six years later, and the cousins became tight even though they lived two thousand miles apart.

He and Andrea had argued about how to respond to their father's dementia. Officially, the staff at Edgewater Cares adhered to "reality orientation," because it was supposed to be beneficial for residents' cognitive development, keep them functioning at a higher level. *Today is Monday, January 11, and we're having split pea soup for lunch. It's snowing outside, Rahm Emanuel is the mayor, and the Bears are playing the Packers this Sunday.* Andrea had been adamant that they follow that approach, and she was quick to correct their father when he said something that was not true.

Unofficially, however, the Edgewater staff practiced what Lamar called "therapeutic fibbing"—they validated the residents' reality or diverted their attention. If his father asked where Celeste was, as he often did, they didn't say she was dead, they said, "She's not here now." It was an easier answer to deliver, and to receive. Correcting the residents could cause distress and agitation.

Lamar felt that was a more compassionate approach, and he tried to practice it. But when Andrea was around, she scolded him. "You're hurting him, not helping him," she would say.

Still, he couldn't believe *that* was a reason for her accusations at the memorial.

He still loved Andrea, even if much of that love was rooted in the past. Not *all* of it was.

Lamar desperately wanted to talk to Julia, but he was relieved Todd told him not to. What would he tell her anyway?

Julia had been with him all morning, in the church and overheated gym, and never pressed him about what Andrea said. The plan had been for her to stay with him that night in Andrea's guest room, but that wasn't happening. He liked Julia. He liked her being by his side. But they were new, still uncertain. It was too much pressure for such a young relationship.

Julia had a friend in Norridge, near the airport, and she suggested it might be better if she spent the night with her friend, then flew home in the morning. Maybe that was for the best, but he missed her.

Heavy times could make any relationship feel deeper, sometimes *be* deeper. It could be a cold, cruel world out there, and who wouldn't want to feel safe and warm in a loving embrace? He remembered one of his clients referring to her "9/11 romance," with a man she'd woken up with for the first time on the morning of the World Trade Center attack. They were sweet and solicitous with each other for many months, until they drifted apart.

Lamar also wished he could talk to his father, though he knew how crazy that was. His father had not been much of a talker, of course, and he had the right to be that way. But it was more than that. He thought talking was unnecessary, even indulgent. He didn't understand why anyone would go to therapy, let alone study and practice it.

As for death, he once said to Lamar, after learning about his hospice training, "Why study death? Yes, we're going to die. Doesn't mean we need to talk about it."

Lamar had eaten enough at the reception that he wasn't hungry, but he went out and bought a bottle of red wine at the corner store. It was bad even by his lax standards, but he drank the whole bottle, and watched old movies on TV until well past midnight.

■ ■ ■

In the morning, he met Todd in a luxuriously appointed conference room on the 26th floor of a glass and steel tower on Lake Street, in downtown Chicago. The sky was gray and the lights in the buildings across the river made it seem like it was still nighttime. Todd had flown the red-eye from Los Angeles, where his firm was headquartered. They also had offices in Chicago, New York, Houston, and Miami.

"Sign on the dotted line first. Then we talk." He slid a single page toward Lamar, who pulled himself up from the soft chair and leaned his elbows on the table. He had been meditating since he woke up and it was helping. He could still feel the anger and anxiety churning through his body. But there was also a thin layer of calm he could take refuge in, like standing under the heat lamp on the Argyle "L" platform, which he had done half an hour earlier.

"The line's not dotted," Lamar said. "Tell me what I'm signing."

Todd, buff and burly, rubbed his eyes. "You're hiring me for one week, for ten dollars. This does not preclude pursuing other options. It means when we talk, it's privileged conversation. I'll bill you later."

After Lamar signed, Todd slipped the paper into his briefcase, and sat. He folded his hands on the table, didn't say anything. It didn't look like he had slept much, but his pink shirt was crisp, his jacket like new, his purple and blue tie knotted tightly. He was a stocky man, a few extra pounds, but a formidable presence. Shorter than Lamar, but he took up a lot more space. The conference room smelled of furniture polish.

"Do you want me to tell you what happened?" asked Lamar.

"No. Better for me not to know. It's not for me to judge."

Lamar had been rehearsing all morning, but now it felt

like a jumble. Didn't Todd want to know if Lamar did it?

"This is quite complicated for me," said Lamar, "because, as you know, I support the idea that people should be able to end their life when the suffering becomes too much. But obviously assisted suicide is against the law and not something we advocate, or I support. So being accused of that is not good. But when I restarted my phone this morning, I had more than twenty messages, some from reporters who wanted to hear my side of the story. There were also about five requests to speak, from organizations, from radio stations. I made a list."

Lamar passed his notepad to Todd, but he waved it away. "Explain how you talking would not backfire and become a disaster."

"As a therapist, I'm well practiced at listening, being deliberate, formulating careful responses on the fly. I have been speaking about the need for more end-of-life options, like the medical-aid-in-dying law you worked on in California. I've got my talking points down."

"Give that to me." Todd took the notepad. "We'll come up with a strategy, find surrogates to do the talking. But the *foundation* of that strategy is you keep a low profile and not say a word."

"I'm going to go crazy if I have to sit and do nothing. I know how not to say too much."

"Anything more than nothing is too much."

12

Accomplished Liar

Edgewater Cares Retirement Community
Apartment 1603
Chicago, Illinois
February 26, 2009

When her mother needed her, Andrea was by her side. Even when it was inconvenient, with her demanding job, and a surly teenager, who was probably taking drugs and watching porn in the rec room. Like today, picking her up for the hour drive to the clinic in Hyde Park. In the snow flurries.

"You're the only one who understands what I'm going through," her mother said, as Andrea walked with her to the elevator. "Your father does not believe in drama. To him, this is just some engineering problem."

At seventy-two, with a history of health and vigor, Andrea's mother started losing weight, sweating through the night, feeling tired even when she slept. When she went to the doctor, they found she had stage 2 chronic lymphocytic leukemia. Not good, but treatable. Andrea took her to every test, every treatment.

Her mother expressed her gratitude effusively, so that helped. No one else seemed to notice how giving Andrea was. Why wasn't her mother's gratitude enough? She reminded herself that the giving was for her, for her karma, for her spirit. It wasn't about getting credit.

Andrea also needed to know what was going on. Her mother might keep things from her. She was like that.

"Dad wants everything simple," Andrea said, "He thinks women make everything complicated."

"Tell me about it. He likes his life to be *efficient*. Like a work project. He's so *rigid*." She spat that last word. Then she composed herself. "Don't you work today?"

"I told you, Mom. This comes first. I can't have you going in for all these serious medical procedures by yourself."

"What would I do without you?"

Andrea chugged up the ramp from the garage, slowly so as not to skid on the thin layer of snow, then turned left on Sheridan. Her mother sighed loudly as they curved onto the Outer Drive. The snow falling on the lake looked so pretty.

"Your father's having an affair with Brigid," she said.

"*What?*" Andrea was tired of her mother's histrionics, but she had to cut her some slack.

"Haven't you seen her flirt with him?"

"Brigid is your best friend," said Andrea. "She's lonely. And Dad—"

"Brigid *was* my best friend. Brigid *was* lonely."

Andrea didn't know whether to take this seriously or not. Brigid was everyone's best friend. When Andrea was at her wit's end with Drew, Brigid was there with a loving ear and a big hug. More than her so-called friends. Not that she had more than a few.

"How do you know?" Andrea asked. "Are you sure?"

"I heard them talking. When they didn't think I could hear."

"What did they say?"

"It's what they didn't say. They talked in code. Half sentences. 'You don't have to.' 'When would we?' 'Celeste has appointments.' I mean, he might be with her now, while we're headed to the doctor. She's four floors below, and there are, you know, all those freight elevators and stairwells."

Andrea could not imagine her father sneaking around while his wife went to the doctor. He wouldn't. "Have you asked Brigid?"

"She is an accomplished liar," she said. "I'm so glad I have you to talk to."

If her father were having an affair, he could keep it a secret. Brigid, not necessarily.

"It doesn't seem like Dad," Andrea said.

"Fine, take your father's side. See how far that gets you."

"I'm not taking Dad's side," she said. "I don't want to get caught between you two."

"You know Brigid plays cards with your father and his friends."

Andrea did know that. Her mother didn't play poker. But what a leap between playing cards and canoodling, or whatever having an affair meant when you were in your seventies.

She had been suspicious about Drew once, that he might be having an affair, but he had been fired and he was afraid to tell her. "What do you want me to do anyway?" she asked.

"You keep talking to your father as if nothing is going on," her mother said. "Until I figure out what to do next."

That was the last she heard of the affair. Several times, she thought of asking, but didn't. And then her mother died.

13

Lost in the Mine

Santa Fe, New Mexico
June 24, 2008

Lamar was grateful he was booked all day. Focusing on his clients' problems instead of his. But his three o'clock canceled, ten minutes after the hour, which pissed him off something fierce. He walked to the plaza for coffee.

The cobblestone alleyway was slick from an early after-noon thunderstorm. The orange trumpet vines climbing the alley walls stretched into the sun, flirting with the bees and butterflies. The air was sweet with a hint of earthworm.

Lamar would have loved to be lazier and see fewer clients, but he couldn't fill his down time. No matter how much yoga and gardening and reading and friends, there were too many hours to brood, to feel lonely, to play the same broken record about Janis.

When he returned to his office, he almost bumped into Skip, his last client of the day, who was standing inside in the waiting room.

Usually, Lamar opened his double doors from inside his

office to greet clients. Before Skip's appointments, he always moved his white leather chairs a couple feet further apart to accommodate Skip's lanky legs. Lamar liked to sit close to clients, but not so close they bumped feet. But he'd forgotten to move the furniture before heading to the plaza, so he tucked his legs under his chair.

Anyone six-and-a-half feet tall was distinctive, but there was a certain blandness to Skip, and he was relatively un-complicated, especially compared to Lamar's other clients, who had built so many layers of rationalization and denial that he needed a post-hole digger to bore his way in.

He was not especially handsome. With his round face, untamed clump of curly brown hair, and big front teeth, he looked like an overgrown kid. Today even more than usual, his bony legs poking out of cargo shorts. A four-day growth of beard would have helped, given him a more rakish, ignoble look.

Skip plunged right in with his dating stories. "There are a couple of developments. One is that I accidentally-on-purpose hooked up with Lonnie, you remember her. Really a pretty and sexy woman. Once upon a time, I wanted to marry her."

Lamar remembered. Skip had started therapy after his divorce and Lonnie had been his first new relationship.

"I sent an email by mistake. On purpose. I sent her this work email, about rescheduling a meeting, and she replied, right away. Looks like a mistake, hope you're well.

"I write back, *oops,* I sent this to Linda, who I'm work-ing with on this launch and I typed it wrong, and you're still in my email memory and it went to you. My email must have been channeling me, I say, because I was think-ing about you, the other day when I passed that Mexican restaurant we used to go to in Eastside, with the fountain, and I remembered how much fun you were."

Skip perched on the front of his chair, his neck upright, his shoulders hunched forward. He chopped the air as he spoke, his voice rising in pitch and his words rumbling into each other.

"I ask her how she's doing, say it would be good to catch up, but I don't ask her out. She gets back to me about the restaurant. Sopa's. Which I knew. I ask her if she'd like to go there for dinner, and we end up at her place making out. She says she wasn't planning on this, and I say neither was I, and we have a great time in bed, but the next day, I'm like, *oh shit*, this seemed like a good idea, but...."

He trailed off.

"This wasn't what you wanted?" It was fine to challenge Skip, Lamar reminded himself, as long as he kept it light.

"It's what I *thought* I wanted. I remembered the great stuff about her, her killer smile when I'm inside her, she's right there, one hundred and twenty percent, eyes wide open, licking her lips. But I'm wrong for her, she's wrong for me, and now I feel like I'm *responsible* for her."

For all his self-deprecating language, Skip's body told another story. Those strutting shoulders—how did he do that while slouching? Skip was burning bright, totally in the moment, not measuring his words. Being real. What Lamar asked of all his clients, and rarely got.

Skip had been coming to Lamar for going on two years and mostly talked about women. It was no wonder Lamar felt like punishing him.

After his divorce, Skip had been a basket case, and Lamar had helped him become a new, more confident man. He was spellbound by Skip's stories, for all the wrong reasons.

Lamar prided himself on his ability to give clients his complete attention. He listened. He watched. He divined the emotions below the surface. He kept his own life, his own problems, locked away.

With Skip, the lock didn't hold. He couldn't help but compare his situation to Skip's. Why was this lightweight scoring left and right, and now center, while Lamar was shriveling up inside?

Without knowing it, Skip had been giving Lamar a primer on dating. He had to kick Skip out of the nest.

But Skip was just warming up. "You remember Charlotte, the woman from Speed-Dating? So we're sleeping together now, and she's earnest about her career, marketing irrigation equipment or something. She raises chickens. She's not a looker, but in the bedroom, she's all sexy and wild."

As Skip grew more animated, Lamar got more agitated. Listening to Skip crow was becoming unbearable. Lamar slipped his hands under his legs, pressed his fingers into the cushion. He had to appear professional, so he studied the aloe plants, jammed together on the window ledge behind Skip.

"She's all gushy about me," Skip said, "what did she say, oh yeah, 'He listens, he makes me laugh, he's got great legs, and he knows how to fuck.' Man, I *love* that shit. The problem is she doesn't know about Talia, and Talia doesn't know about Charlotte, and now there's Lonnie. What a *mess*."

Skip leaned back in the chair, stretched his legs, and kicked Lamar's shin.

Lamar jumped up. "*What the—!*" he snapped.

Skip flinched, shrank back into his chair. "Hey, it was an accident. Sorry, I—"

Lamar glared at Skip, his fingernails digging into his palms. As if he were about to pounce.

"*Hey*, I said I was sorry." Skip *sounded* contrite. "It was an accident."

Lamar inhaled through his nose until he couldn't take any

more air in. Calm down, he told himself. He exhaled slowly, deliberately. "You're right," he said. "I overreacted."

He moved behind his chair, pulled it back two feet. How could he have let Skip get to him like this? Breaking into a tantrum during a session?

"Seems to me," Lamar spoke calmly, coldly, with minimal affect, as he lowered himself ever so slowly into his chair, "that you're looking for help with a situation that you *wanted* and *sought out*, and that many men would love to be in."

"I'm just processing."

"Processing? No, it's locker-room bragging." He softened his tone. "Why do you think you need to do that?"

Skip didn't seem fazed. "I want to be able to talk this through. I'm talking to you because I can't talk to them. I feel, you know, distance. I feel alone."

"Can you hear yourself?" said Lamar. "You want to bed these two women, or three if I have my math right, and *then* you want to be able to talk to *each of them*, about the others, so you don't feel so alone?"

Skip grimaced. "Why are you angry? I didn't *mean* to kick you. This all sounds better than it is."

"Sounds better than it is?" Lamar said, sharp and vicious. "Then why the bragging? Are you that insecure?"

Skip was torturing him and he had no idea. He should have referred Skip to another therapist months ago. This was over the line. Unprofessional. He was being cruel, not therapeutic. He had to pull it together.

Skip seemed to get that he had touched a nerve. "You encouraged me to be honest," he said, his voice an octave higher, "to go into detail. Now you're saying I've said too much."

Lamar *had* encouraged the detail. He *had* urged Skip not

to measure his words. That was why he was patient with clients repeating themselves. Sooner or later they heard themselves, and all Lamar needed to do was get out of the way and let them figure things out on their own. But it wasn't supposed to be *voyeurism*, it was *supposed to be* in the best interests of the clients.

"I guess I'm exaggerating the good parts," said Skip. "I mean, sometimes the actual sex is not so great. Like with Charlotte, when I come, it's not intense like it used to be. My orgasms pale compared to hers, which are like *earthquakes*, all these aftershocks. I feel left out, like—"

"*What?!?* Your orgasms aren't *intense* enough?" He couldn't bear to listen to Skip another second. "You are unbelievable."

"I said I was sorry."

Lamar bolted up, clutched his stomach, burst through the doors, and raced to the bathroom. "I have to go."

Behind him, he heard Skip's plaintive, "Are you OK?"

Bile bubbled in his stomach. About to erupt.

He splashed his face with cold water and leaned on the sink, panting as if he'd run from a rabid dog.

No, I'm not OK, he wanted to tell Skip. *I'm fucking suffocating in a stale and hostile marriage to a severely depressed woman and I want to leave so badly I can taste it. I'm dying to meet women, to resuscitate my libido, and pardon my bluntness, it is fucking excruciating to listen to you whine about your overabundance of riches while I'm drying up inside.*

That might have shut Skip up.

Not that it was Skip's fault. This was all on Lamar.

The bathroom was small and windowless, but the mirror covered the whole wall above the sink and the three globe lights and the glossy green walls gave the room a bright cheerful feel. The mirror was framed on three sides by colorful glass tiles. Lamar felt human again. That was a panic attack, a *textbook* panic attack.

You cowardly shithead. If you weren't so afraid to leave Janis and take control of your life, none of this would have happened. The one thing you have going for you—being a halfway decent, empathetic, wise therapist—now you're fucking that up too. And get yourself a shrink. That's where you're the biggest coward of all.

He went back to his office and with as much gentle professionalism as he could muster, told Skip he was ending the session.

Skip stopped in the doorway. "Hey doc, I'm sorry. I *was* bragging. The thing is that, well, maybe I'm not exactly getting as much action as it would appear."

"As it would appear? You mean, as you told me."

"I *exaggerated* a bit."

"You haven't had all the dates and sex you said you did?"

"Well I, no— " Here he threw up his hands in surrender, as if Lamar had been grilling him under a hot light. "Some of the dating stories are true, some not so much."

"Are you shitting me?"

"You were pumping me for these stories. The more I talked about sex the more engrossed you seemed to be."

"You made up stories because I was more attentive? *Unbelievable.*"

"The problem is, I don't have that deeper connection, the intimacy of sleeping together for years, like someone who's been married a long time, like you, where you have a soulmate."

"*Stop.*"

"I'm more messed up than you could possibly imagine," said Skip.

■ ■ ■

Lamar usually drove home from Santa Fe on Interstate 25 to the Coal Avenue exit in central Albuquerque. Still berating himself for his unprofessional outburst, he stayed on Cerrillos as it turned into the old, sparsely traveled mining road meandering along the base of the Sangre de Cristo Mountains. New Mexico State Highway 14. The Turquoise Trail. He needed to clear his head for the task at hand. Leaving Janis.

His father hated to drive the interstate—"freeways are for speed freaks," he would snarl, though with a hint of a smile—and so over the years, when Lamar wanted to slow down, he chose this more circuitous route. He and his father didn't have a lot in common, but they both liked the Turquoise Trail.

When he was in middle school in Los Alamos, Lamar's scout troop took a field trip to an abandoned mine off the Turquoise Trail, and he got separated from the group, lost for hours. He had learned that when you're lost with a group, you should stay put and let the others find you, but in the mine, he panicked and kept moving, further and further into the mine and away from the search party.

As the road veered westward, he drove into the soon-to-be-setting sun and wondered if he'd been foolishly abiding by that same directive that he had ignored in the mine forty years earlier. He was staying put, waiting for someone to find him. Panicking and getting more lost was a risk, but so was waiting for a search party that was never coming.

Lamar stopped in Madrid, a ghost town that had reincarnated itself as a quirky, ramshackle art colony, full of wooden houses disassembled and shipped by train from Kansas during the mining boom. He'd learned from a client that Madrid's water had to be trucked in, because of all the suspended coal and turquoise particles swimming around in the underground streams. Well, he wasn't here to drink the water.

Parking his gray Volvo next to a pair of grand old Harley Davidsons, shining in the evening sun, he walked gingerly into the Mine Shaft Tavern, where the sign above the fireplace said, "Madrid has no town drunk. We all take turns." He and Janis had eaten at the tavern several times over the years, back when she was social. It was a friendly, boisterous place where they often ended up in conversations with other patrons.

Tonight he sought out a quiet corner, and ordered a chili relleno with sopapillas, and a Dos Equis with lime. He would pour himself a stronger drink when he got home to break up with Janis.

His stomach was better, and his headache was dull instead of sharp, but he was nowhere near OK.

On the balcony, a group of old bikers in jean jackets and vests were talking loudly. All at once, so Lamar only heard snatches. One big guy was taking his mates to task for knowing nothing about native plants or landscaping with rocks. Built like a former football player who had hit the cookie jar, he had a grizzled face, pink and plump, peeking out from behind a long white beard. He peppered his lecture with "fucking" and "you hear what I'm saying," and "dude," so he didn't exactly sound like a horticulture professor.

Lamar left the tavern. Sat in his car.

He stuck the keys in the ignition, and then rested his head on the steering wheel. He could hear the bikers laughing on the balcony.

Janis had not always been depressed. When he first met

her, she had been wild, manic, enthusiastic, sexy. Full of energy. Extremely bright. She had been seeing someone, but he was determined to win her, and he did, hurting both his partner and hers. They married. Had a daughter.

Janis got depressed after giving birth, severe enough that she spent a month in the psych ward. She got better. Until she had a miscarriage that she blamed on Lamar, claiming it was caused by the stress and conflict he created.

That wasn't the end of their marriage, but the beginning of the end.

Janis took her meds while Sierra was young, saw a therapist, and nurtured her practice. Now and then, she even acted like a loving wife. But she let it fall apart as their daughter grew older.

Lamar helped her at first, or tried to. Did you take your meds? Is there anything I can do? He thought he was being sensitive, but she didn't. Somewhere along the way, he gave up, but not until long after she had.

He'd lost respect for Janis. She didn't try. But wasn't that what severe depression was, a disease that sapped even your ability to fight for your own life?

Over the years, Lamar had advised clients who were flattened by a deep hurt to comfort themselves as if the part of them that was suffering was their own child. That was what he did, leaning back in the driver's seat, his eyes closed, his hands clasped in his lap.

His daughter was grown and launched, but as an infant, before she could do much for herself, she wailed incessantly. Many nights, he held her in his arms in the rocking chair in the quiet of the night, telling her it was going to be alright.

I took care of her, now it's time to take care of that wounded and scared boy inside me, tell him it's going to be alright. He wants to fly, but he can't seem to flap his wings.

I'm here for you. I'm with you. We're going to get through this together.

Lamar squeezed the tears from his eyes, as if there were gunk clogging the pipes that had to be cleared out first, and then they started gushing.

He felt better, but then, maybe because he was on the Turquoise Trail, he thought about what his father would say. Well, he probably wouldn't have said anything, just pursed his lips and narrowed his eyes in disapproval.

Men didn't cry in his father's world. They dealt with whatever was in front of them. There was no need to get emotional.

OK, Lamar told himself, he'd had himself a good cry. Now he would do what he had to do. Deal with what was in front of him. He wiped his face, took the key out of the ignition.

One more drink, then I head home to tell Janis I'm leaving. I need it. I deserve it.

Back in the bar, after gulping down a Scotch, he waved over the xeriscaping biker, whose name was Jeff, and offered to buy him a drink if he'd recommend a fast-growing cactus for his front yard in Albuquerque.

He woke up the next morning sprawled on his back, sunk deep into a spongy green couch that was way too soft, the sun streaming through the window. The air smelled of ash and sand, and his mouth was as dry as the Madrid water tower.

14

I Can't Sit Back and Say Nothing

Freedom Channel TV Studio
Chicago, Illinois
January 18, 2016

"It's disconcerting," Paula said. "Like being on the phone, but different. You're in the room by yourself, with the camera patched into the studio, and you want to look directly at the camera."

Andrea and Paula sat side-by-side on a gold couch.

"When the light's red, you're on, but you have to *assume* it's *always* on. No biting your nails."

Andrea pulled her finger from her mouth, tucked it under her leg. "You told me all this already," she said. "Why do they call this a green room? The walls are white. Like my doctor's office."

"Focus, Andrea. Keep your answers simple, and put all the evidence in one soundbite. You're going to hit it out of the park if you stick with what we went over. Do you need to practice again?"

The three days since the memorial and Andrea's

church-pulpit accusation and TV interview had been crazy busy.

That first day, she had felt so exhilarated she was light-headed. She couldn't help but replay her dramatic charge over and over again. She could still hear her words echoing in the cavernous church. Every eye locked on her. Every ear waiting on her next sentence.

She had pushed through her fear, spoken truth to power. This was the new Andrea. No more complaining. No more victim. Andrea reborn. She had never felt so powerful before.

Her WLS interview outside the church was all over her Facebook, her email. Long-lost friends reached out. Strangers walked up to her in the supermarket. She'd never had her voicemail box full before. Lamar wouldn't stop calling her. She wouldn't answer his calls. She couldn't.

Paula had taken charge of who to respond to and why, and now here she was about to be interviewed by Alice Ketting on the Freedom Channel.

Paula said Alice Ketting fancied herself a street fighter, the Rachel Maddow of the right. Her promos showed her at demonstrations or outside town hall meetings, wearing combat boots with steel toes, not heels. The better, she claimed, to stomp out evil.

After Alice Ketting, from her New York studio, introduced her, and set the scene, the first question was why she was certain her brother had killed their father.

"First off, he was here, in town, in Chicago—he lives in Albuquerque—and he had just visited and was heading back home, and he said something about how tiring it was to be flying back and forth so often."

She was looking directly into the camera and speaking slowly and clearly, but this wasn't how she planned to start. With her weakest argument.

She took a breath, started again.

"First off, we have my brother's web browsing history, and he's been researching death cult websites, including sites that sell suicide kits, instruments and drugs to do that kind of thing. Second, we know at least three people at Edgewater who heard my father asking Lamar to help him die. We already have this much damning evidence from two days of investigation. There's also an autopsy in the works, and the district attorney's office is reviewing potential charges."

Nailed it! She could see Alice Ketting on the monitor nodding her head, her eyes blazing. As if they were in the same room. She held up her finger when Andrea stopped.

"You lost your mother a few years ago, your father a few days ago, and now you're accusing your brother of murder. Don't you fear you're going to lose him as well?"

Paula had told her the questions would be supportive, like slow-pitch softball, but this one sure as hell wasn't.

She hesitated, practiced her response in her head. Paula said not to worry about being too slow.

"I can't sit back and say nothing."

Alice Ketting kept boring in about her father wanting to die. As if that made what Lamar did right. The lights were bright and hot, and too close, and she had too many layers on. But she couldn't take off her sweater. She wanted a drink of water, but that would make her look nervous so she sat up straight and looked directly into the camera. Paula said they sometimes did a split screen so viewers might see her even when she wasn't talking.

"Lamar *acted* as if he wanted to end my father's suffering," Andrea said. "But we were giving him drugs for the pain. This was about *Lamar's* suffering, *Lamar's* inconvenience."

Why was she harping on inconvenience again? How

could she be so lame? Her armpits were dripping with sweat. She could smell herself and it was not pleasant.

"His supporters," said Alice Ketting, "claim he's a skilled and caring psychologist who is a comfort to people who are dying."

"My brother is a smug and sanctimonious man who has deluded himself into believing he's kind, a do-gooder, and that killing my father was the right thing to do."

"How do you *know* he did it?"

"He *told* me. He *admitted* it."

When the red light went off, the producer in New York clapped and said, "That was great television." She never saw the producer, or her face.

"Thank you," said Andrea. "It's my first time on TV, other than, you know, webinars."

Paula stood when Andrea walked back into the green room. No smile.

"I think I did well," Andrea said. "Curry Wood, you know, the producer on the other end, she said it was great television."

"She says that to everyone."

Then silence.

That was not reassuring. High a second ago, now Andrea felt tense and sour, as if that champagne bath had turned to vinegar.

Paula motioned for Andrea to follow her. Hurry, her impatient fingers said. Back to the car. Bundle up for the cold.

"She kept goading me," Andrea said, "trying to trip me up."

"Andrea, we'll talk in the car."

Paula didn't say anything until they pulled onto La Salle. She kept one hand at the top of the steering wheel and the other on the right. Her black leather gloves had that rich warmth of aging. Leather aged better than people, that was for sure.

"That stuff about your brother and his sanctimoniousness makes you look mean-spirited and vindictive," said Paula. "Maybe that's great for a soap opera, but we have to make a strong case that *we're* the good guys and your brother and his death-cult buddies are wearing the black hats. Being a bitchy sister does not help."

Andrea turned away from Paula and squeezed her eyes shut.

She had to work late this evening. She was falling too far behind. Work was no more stressful than usual, but on top of this "crusade," as Drew called it, she was ragged. But the interview had been *exciting*. She had been articulate and forceful. No church mouse.

"It was my first time. I was passionate."

"We'll see how they edit this, but I fear we'll see more pouting, angry, hurt Andrea than grieving daughter. You made it about *you*, not about your father."

"You told me to tell my story. That *was* my story."

"You hardly mentioned Robert."

"I *did*."

She had. She was doing this *for* her father. She certainly didn't covet the limelight.

"Stick with the script next time or we're done," Paula said.

Andrea was not going to back down. "Caution is for space travel, not for TV. Train wrecks lead the news. You wanted fireworks, we got fireworks." She had hit her mark. Paula was a control freak.

"Lamar is the one who has to watch what he says," Andrea added, "He's the one in trouble. I have nothing to lose by telling the truth."

■ ■ ■

Alice Ketting aired at nine that night. Andrea didn't even know if they got the Freedom Channel at home, but she found it. She asked Drew to watch with her.

Such torture to see herself on the screen. She shook as they watched. Her hair was bad. She needed to lose weight. She couldn't stop seeing her double chin, that wiggle under her jaw as she talked. Drew, as usual, said nothing.

But she was raw, riveting. She had opened her heart and poured it out. Maybe she was rough on Lamar. Maybe she was shrill. Maybe next time she could dial it back.

It ran eight minutes. She'd been in the studio half an hour.

Drew didn't say a word until she turned off the TV.

"You've got to drop this," he said. "You say cruel things about your brother. Are you trying to destroy what little family we have left?"

"Don't you pin this on me. Lamar started this by killing Dad."

Drew shook his head. "He didn't do this to hurt *you*. If indeed he did do it."

"Whose side are you on, anyway?"

"I would just as soon not take a side."

"You have to understand—"

He cut her off. "Watch what you're saying. I'm doing you a favor right now—I'm taking a shower and going to bed."

15

I Can Do That

Coal Avenue
Albuquerque, New Mexico
June 24, 2008

Lamar drove home the morning after spending the night on Jeff's couch in Madrid. He parked across the street from his house. As if he were a visitor.

He could see the glow of the TV through the blinds.

As he approached the front door, he steeled himself. Why now? He was upset—still shaken by yesterday's explosion with Skip. Still hung over. Shouldn't he wait until his head was cooler? Clearer? This was a life-changing event he was about to engage in.

No. He had waited too long already. Patience was a virtue, but also a trap.

Caro barked and bounded toward the door. Too late to turn back now.

When he opened the door, she poked her head between his legs, her tail wagging furiously. He used to have to raise his knee to keep her from jumping, but now, with her hip dysplasia, she couldn't push off with her hind legs.

Caro followed him into the living room, where Janis sat in her chair, watching Oprah.

"Turn that off, please," he said, standing in front of the screen. Caro sat alert in front of Janis, as if she were equally mesmerized by Oprah.

The remote lay on the arm of the chair. Janis made no effort to reach for it, but twisted her torso to look around Lamar. He reached down to the power strip poking out from under the cabinet and flipped the switch off. Not as dramatic as yanking out the plug, but it did the trick.

Janis grabbed the remote and pointed it at him, pushing buttons. Her big blue eyes were wide open. She seemed more awake than she'd been in weeks. She knew what was coming.

"I slept on a couch last night in Madrid," he said, his heels digging into the pile of the carpet. "A man I met at the Mine Shaft put me up because I was too drunk to drive home. I was depressed. You might know the feeling. Not the deep darkness of the soul you're trapped in, but dark enough."

Janis stared at him. Caro, her eyes on Janis, raised herself slowly and took a couple steps toward Lamar, rubbed against his leg. A clump of her chocolate brown fur came off in his hand. Someone needed brushing.

"I'm going to live somewhere else for a while," he said, absently petting Caro. "I need, I want a break from us."

Her eyes closed, then blinked open, but he couldn't hold them. She almost seemed to be smiling. He wasn't going to let her get away with her helpless act. Caro went back to Janis, resting her head on her knee. Maybe Caro could come back in her next life as a marriage counselor.

Janis sat still and expressionless, pushing buttons on the

remote again. He could have been speaking another language for all the emotion she showed.

"I will be here three days a week to see clients in our office downstairs," he said, "and I will say hello and goodbye and keep up with the chores. I'll hire a housekeeper or gardener, if need be. I assume you want to keep Caro here, but you'll need to feed her and take her out."

"I can do that."

He listened for baiting, or pouting, or any of her usual passive-aggressive posturing, but she sounded like one of those computer voices that talk with no affect. *I can do that.* An easy sentence. Four one-syllable words. No rhythm to trip on. Finally, she noticed Caro, who had been waiting for her to pay attention, and she petted her head.

"I'll walk her when I'm here," he said. "I'd be happy to take her with me, if you want."

"You'd take her?"

"I'd like to. But you'd be better off with her here. She knows how to be a friend better than I do. And it will be easier for me to find a place without a pet."

He could see Janis' brain spinning—let's see, if he doesn't want the dog, maybe I should make him take her? She set the remote down and narrowed her eyes, as if she was giving his last statement more thought.

Caro was back by his side now. She knew something was going on—she kept moving nervously between them looking to be petted. As if that would bring them back together. He would miss her. Caro, that is.

"There's the *Journal* too," he continued. "It's paid through August. We can keep it coming, but you need to take it in every day, even if you don't read it."

"I'll keep the dog and the newspaper," she said.

"Do you want to talk more about this?"

"No," she said. "You've made yourself clear. Turn Oprah back on."

"I'm going to pack now. I've got clients this afternoon, but we can eat lunch together."

"I'm not hungry in the middle of the day."

"I'll eat then. We can talk more about what all this means."

"I know what it means. I'm surprised you stayed this long."

16

Smug and Sanctimonious

Coal Avenue
Albuquerque, New Mexico
January 19, 2016

Begrudgingly, Lamar followed Todd's advice and kept his mouth shut. The day after their meeting, he flew back to Albuquerque and kept to himself except for seeing clients, who either hadn't heard anything about his sister's accusation or were too caught up in their own troubles to care. At home, he read, watched movies, drank wine. He didn't even call Julia.

Todd had warned him that there might be reporters coming to his house, so he stayed out of his living room, spent all his time in his kitchen and basement office. But it seemed that his notoriety hadn't followed him to New Mexico.

He hoped Andrea's accusation at the church would get it out of her system, that the furor might fade, and, for a few days, it seemed like that was happening. But Tuesday morning, when he looked at his phone, there were more than twenty emails, ten voicemails, one death threat, and two appeals to help someone die.

It didn't take long to find clips of Andrea's appearance on the Alice Ketting show. There was one photo of him, his professional headshot, spliced into the footage while Andrea attacked him. At least he looked respectable, even distinguished.

He could not believe what he was watching. This couldn't be. She was his sister and she was making him out to be a selfish, horrible person.

He called her. Again. Of course she didn't answer. He was tempted to rail at her, but she was unhinged enough to send his voicemail to Alice Ketting, so he left as polite a message as he could muster.

He called her three more times before he finished his coffee.

How could she be so spiteful? Why was she after him with such a white-hot vengeance?

He wanted to strangle her, but there had been too much dying already.

Would he ever be able to practice psychotherapy again? That is, in the unlikely event he had to earn a living because he was not in prison.

It was one thing to accuse him of killing their father—that at least was true—but the way she attacked him—when did she get so mean? She couldn't have been *that* crushed by their father's death. She didn't even like him that much. She had told Lamar that any number of times.

He tried to make excuses for her—the reporter baited her and she didn't have a lot of experience doing TV—but where did all that anger toward him come from?

Sanctimonious and smug? That was not him at all.

Maybe that time he suggested Andrea consider therapy and she said she had, but it was useless for her, and he had said something like, "well, not everyone is as blessed as you are, with perfect mental health." But that was more snarky than smug.

As for what he did for his father, that had been the right thing to do, the only thing an enlightened loving son could do. He certainly hadn't been self-righteous about it.

Lamar aspired to be humble, curious, empathetic, and while he fell short of a perfect score, he was the opposite of smug and sanctimonious. He wasn't deluding himself, was he?

But if that were the case, why couldn't he ignore what she said? Maybe she thought that having the courage of his convictions was somehow smug.

Stop it, he told himself. This was about her, not him. Poor Andrea. She said mean things about him, but he felt sorry for her anyway. Her desperation, her thin skin, it was palpable, even in the tiny video on his phone.

Every time he heard Andrea accuse him of killing their father because it was *convenient*, he winced. As much for Andrea as for himself. She came across as so *unlikable*. Did she know that? He suspected she didn't.

She had been so bereft after their mother died. Lamar remembered one visit, maybe a year later, watching Andrea when she didn't know he was watching, and she looked so defeated, deflated, with her shoulders sagging and her jaw clenched.

Her relationship with their mother had been unhealthy— they were a textbook example of co-dependence. Better that than being estranged, but still. Lamar missed his mother too, but she hadn't been part of his daily life. Andrea and their mother had talked every day, sometimes several times a day, for decades.

Once, Lamar had an oblique conversation with Drew

about the too-tight connection between mother and daughter. Drew minimized it, but he didn't *seem* to believe what he was saying. Lamar tried to draw him out, but Drew clammed up.

At least Lamar wasn't depressed. He was in too much trouble for that.

His father had never been a complainer, so his angst and agony about losing his mind carried weight. But his moments of lucidity had been more and more infrequent.

He had still been able to go to the bathroom on his own, though he needed help more often. He would have rather died than wear diapers. Lamar remembered when his dog Caro was unable to move her back legs anymore and had to poop on the tarp in the living room. She had been so distressed. Her eyes so tired. But Lamar didn't have to take the matter into his own hands. He only needed to make a phone call. He didn't have to hide in a janitor's closet.

That had been such a wrenching time, Caro's death. After he had called the vet to come to the house, Janis sat on the tarp and fed Caro raw hamburger from the palm of her hand. She hadn't lost her appetite. When the vet arrived, Janis retreated to her room.

Lamar buried Caro in the back yard, dug the hole himself. It took hours. He had to rest frequently because of the exertion and also because he could barely see what he was digging through the tears. Losing Caro was sad, of course, but he cried as much for the loss of his marriage. He couldn't separate the tears for Caro from the tears for himself.

He remembered he had called Andrea, and she had been so sympathetic. But he had only told her about Caro, not about Janis.

He waited until nine to skype Todd, who was back home in Los Angeles, where it was an hour earlier. He was wearing a white V-neck undershirt and the sun hit the side of his face. Todd had seen the same clips as Lamar. He told Todd about all the messages he had received.

"One of the voicemails was from this simpatico reporter—we've talked before—and he said that if I say nothing, the only narrative anyone hears is Andrea's. He said he would help me get my story out there."

"I'm sure he was friendly," said Todd, "but he is *not* your friend. Reporters, cops—that's what they do. Last week, we agreed to you saying nothing."

"I may be acting calm," said Lamar, "but I'm going out of my mind keeping silent. Andrea is batshit crazy. I have to set Andrea straight. I have to bring her down. It's one thing to accuse me, that's bad enough, going on right-wing TV—I mean, how could she do that?—but she was almost gleeful the way she assassinated my character."

Todd set his jaw, and then looked down at his pad and wrote some notes. Todd was not an easy man to read.

"My life was not so perfect before," Lamar said, "but now I want that life back."

Now Todd looked up, waited. He was good at that suspenseful pause. He held it for a couple seconds, so Lamar was tempted to jump in again.

Lamar had experience talking in front of people—he'd taught a buddhism/therapy class at Central New Mexico Community College. He had prepared conscientiously and received good feedback. He knew he was not dripping with charisma, but he could think on his feet. Ride the rapids when they came up.

Finally Todd spoke. "I'm sure attacking Andrea would make you feel better, but it would be the *worst* possible thing you could do. Think about it."

Now Lamar waited. Todd was right, of course. He had

to take the high road, even if he didn't want to. What kind of pain must Andrea be in, he wondered, that she would hurt him like this?

"You make a valid point," he said. "I promise not to get into a public shouting match with my sister, but I have to address her accusations. In a calm, non-defensive, non-attacking kind of way.

"How do you propose to go about this?"

"First, we find friendly venues," Lamar said. "There's the hospice program in Santa Fe, where I know the guy, Terry. They have public forums—I was on a panel a year ago—they would be the right audience."

"And what would you say?"

"I start by denying that I had anything to do with my father's death. And that I can't say anymore or my lawyer will kill me."

Todd didn't laugh. "You don't want to joke about that, even with me. They're going to press you with questions no matter what you say."

"I would talk about DBC, the importance of talking about end-of-life stuff, the hospice movement, palliative care, consultation with your medical team, how much we can learn about life from death. It's a great opportunity. At the same time, I demonstrate that I'm a grounded and reasonable person, not the monster she's made me out to be. "

"Your sister made strong accusations. She says you admitted it to her."

"Not true. She didn't even talk to me before this *attack*. I mean, she could have confronted me privately. She won't do that—I've been calling her and she won't answer."

He started to tell Todd about Andrea's complicated relationship with their father, but stopped. If Andrea wasn't going to answer his calls, he would have to confront her in person.

"You don't see how risky this is?"

"I do. I've given it a lot of thought. I can do this. You know when I was on the comms committee, we struggled to get speaking gigs and audiences. Now they're coming to us."

"Sure, they smell blood. Look, as a DBC board member, I understand that we could benefit from more visibility, but as your lawyer, I need to protect you from all those people whose job it is to knock you off your stride. If I allow you to speak, I will be pilloried for shirking my duty as your lawyer. You're a murder suspect, after all, and hiding out is the normal strategy."

"We could arrange for a talk at the Unitarian Church, in Albuquerque, where I've spoken before."

"You're not listening," said Todd. "You are *working* for Dying By Choice, as a volunteer, whether you like it or not. You can say, I'm speaking as myself, not as a spokesperson for DBC, but no one will hear that. If you fuck up, you hurt yourself, *and* you hurt DBC, maybe even me, maybe even my reputation, which I have been working to rehabilitate for years."

"It is tricky. I get that. But this bully pulpit doesn't come around every day, and I am willing to be exploited on behalf of DBC, if that's what you're concerned about." Todd was wavering, Lamar could tell. Murder suspect? Had Andrea used the word "murder"?

"Send everything to me," said Todd. "I'll ask Lansing, my assistant—she handles all my email—to track down the best leads and *maybe* we get you out there with a muzzle and a leg iron. No promises. This is not a green light, this a yellow light. Proceed with caution. I hope I won't regret this.

"And just so you know," added Todd, taking a softer

tone. "I've been in your shoes. Some of my friends who had AIDS. The dying was excruciating. We found ways to make the end come quicker. But no one came after us. And no one will. I'm the only one left."

17

Shotgun Shack

Madrid, New Mexico
June 26, 2008

Within ten minutes of breaking up with Janis, Lamar was downstairs in front of his computer, reviewing, one more time, his emails to prospective dates.

He had promised himself he wouldn't contact any women until he talked to Janis. Now he had.

He sent the first five.

He also sent a note to Jeff, the xeriscaping Madrid biker, thanking him for his hospitality the previous night, and asking him about the nearby place he mentioned that might be for rent.

That evening, after he checked into the Clarion Hotel, up near Balloon Fiesta Park, he sent his second foray of emails to five more prospects.

He started looking for apartments, but he kept checking his email every few minutes. Then he made himself wait before checking again. Fifteen minutes.

Still nothing.

Calm down, he told himself. You want a woman who has a life, not someone checking her inbox every second.

One of Lamar's woman clients who had done internet dating used to complain about how disappointed she was with most of her email overtures. They were more like grunts than letters, she said. *You look cute. Check out my ad.*

Lamar had poured his heart and soul into the emails he sent, and he wanted to be earnest, not desperate.

He wanted his prospective dates to feel like he wrote because of something *special* about them, but he didn't want to go overboard, into the creepy stalker realm, studying their profiles in depth, highlighting key phrases, sweating over multiple drafts as if his life depended on it.

That was too close to the truth.

The first email to pop up was not from one of his dating prospects but Jeff, who explained that his friend Greta had a rundown cabin, but the roof didn't leak. He said Madrid was cool, good for a new start. If Lamar remembered correctly from the loud and drunken conversation at the tavern, Jeff had settled in Madrid after he got out of prison, and had managed to stay out of trouble.

Madrid would be inconvenient. Staying in town, close to his house, his office, made far more sense. Did he want to be doing all that driving? Well, he already drove to Santa Fe twice a week, and Madrid was, what, twenty minutes closer? He was never going to find a commute as easy as walking down the stairs from his kitchen.

He wanted to make changes, didn't he? Everyone had seemed so friendly at the tavern. Maybe a shack in Madrid might be exactly what the doctor ordered.

■■■

The next afternoon, after his last client in Santa Fe, Lamar took the Turquoise Trail to Madrid, turned up the hill on Back Road to Grasshopper Lane. "Follow the road to the 'mailbox jungle,'" Greta had said. "You'll know it when you see it. Next door is a whitewashed cabin with a sagging roof."

The jungle was impossible to miss. Behind a low pinion fence were rows of tunnel-shaped pounded-metal mailboxes on black posts, painted in psychedelic colors, ornamented with stones, with cartoon faces on the latching doors. A yard of wild robot animals.

The fuchsia and chartreuse mailbox in the front had a price tag of $300. Steep, but not your neighbor's mailbox.

As for the cabin, it was a dump. The porch roof looked like it would collapse if you hiccuped. He couldn't imagine bringing a woman here, even with a song-and-dance apology in advance. Some ramshackle cabins had charm. This one didn't.

As he climbed out of his car, he saw a woman with long gray hair, paint-stained overalls, and an unzipped fleece vest emerge from behind the mailboxes. She walked with a limp, one leg stiff and dragging, then swinging to the front, her torso leaning forward to help it along. She waved at him. He paused a few steps from the weather-beaten porch to wait for her. She gave him a beaming smile and reached out her hand.

"Lamar Rose? I'm Greta. Greta Lang." With her good leg, she started up the stairs, then paused and turned to him. "Are you ready for this?"

"Ready for anything, I'd like to think." He wasn't sure he was. "Are you the artist who does those?" He pointed to the mailbox creatures.

She shook her head no. "Wish I was. This cabin is more

spartan than you're expecting."

"Oh, I think the low rent and sagging roof give me a pretty good idea." He said it with a smile, then grimaced, hoping he hadn't offended her.

She squinted behind thick glasses and gave him a sheepish half-smile. "Don't say I didn't warn you. There are repairs, painting. I've been meaning to have it done since, well, a long time." On the phone, she said best-case scenario it would be available in July. "Some of the nice, colorful houses down the hill *used* to look like this."

Inside, the walls were wooden slats like the outside, but vertical instead of horizontal. The floor was also wooden, more scuffed and worn than the walls. It was all one room except for a bathroom in the far corner. In the other corner was a refrigerator and stove, and an L-shaped tin counter. The only furniture was a square red table with two folding chairs. Spartan indeed. But he had more than enough furniture in his garage on Coal Avenue.

"You met Jeff," said Greta.

"Yeah, and a few of his, uh, colleagues," Lamar said.

"I was expecting someone more like them," she said.

He immediately decided he wanted to live here—he was enchanted by how the windows *pulled in* the light. Once she assured him that internet and cable were easy via satellite—she pointed to a dish behind the mailboxes—he was sold.

They made a deal. He would front first and last month's rent—$600 total—and then she'd give him three months free for painting the house inside and out and handling the repairs. She'd pay for the supplies and rewiring. He could move in as soon as he wanted.

"You live near here?" Lamar asked.

She pointed down the road, past the mailbox jungle.

"Going on twenty years. Buried two husbands here. This place used to be a ghost town. For me, it's a ghost town again."

"A question about the house? Do I have to paint the outside purple or gold or red?" he asked. Partly to tease, but he also needed to know.

"In Madrid, you do whatever you want," she said, "even paint your house gray."

On his drive back to his hotel in town, he called his sister. Andrea had just finished dinner.

"I've left Janis," he said. "I'm going to call Mom, but I haven't. Oh, hello. I forgot to say hello."

Andrea didn't say anything.

"Dad too, of course, but I'll talk to Mom first. She might put me on speaker though. Please don't say anything until I call them. I know she'll worry or try to talk me out of it. She likes Janis."

"So do I," Andrea said. He had taken a long curve on the Turquoise Trail and was now driving directly into the late afternoon sun. He lifted his foot from the gas and flipped down the shade.

"That's the problem," he said. "Janis sucks it up for family gatherings, and, you know, back-to-school nights—she can be charming when she wants to—so everyone thinks I'm being selfish, having a midlife crisis, and maybe I am, but the Janis I live with does *not* suck it up for me. I put up a good front too, so people on the outside do not have a clue as to how bad things have been. I had to leave."

Andrea was quick to judge first, listen later, but here she was not telling him what was wrong with him or how to fix his life. She just hummed. Un huh, un huh, un huh.

Like he did.

"Call Mom right away," Andrea said. "I talk to her every day and I don't want to have to pretend."

18

Dead Battery

University of Chicago Medical Center
March 18, 2009

Andrea wanted to be there for her mother, but she was haggard, still fighting the flu.

The whole family had gathered at the clinic. Lamar had flown in on the redeye. Brigid was there too. But Brigid was part of the family now, wasn't she?

Her mother's radiation treatments had made her nauseous and hadn't knocked out more than a few cancer cells, so now they were onto chemo. The first round of treatment had been mild and she was only sick for a day. The doctor recommended amping up the second round.

They installed a port in her chest to make it easier to deliver drugs into a large vein. The doctor said she had a good track record with this particular chemo cocktail, and the last patient who had gone through it was now cancer free. Of course there were risks—the idea was to pump enough of this poison into her bloodstream to kill the cancer cells without killing her. It could be routine. It might not be.

Andrea could not lose her mother. She could not.

Once her mother was wheeled into the treatment area, Andrea announced she needed to sleep. Lamar suggested she stay in his guest apartment at Edgewater.

"Nonsense," she said. "There are couches in the waiting room. Besides, what about your sheets? I'm sick." Her body ached for a bed, but she felt like she would betray her mother by leaving.

"I came straight from the airport," Lamar said. "The sheets are fresh, and you need to rest. With the flu you have, this is not the best place to be. It's only thirty minutes by cab."

There he was, with his judging again. "I can take care of myself, thank you. Besides, your sheets will have all my germs."

"I'll call for clean sheets. I leave generous tips and word gets around."

Andrea couldn't come up with a reason not to go.

"Let me call Edgewater," Lamar said. "But I need to use your phone. Mine's out of juice."

"Call me if anything happens," she said as she left.

She woke up in the dark sweating. Reached for her phone. It was dead. To see the little red digits of the clock radio, she had to contort her upper body and twist her neck. 8:18. She'd lost the whole day. She didn't feel good, but her head wasn't as clogged. While she slept, a wind had roared in and swept away the cobwebs.

She plugged her phone in, tapping her toes waiting for it to boot. It took forever. Goddamn her brother for sapping her batteries.

There were seven messages and ten texts.

Call.

Come.

Now.

Oh shit!

She called her father.

"We've been trying to reach you." His voice was raspy. "Your mom is in trouble."

"What do you mean?"

"Her body shut down, a reaction to the treatment, shock, organ failure. I don't understand, but it's bad. They moved her next door to the hospital and she's tied up with tubes. She's asking for you."

"I just woke up. My phone was dead."

"Your mother could die."

No. *No.*

"I'll be there as soon as I can."

Shit, shit, *shit*. She was awake now. She should *never* have left her mother's side.

She had a phone charger for her car, but it wasn't *in* her car, so she left for the hospital with her phone at 2 percent charge.

While she was parking the car, her phone jangled. Her brother.

"Hello, I'm parking the car."

"Andrea. She's—" The connection broke. The phone died. She screamed and lurched the car forward, hitting the blue Lexus in front of her. Her airbags inflated, pushing her back against her seat. Both car alarms blared.

She shrieked, fought to free her arms, and grabbed a nail file from her purse to puncture the airbag. Then she squeezed out and raced into the hospital.

Her mother was dead by the time she arrived at her bedside.

19

Operates Power Tools with Painted Nails

Flying Star Cafe
Albuquerque, New Mexico
June 28, 2008

Saturday morning, Lamar met Diana, a.k.a. Paradoxical Dreamer, at the Flying Star Cafe. She said she'd be wearing a red top, and her hair was red too, but more like rust.

While waiting, and studying the tile on the walls, Lamar did some seated yoga—squeezing his glutes and kegels. His yoga teacher called kegel squeezes by their Sanskrit name—mula bandha—and said they were beneficial for women preparing for childbirth, and men who wanted better ejaculatory control.

Just in case he ever had sex again.

He wore his contacts. He had to get new glasses. The wire rims he had, well, a colleague said he looked like Gandhi. Sure, Gandhi was a hero and all, but that was not the look Lamar wanted to cultivate. Maybe if he was accepting the Nobel Peace Prize, but not for dating.

Diana was his first date in thirty years. Since he met

Janis. He had received three responses from his initial ten email forays, and the other two seemed wary about meeting in person, wanted more back and forth on email. Three for ten was excellent for a baseball hitter. Diana said she had been charmed by his note.

There she was. Red top. Red hair. The top brighter, redder than her hair, which was thick and unruly and sexy. He waved, stood to greet her.

In her profile, she had been more honest than most, admitting to being world-weary and rundown. "I look better with my clothes on than when I'm naked, but I'm still alive and laughing in between my aches and pains. I feel hot, but it could be menopause."

Her tagline was, "You must be present to win."

She was way overdressed for a balmy day—long sleeves, leg warmers under her skirt. Like they were going out to a meat locker. But she was tall and pretty and lively. That was enough.

No coffee, she said—her stomach couldn't handle the caffeine. No dairy, no wheat. On the phone, she'd stressed that eating in restaurants could be an adventure because she had "food issues." She ordered fresh-squeezed orange juice and Lamar asked for a latte.

"All this talk about food reminds me of one of my daughter's favorite stories, about two cannibals eating a clown. One asks the other, 'Does this taste funny to you?'"

What was he doing telling jokes? He'd already told her he had a grown daughter, but here it was again, in case she forgot. Of course, it had been a decade since Sierra told that joke. Probably longer.

"You're a comedian."

"Obviously not," he said, studying the menu board behind the counter. "But some people laugh at that."

"No, it's good. I don't hear enough jokes. You said you have a dog. What kind?"

They leaned against the wall waiting for their drinks. "A mutt. Half-lab, half shepherd, half we don't know. A dog and a half. She's living with my ex-wife, but I still think of her as my dog. I miss her." He stopped before he said, "more than my wife."

"I'm allergic to dogs. Cats too. I would drive you crazy."

He tried to pay for her drink, but she wouldn't let him. She thanked him when he pulled out her chair.

"You know, your letter," she said, "as much as one can be seen in a letter from a stranger, I felt seen. Like you read between the lines. I mean, I didn't say I was intense, but you got that. You used that word."

"It came across. In person even more."

"You're a psychologist. You pick up stuff like that? Do you use your psychology tricks for dating?"

"You mean, like listening?"

"I don't like to be judged. Live and let live."

"I would say that one of the most important qualities in being an empathetic therapist is not to judge. To accept. To see."

"Smart answer. You're doing great." She looked up as if seeking inspiration from the pendants hanging from the ceiling, then met his eyes as she finished her thought.

"I liked the line in your profile," he said, "about how you were remarkably honest and straightforward, except when you were too scared to be. That's honest. That's straightforward. Do you really operate power tools with painted nails?"

"Does a blender count?" she asked. "I do know my way around saws and drills, though I generally wear gloves."

They blabbed and bantered with an ease that was a

revelation to Lamar. He laughed more than he had in months. She talked about her work—she was a financial watchdog for the city. He wondered if she knew Sierra, who had been appointed to some city commission.

Diana ran her fingers through her hair, licked her lips. Lamar kept thinking of complimenting her on her hair, but he didn't want her to think he only cared about how she looked.

"So, you were married?" she asked.

"Twenty-seven years. I moved out last week. But like I said in my note, we've been separated for many years while living under the same roof."

"You didn't say *last week*."

"I said *recently*. Last week is recent."

"How many days ago?"

"What, you're worried it's too soon," he said, "that I want meaningless sex and I'm not ready for a meaningful relationship?"

"That's one way to say it."

"Look, I'm grateful to be talking to someone who makes talking fun. I'm not in a hurry."

He didn't need to go fast, as long as he was headed in the right direction.

"I've been doing this for too many years," she said, "and have met too many louses disguised as charming men."

Was she calling him charming? Or a louse? Didn't matter. He was here. They were talking. She was smiling, even if she was dressed for winter.

Then she stood up abruptly and said she had to go. He didn't want her to leave.

20

Drinking Poison and Expecting the Other Person to Die

Northbound Metra Commuter Train
Chicago, Illinois
January 20, 2016
5:50 pm

Andrea stepped off the escalator and there was the train, pulling to a stop. *What a horrible day at work.* She couldn't wait to get home and pour herself a vodka.

There, look, a window seat near the doors. She plopped herself down, pulled off her glasses, rubbed her eyes.

A man slid into the seat next to her.

"Hi Andrea. How are you doing? I've been trying to reach you."

Oh. My. God! Her brother. With his suitcase in his lap, trapping her in her seat. The suitcase wheels at her knees, wheels that had rolled through every flavor of filth. He had that phony kind-hearted look that he could turn off and on like a lightswitch. *What the hell was he doing here?*

She was *not* going to talk to him. That was the only way. She had been ignoring his calls, but never imagined he would stalk her on the train.

"I saw you on TV the other day," he said. She didn't detect any anger in his voice. Yet. "It would have been engaging if you hadn't been so *vicious* attacking your brother. The poor guy."

The woman in front of her had headphones over her ears. In front of Lamar was a man reading a magazine. *The Economist*, it looked like. Headlines in bright red type. She leaned toward Lamar.

"I'm not talking to you."

"That's going to make things better?"

"What are you doing here? On this train?"

"I'm here to see you," he said.

The train stopped at Clybourn and now it filled up. A large woman wearing a burka stood next to Lamar. Looked like she was pregnant. Andrea willed Lamar to stand up, give the woman his seat. He *would* if he were a gentleman.

The man reading *The Economist* stood, smiled, gesturing to his seat. The woman took it. The train picked up speed.

"You can't stay with us," Andrea said.

"I'm headed home tonight."

"Don't you fly from Midway?" Andrea asked. "This train is going to Barrington."

"Guess I'll need to switch trains," he said. "You must be missing Dad something fierce. I certainly am."

"I know—" Then she stopped, looked around. No one was paying them any attention. "I know what you did, and we'll be getting autopsy results any day now." They had warned her that the full results might take weeks, but Lamar didn't need to know that.

He didn't respond. But he heard. The train stopped again.

She couldn't stop recoiling from the suitcase wheels. There was no room on her right to move her knees. If she were nimble enough, she'd climb over him and his suitcase and bolt. But he would block her.

But really, Lamar was the one who was trapped. She was in control now. He couldn't bully her any more. With his suitcase or his lies.

"Those wheels," she said, pointing to his suitcase. "They're filthy and my work clothes are—"

"You want me to turn it around?" he asked. Which he did. As if he were doing her some big favor.

"Look, we miss Dad," he said, "but it's a blessing he didn't linger. He would have hated that."

"Blessing? For who? You're the one who couldn't stand it. He was fine a few weeks ago. We were talking about movies when we were on the treadmill. The Benjamin Button movie they showed at Edgewater, about the man who lives his life backwards. Dad got it. He understood it. He enjoyed it."

"So you think making my life more difficult is going to make yours better?"

"As a matter of fact, I do. I'm not going to say any more."

"I'm glad you saw that movie with Dad," Lamar said. "That he enjoyed it. Did you know that the movie is based on a short story by F. Scott Fitzgerald? It—"

"Do you know how condescending you are?" she asked. "Everytime you open your mouth. You think you're better than me, with your doctorate and your journals and your high-brow speaking engagements for that death cult you're in. I know my F. Scott Fitgerald. You don't know what it's like to struggle. You have it easy. You—"

"What?" Lamar was too loud. The pregnant woman adjusted her scarf. "Where do you get this idea that *I* have it easy?" Now he whispered. "Look, I'm a flawed person and I'm disappointed with how my life has played out. My daughter blames me for Janis, and now you—"

"Don't you play the victim game with me. Maybe if you had treated her better."

Lamar twitched. His knuckles whitened as he squeezed his hands together on top of his suitcase. "You may have heard the line," he said, through clenched teeth, "about how holding onto anger is like drinking poison and expecting the other person to die." He took a breath. "It's often attributed to Buddha, but he never said it."

He was livid, and trying to hide it. She was rarely successful piercing Lamar's more-serene-than-thou demeanor. She got him this time. But she was being unfair, she had to admit that.

"It wasn't your fault," said Andrea. "Janis was troubled. Sierra doesn't blame you. Neither do I."

There, that was better. See, she wasn't a mean person.

The announcer called the next stop. Norwood. "This is silly," he said. "Who has it worse? It's not a competition. Can't we agree it's tough to lose our parents? We're orphans. Do we need to make it worse by losing each other?"

"Worse for you, maybe. Better for me."

The train pulled into Edison Park. Two squat women huddled on the platform. A lone pigeon stood watch on the snow-covered roof.

"You know, if you're so certain I did it," he said, "why did you lie and say I admitted it to you? On TV. You know I didn't."

There he was with his word games again. What was he saying he didn't do? Admit it? Or that he didn't kill their father? What was he denying?

"You don't understand," Andrea said. "Dad and I were

closer than we'd ever been. I mean, you know, he was always so controlled, so tight, and he wasn't that way anymore."

"I do understand. I felt the same way. He became a different man. Not so closed."

There was her brother trying to pull her in again, but she wasn't going to let him.

"We have an investigator who's going to ferret out all the evidence," she said. "We know all about that conversation you had with the social worker, when you asked if they might *hasten* the end along for Dad. I believe that's called 'premeditation.'"

Lamar opened his mouth to respond, then slowly closed it. His Adam's apple wobbled.

"Evidence?" he asked. "Are you imagining some kind of trial? Put our family grief on public display? Do you want to hurt me that much? *And* yourself?"

She wasn't going to tell him anything more. He never took her seriously. He thought he could talk his way out of anything. Not this time.

"I believe this is my stop," he said, and stood up. Then he changed his tone, like nothing had happened. "You know, Andrea, you might want to do a bit more research about your friend Paula Merrill. You know her church is unapologetically anti-abortion, anti-choice. But I'm sure you know that. I'm sure you've done your homework."

"How do you know about her?" She *had* looked up Paula, and the church, but she wasn't converting or anything. It was a strategic alliance.

He wheeled his suitcase down the aisle, then turn back to her.

"You're not the only one with an investigator."

PART THREE

Luck Disguised as Ordinary Life

21

Bathroom Violations

Oakland, California
June 16, 2015

Kira woke with pain in her lower back, like most mornings, and she took long, deep breaths. Trying, hard as she could, to find ten seconds of peace to start her day. Before the accident, she prided herself on how much pain she could endure when she powered up steep Cool Springs Drive on her road bike. That was different pain. She chose it. Her legs had been lean and strong.

She gave up after a few minutes. Too much to do. Too many changes she had to make. Too sharp a pain to blot out with breathing.

Wennie, asleep beside her, would jump awake as soon as Kira stirred. She wished she could slip out of bed without rousing her.

She was so finished with Wennie. Why did she let this woman into her life? How was she going to get rid of her?

Kira went through four assistants before Wennie, and none lasted more than a month, and Wennie was, she had to admit, hard-working and ambitious. She made more money with Wennie than any of the others, even though there was no more low-hanging fruit.

She should *never* have let Wennie into her bed. That was her big mistake.

Wennie was no beauty queen. She was squat and chubby, but she had a flawless complexion and a can-do attitude. With her succinct answers and confidence, she had fooled Kira during her interview. Soon enough, Kira found out how limited her experience with paraplegics was, but by then she'd been hired, and she learned quickly.

There had been nothing premeditated about their romance, if that's what it was. Wennie was a tender masseuse—she didn't lie about that—and Kira soaked up her touching and affection like a dry sponge, and well, neither of them identified as lesbians, but who cared about labels anyway? The main thing was that Kira didn't want to be so dependent on Wennie.

Time to do her exercises. Find some distraction to keep her from emptying the medicine chest into a blender and ending it all.

She slid herself into the wheelchair on her own, but Wennie was out of bed before she'd righted herself. "Go back to sleep," Kira said. "I can get to my mat myself. I'll call for you if I need help."

"No, I'm ready to go. I'll make breakfast."

The doctors warned Kira that her legs would eventually get flabby, but that the muscles she'd grown from bicycling wouldn't disappear overnight. She had enjoyed being called a tall drink of water, and she used to wear skimpy dresses to show off her legs. Now she covered them up even when it was hot, because of the scars.

Wennie had taken advantage of her vulnerability, her

loneliness. Wennie had asked, "Do you like this? Do you want me to do more of this?" Part of her wanted to shout no, but instead she whispered, "Yes, *please.*" She had never had sex with a woman before and it was different. Not as exciting or ferocious as with a man, but in her condition, gentle was best. She couldn't move her lower body, but she could feel it.

What troubled her most about the relationship was that Wennie worked for Kira, and yet somehow she had the power in the relationship. That never happened with her other assistants. They feared Kira.

Today they were driving two hours to Brentwood, looking for restaurants and beauty parlors to sue. Wennie had four pages of printouts. It was more of a wild goose chase these days. The only places left were far away, and every dollar they earned in damages came with hostility, sob stories, or both. Not to mention hours in traffic.

They were on Highway 4 between Pittsburg and Antioch when Kira reached over and turned the radio off. "We have to talk," she said. "This is not working out."

Wennie kept her eyes on the road, but Kira saw her elbows lock, her jaw clench. "I'm right here, not going any-where," said Wennie. "Except Brentwood."

"That's the problem. You not going anywhere." Kira waited, but Wennie didn't say anything. She waited some more.

Wennie reached over to turn the radio back on. "I'm not going to do this for you."

Kira grabbed her hand before it reached the dashboard. "You drive. And listen." Wennie sat up straight and lifted her chin. She was a proud woman. This was not going to be easy.

The grass in the hills was still green, but not that deep

emerald it had been in February. Kira used to love this time of year the best, when the days were getting warmer and longer, but the hills were still verdant. Perfect biking weather.

"You know how hard this is for me," she said, "to be paralyzed, to be dependent, to have to squeeze out my livelihood from these poor saps who are barely hanging on. I'm a proud person, like you, and I made a mistake letting you in. To my bed, to my life, to my livelihood. You're smart and capable. You don't need me. You don't need me and I don't need you. I'm going to find someone new."

"You won't find anyone as good."

"I'm sure."

Kira told herself that she *could* move back home with her mother, but no, she couldn't. Her mother had bragged about her when she won that track race in Reno, as if she were the one on the bike. It was all about *her,* always. When they passed out the mothering genes, she had skipped out for a drink.

They were slowing down now, as they passed through Antioch, where a couple weeks earlier, they had found a strip mall without the legally required three feet of access next to the handicapped parking space. It was an ugly fight for a thousand dollars. They had to drive out there three times, plus two trips to the courthouse in Martinez. Wennie reminded her that all their driving was deductible.

They took the Lone Tree exit and started on the restaurants and small businesses near the big box stores. Brentwood was a newish bedroom community, built on the alluvial plain of the delta and surrounded by cherry and peach orchards, and the ubiquitous fields of corn.

They had their routine down. First, they'd check out the parking, but in Brentwood, the pickings were slim. Then

Wennie would push Kira into a restaurant in her wheelchair, where they'd order coffee and ask to use the bathroom. That was their bread and butter.

The first four establishments didn't yield anything, but the fifth, a Mexican restaurant where they ordered enchiladas for lunch, did. Wennie was able to wheel Kira into the bathroom, but once inside, there was no room to turn the chair around. Kira was reaching for her camera when she heard the click of Wennie's phone.

"I want you to try to get out of the chair onto the toilet," she said.

"You enjoy this, don't you?" said Kira.

"We're helping enforce the law, like you say."

Kira could explain, in a minute, how the success of the Americans with Disabilities Act depended on people like her bringing suit to enforce it, but Wennie knew that already. But the way Wennie rejoiced when they found a violation made Kira shudder. Wasn't the point *not* to find any violations because everyone was obeying the law?

But that wasn't it. It wasn't what Wennie was saying or not saying. It wasn't Wennie's enthusiasm for the tedious job. It was Wennie herself. How deeply she had insinuated herself into Kira's life. That's what she could no longer stand for. Or sit for. Whatever.

"This is a family business," said Kira. "The kids are working the kitchen. They're going to spend money they don't have to fix this and they're going to hate us, and—"

"You're doing that self-loathing crap again. Stop. This is why you need me."

"I have a right to question my actions," said Kira. "It's not like this is our only option."

"This is what you hired me for."

"No, I hired you to be my assistant, and you've taken

this on like a crusade. Like you single-handedly are going to make the world better for gimps."

"Smile for the camera." She took two more photos. Kira didn't smile, but it was better that way. Wennie said that just to goad her.

"You're going to do well in law school," Kira said. "I'll give you that."

The owner, a wiry and fidgety man with graying hair and smooth English, brought them their enchiladas and introduced himself. "First time here?"

He smiled broadly when Kira answered him in Spanish. The food was forgettable, but Kira left a large tip.

22

Mr. Graduate Student Big Shot

Schaumburg, Illinois
January 20, 2016
7:05 pm

Andrea bundled up for the two-minute walk from the Barrington Station to her car, but couldn't avoid getting the shivers. And then, when she got home, she couldn't get the damn garage door open. It was frozen closed. She had to call Drew, who had already put his mukluks on, and then wait until he got dressed in all his layers, and it took him forever with that long-handled scraper to dislodge enough ice to open the door.

Once inside, she was not in the mood for being interrogated. Drew had been asking questions, trying to undermine her confidence. Repeating the qualms about tearing the family apart.

He had cooked a pizza from the freezer and pulled it from the oven hot and steamy. He asked her how her day was. She could handle that kind of question. Though she was not about to tell him about being trapped by Lamar on the Metra.

"Roger, my asshole boss, went behind my back and assigned Adarsh, one of my people, a project, and I marched into his office and confronted him. Politely, even though I was furious. He waved off my concern. 'Oh, I'm sure I mentioned it. We're on fast track. All hands on deck.' Then he gets all gentle and leans over his desk and says, 'I want to say again how *sorry* I am for your loss.' What a manipulative bastard. Feign compassion, and, oh, look, now we've changed the subject.

"No, he had not mentioned the assignment to me, and he knew it."

Drew didn't listen to her complaints about work. He let her vent, she gave him credit for that. The cocky youngsters had no use for her, as if she weren't their boss. They called her a dinosaur behind her back. They didn't care how hard she worked, how loyal she had been, how many new security protocols she'd learned. They couldn't wait to get rid of her, but she had to hang on for five more years.

She heard the familiar Bach Inventions ditty on the iPad—a call from Sully. Of course, Drew put him up to this. So his way. Passive-aggressive.

Drew set up the iPad on the kitchen table. Their son's face took up most of the screen, his big hair hanging over his forehead, ears. Closer on the tablet than they ever talked in real life. She had a hard enough time getting him to cut his hair when he lived at home. Now it was hopeless.

"How you doing, Doctor Glenn?" Drew said.

"I said I *might* do the PhD. First, the Master's." Sullivan, their twenty-five-year-old son, was a graduate student in electrical engineering at the University of Illinois in Champaign-Urbana, where Drew had gone as an undergrad. He was a good kid, though not good at being humble. With a Master's in electrical engineering, he was going places, and he made sure everyone knew.

"Mom, *what* is going on?" he said. "All of a sudden, you're going reality TV on us, and it's our family, our reality. We're all over the news. And Dad said you hired an investigator to go after Uncle Lamar. I mean, *what the fuck?*"

"Stop." She hit the mute button and turned the iPad screen upside down on the table. Grabbed Drew on the arm. "What the hell are you doing, turning Sully against me? You have no right."

"He's asking you a question. If your skin is so thin, if you can't handle a question from your son, you're certainly not prepared to do battle out there in the cruel world."

"'What the fuck' is not a question."

"Tell him the truth. Tell *me* the truth. It's not like we can stop you from hurting yourself and everyone around you if that's what you're determined to do."

Andrea felt cornered. But Drew was right about the thick skin. It wasn't as if she was a stranger to criticism. She weathered it at work all the time. She poured another glass of red wine, took a generous gulp, then turned the iPad over and unmuted it.

"Let me explain," she said. "You know, of course, that your grandfather was suffering. The cancer, for sure—the pain was so intense sometimes, it would immobilize him. But he had drugs that helped with that. It was the dementia he struggled with the most. I was helping him with that. We got him a good social worker, arranged plenty of visits from his friends. More recently, the hospice people came to visit. Your father and I, *and* your uncle, spent a lot of time with him. Sierra came to see him before Christmas. He was only disoriented *some* of the time. We watched movies and he was able to pay attention to them, noticed things I didn't even notice. You know the first Harry Potter movie. He said to me, why didn't Harry do whatever, I can't remember. The plot was too complicated for me. He found a hole in the plot I hadn't noticed."

"I was there, Mom, I know. It was *me*, not Grandpa who brought that up. But what does this have to do with Lamar? You don't really believe that—?"

"Yes, I do. We have four pieces of evidence that, together, add up to a very convincing case. Already. He was the last person to see Dad, and they usually check on everyone after the visitors leave, but it was that polar vortex week and some of the staff didn't make it in, so there's that. Two— you haven't heard this on the news—is that the police found your uncle wandering down Winthrop in the middle of the night, disoriented, not even aware that it was twenty below. The night Grandpa died. Which is consistent with dissociation, the result of doing something that puts you into shock. He snapped out of it, but—"

"Mom, you got nothing. I assume you're saving your best cards."

"OK, well, the most damning thing is that, well, there's several pieces to this. One is, I was able to get his browsing history, because, long story, but you know how Chrome saves the cookies and you can find the history even from another machine. So the history had these visits to this Australian site that sells nitrogen tanks for euthanasia—"

Sully broke in. "I heard all that—on that Freedom Channel clip. You—"

"They say it's for making beer, the nitrogen, but that's a front. Now we're looking for credit card bills—"

"But Mom, how did you get Lamar's browsing history? Wouldn't you—oh, never mind. It doesn't matter."

"Would you believe I was able to guess his password?

Our address in Los Alamos."

"Mom, I don't mean to tell you what to do," said Sully, "but you can't just make these accusations and think there aren't going to be consequences, for the family at the least."

"New rule, Mr. Graduate Student Big Shot. Saying 'I don't mean to tell you what to do' does *not* give you license to tell me what to do."

She was proud of her son, and he had a bright future, though she worried that, despite his high opinion of himself, he hadn't had a girlfriend for some time. She wondered if that had anything to do with her.

"You're a long way from here," she said, "and you didn't grow up with your uncle, like I did. Oh, there's also the security camera from the loading dock, showing a man bundled up against the cold leaving the building at two something in the morning. Besides, the train has left the station. Even if I backed off, it would keep on rolling.

"Your uncle left me to deal with your grandfather on my own, and that was no picnic. I would visit him and try to make conversation and ask him questions and he would clam up and not say anything. He never asked about me or my life. He thought I was just an emotional ninny, that expressing your feelings was a sign of weakness. He only let down his guard because of the dementia. If it would have been up to him, he would have stayed cold like a statue till the end."

"But Mom, I don't get why you're attacking Lamar. Back off. You can—" He stopped, scratched his head, and leaned back so now she could see his upper body, not just his face. He was wearing that Cubs sweatshirt she bought him for Christmas. Well, that was something. A small victory. When he moved out for college and she cleaned out his closet, she found four or five presents that she had given him still in the original box. Never opened. Never worn.

"I thought I should at least try," he said, his voice resigned. "I just don't want this to turn into a civil war in our family. I don't want to mess up my relationship with Sierra. Now, if you don't mind, I've got a linear dynamics lecture to unpack. Love to you both. Over and out."

Drew didn't say anything, but he left the kitchen table, and went upstairs to take a shower. At least he was clean.

23

Splatter

Madrid, New Mexico
June 28, 2008

Lamar planned to wash the walls and ceiling of his Madrid cabin before painting them, but the woman at the paint store said that wasn't necessary. Today's paints, she said, would cover most surfaces unless they were greasy or chalky.

He wiped the surfaces with a damp rag, covered the floor with drop cloths, then stood on a chair and glided a roller of eggshell white above his head. A little luster.

He found CDs he forgot he had and played them loud. The Ramones. The Police. Not his usual, soothing classical sounds.

He was in such high spirits. He couldn't remember the last time he felt this light, this bouncy. He felt guilty at first, but what was wrong with feeling good? Painting the ceiling was tough on his neck, but it was quick work, and didn't require his full attention, so he could replay his date with Diana that morning.

Pretty great, he told himself. Better even than his inflated expectations. Lamar Rose on a date with a lovely and intelligent woman.

No, it was not love across a crowded café, and yes, she had her prickly moments, but they kept up their lively conversation, and there *seemed* to be a genuine connection, an attraction that, if not mutual, *might* be. She couldn't have faked *all* those smiles.

Sure, she was on the lookout for danger signs, walking through her checklist. Women had to be cautious. Of course she was suspicious of how recent his breakup was. But what was he supposed to do, sit around and wait? He'd been waiting for years.

He didn't want to get ahead of himself. One step at a time. Did he want to see her again? Yes. That was enough for now. He would write a brief thank you email, then call her in a day or two. He didn't want to appear too anxious.

As happy as he was about Diana, and excited about painting his new home, he couldn't stop worrying about the phone calls he had to make to his daughter and his parents. He had put them off too long.

As soon as he finished the ceiling, he put on his headset, made a few quick passes on the rough wood walls with a thick-napped roller, and called Sierra.

He took a deep breath and inhaled the sweet smell of wet paint. There was something promising about that smell. A new beginning. A clean slate.

He had rehearsed what he was going to say—it was a damn big effing deal, telling her he left her mother. No mystery why he'd been avoiding the call.

Maybe his life needed work, but he still had the discipline to push himself through.

Through was the only way. There was no going *around* this conversation.

Sierra didn't even say hello. "I call the house to tell you guys I'm coming home and Mom says, 'He left.' 'What do you mean, left?' I say, 'Left you?' She says yes, that you were supposed to tell me."

"That's why I'm calling," he said, "but wait, what's this about you coming home?"

He had planned to keep on painting, but he had to concentrate—his daughter could be pretty intense—so he put the roller in the pan and found a spot on the dropcloth to sit.

"Don't change the subject," she said.

"It's a long story and I—"

"I don't have time to talk now. You and Mom didn't even argue."

"We did," he said, "but arguing was not the problem. It was showing up and—"

"I *am* coming home, and *you* have some major explaining to do. But not now."

She told him about her new job, something about working for Barack Obama, not for him per se, but for some coalition that supported him. She started in a week. Now that she was talking, and he didn't have to be on guard, he went back to the painting. Didn't want the paint to dry on the roller. Sierra spoke fast, as she often did, but still enunciated every consonant.

"You cannot dump Mom on me," she continued. "This is a 24-7 job I've signed on for. I will not be available to babysit. I *was* going to stay with you guys. I thought that would make things easier. Now you won't be there. Now—"

"You don't have to stay with Mom. You—"

"I have a deadline, like, yesterday. I can't talk now. Why didn't you tell me what was going on?"

He scrunched his face in the most incredulous look as he

could muster, but of course, she was on the phone, thousands of miles away. "When have you ever made it easy for me to tell you anything?" he said.

"Well, now you have. Except you didn't. Mom did. With no warning."

She didn't even ask where he was staying. She was a great kid, but sometimes way too caught up in herself.

"Oh, there were so many warnings," he said.

After the call with Sierra, he finished the fourth wall and now the first one was dry. He stood three feet from the wall, dipped an old toothbrush into a yogurt container, one part clear glaze, one part warm olive green. Then he flicked his wrist.

Before Sierra was born, he and Janis had splatter-painted her nursery, and he was excited to be doing it again. Making his vanilla cabin bright and lively.

He called his parents before he could talk himself out of it.

His mother answered. He barely let her say hello. "Hi Mom, I left Janis and moved out."

Then he waited. Dipped the toothbrush and spattered.

"Oh my goodness." He could hear her sigh.

"That's the short version," he added.

"What about Janis? How is she? I mean, if things are so bad you have to leave, how will she manage?"

His mother cared about Janis. His parents had moved to Illinois before Sierra was born, but his mom came to stay in New Mexico for more than a month, and witnessed first hand how depressed Janis was after her delivery. In many ways, Janis bonded with her mother-in-law better than with her new daughter. But then a baby has no sympathy for a depressed mother.

"I know what you're saying, Mom. I do. I intend to

continue looking after her. But I'm not going to be married to her anymore. I'm not going to live with her anymore."

"You're not going out with other women?" Sort of a question, sort of a reprimand.

"I had a coffee date yesterday. My first."

He had not intended to talk about his dating, but it was best that she understood, even if she disapproved. Honesty was *usually* the best path.

"I know you've put in a lot of years without getting much back," she said. "But it's too soon. You don't want to rush into anything foolish."

"Rush? Mom, I've postponed this for years. Decades."

"You didn't tell me things were *that* bad."

"I guess I didn't. But I told you it's been tough. A couple times."

He had, but he had framed it more as a challenge he had to struggle with, not something he had to escape from. Mostly, he had kept his despair to himself, not wanting to worry his parents, not wanting anyone to talk him out of his decision to leave.

"I need you in my corner, Mom. It's one date I've been on. One cup of coffee. One hour. I appreciate that you care for Janis. I do. I care for her too. Enough about me. How are you? How's Dad?"

"That's a good question." At first, he thought she sounded angry, but it was more annoyed.

"Is Dad there? I want to tell him too." He didn't know what his father would say, if anything.

"I'll tell him," she said, "when he gets home."

"That's not *your* responsibility, to be the bearer of my news. When will he be home?"

"To tell you the truth," she said, "I don't know. He does that math tutoring thing in the afternoon, but that was over hours ago. And you know your father—he doesn't, well, even when he's here, he's not here."

For a moment, he considered probing deeper—years earlier, more than once, he had drawn his mother out about how distant his father was. Even over the phone, Lamar could smell trouble. But he didn't have any empathy left in the tank.

24

We Never Meant to Hurt You

Schaumburg, Illinois
January 23, 2016

Andrea called in sick, slept late, holed up at home.

Outside, it was sunny, but still cold. The barren trees glistened in the sun. Ice was everywhere.

After breakfast, she bundled up and padded in her furry slippers and wool socks to the sun room, where it was at least ten degrees colder, and planted broccoli, bok choy, tomato, melon, squash, and pumpkin seedlings in egg cartons. She had ordered seeds early in the new year, and every few days another box of seed packets arrived, and she tossed them in the gray bucket in the corner.

Sully had claimed the sun room when he was a teenager, and hung out here with his friends, but once he left for college, Andrea took it over for her garden. Most years, she didn't start planting until March.

She ignored her phone messages and emails. The requests for interviews and TV spots kept coming in. But the media had done fine without her for fifty years. They could do without her this morning.

After an hour planting seeds, she traipsed back into the warm house and sat down with a box of her father's papers. She'd had them since he moved from his apartment into the memory care unit, but she hadn't sorted through even half of them. It hadn't felt right going through his papers while he was still alive.

Most of the papers were not personal, and not even her father's. There were as many of her mother's papers in the box as his. But even reading their bank statements, she got emotional, felt closer to her parents.

As she tossed more papers in the bag for shredding, she found a card from Brigid to her mother. No date.

> *Celeste, my best friend in the world.*
> *I'm sorry. We never meant to hurt you.*
> *Love, Brigid.*

The photo on the card showed two elephant calves entangled with each other in a mud puddle. So sweet it could make you diabetic. Her mother would have loved the card. The photo anyway.

We never meant to hurt you. It sounded like Brigid and her father had an affair, which her mother had claimed one morning many years earlier, then never mentioned again.

Andrea was going to get some answers. She drove to Edgewater.

Brigid gave Andrea a big hug when she opened the door, but there was a wariness there, too. Like, what the hell are you doing here?

This had been her parents' apartment, on the 16th floor, with a sliver of a lake view. After her mother died, her father lived in the apartment himself for a couple years before Brigid moved in with him. Most of the windows faced south and southwest, so the big, airy living room could be blazing hot on summer afternoons. Not today.

"You know I've been trying to organize, purge Dad's papers," Andrea said, standing with her coat on, her hands gripping the back of a kitchen chair. "I am his executor and I found some letters of Mom's. That he kept. Letters *to* Mom. I don't know if he ever dug through the boxes like I'm doing. Anyway, there's a letter from you that I can't stop thinking about."

Andrea studied Brigid's shoulders as she scooped coffee into a filter. She thought she saw a momentary shiver, but Brigid quickly busied herself with rinsing out the carafe and filling it with cold water.

"I don't remember your mother and I writing letters." Andrea couldn't see Brigid's face. She seemed to be pouring the water into the coffeemaker as slowly as possible. "We were so close. Same building. Same wing."

"You had an affair."

"With Robert? Never." She laughed. "I mean, not back then. Not while Celeste was alive."

She spoke without hesitation, but Andrea could tell she was lying. There was a confidence that didn't seem right. She wished she had confronted her father about this, back when her mother had made the accusation. Not that he would have answered.

Andrea pulled out the card and placed it on the table. Facing Brigid. Unopened. The coffeemaker gurgled.

On the kitchen wall was a black-and-white print in a sil ver frame. Lamar and Andrea as kids. Mud on their cheeks. Hair sticking up like punk rockers. Silly grins on their faces. Andrea must have been about four. She'd seen the photo a million times, but had no memory of that day. Brigid hadn't moved any of the family photos, but then she had decorated the apartment long before she moved in.

Brigid sat down slowly, picked up the card and smiled at the elephants on the front, then opened it. Andrea took off her coat and put it over the chair.

"My sweet Andrea," said Brigid. "I imagine you perceived your parents had a good marriage, and they did, but it was not all chocolate and roses. Your mother told me a lot. We were all friends, the three of us—Dick had died by the time your parents moved here—and your mother was my *best* friend in the world. I would *never* have betrayed Celeste. And I would *never* lie to you."

Brigid got up again, and poured coffee into a red mug with a small gold butterfly. "This was your mother's. The cup. I bet you miss your mom even more than I do."

"There's no one else I can talk to like I talked to her," Andrea said. Of course she missed her mother. But she wasn't going to let Brigid squirm out of this by changing the subject. "There was this one time when Mom said—"

Brigid jumped up. "Let's go to Celia's. It was your mother's favorite place."

"But our coffee—"

"I'm hungry. Besides, it's practically balmy outside."

At first Andrea felt relieved. They would be in public. She wouldn't break down. But she wanted to talk privately. Brigid was putting on her coat. Well, Celia's was noisy. No one would hear them.

As the waitress led them to their table, someone tugged at Andrea's coat sleeve.

"Excuse me, I'm sorry to bother you." It was a small elderly woman. "I saw you on the television a couple days ago and I want to express my condolences. How horrible for you that your father was murdered. I appreciate what you're doing—this killing old people is going too far."

"Thank you," said Andrea, then she rushed to catch up with Brigid.

Andrea waited until after the waiter handed them their menus. "That was nice to hear," she said. "Someone complimenting me. About what I said on TV. Mostly what I'm hearing is people telling me how terrible I am."

"People?" Brigid peeked over the top of the menu.

"My husband. My son. My brother."

"Telling you how terrible you are."

"Yes. Paula, too. The woman from the church in Barrington. I don't know why I agreed to this. They're taking my grief and turning it into clicks and donations. There's a photo of me, poor little orphan me, on the home page of the Force for Life site—the group Paula works for. At first, I thought she was a volunteer, helping me, but no, she's staff. She gave me the impression she would be working for me, but it feels like the other way around. I haven't been answering her calls. They want me to do more TV. I owe it to Dad to see this through."

"You have a right to be upset," said Brigid, then the waiter approached. They gave him their orders. Which included a bottle of chianti.

Brigid reached across the table and placed her hands on Andrea's. "How honest do you want me to be?"

"So you agree Lamar did it," said Andrea.

"I don't believe your father would enjoy seeing his children at war," said Brigid. "Do you?" For the first time, Brigid looked annoyed instead of sympathetic. Andrea wasn't sure. Brigid was holding her wine glass in front of her mouth.

"Mom would have supported me," Andrea said.

Brigid kept her eyes on her bowl and chewed her linguine slowly. She claimed she didn't take sides, but

Andrea knew she favored Lamar.

After she put down her fork, drank her wine, and checked the nearby tables, Brigid leaned forward.

"So this *affair*," she said, "it was a lot more complicated—"

"*Affair?* You said you would never lie to me—"

"I *did* have an affair with Robert, sort of, but if only it were that simple. First of all, you have to keep any lurid thoughts at bay. It was not about the sex. I'm not an adventurous person. I found your parents, latched on. Are you sure you want to hear this?"

Andrea nodded. Poured more wine into her glass.

"They weren't having sex with each other, your parents, for a good while. They *were* in their sixties, and, you know, couples get out of the habit. Not that I'm an expert. Anyway, I was *recruited*, in some *strange, unspoken* way, to bring them back together. It didn't work out, because Celeste got sick and died, so she and your father did not live happily ever after."

"You had sex with my dad?" Andrea said. She was having trouble taking this in.

"I can't tell you how it came about, because it's fuzzy to me, but it started when Robert was sleeping on my couch. He said he needed a break, but I believe Celeste threw him out. She never admitted that. I connected the dots. Where else could he go? He didn't have friends."

"Mom kicked Dad out and you had sex with him?"

"Oh, honey, it was two old friends being a little more than friendly. It probably didn't even count as sex, but it *was* lovemaking, or it felt like it. Whatever we did, whatever you want to call it, it was *special*. There was jealousy, but not as much as you might think. Celeste knew I liked Robert."

"Mom knew?"

Andrea was more upset now than when she stormed out

of her house, but now Brigid said she was tired and didn't want to talk about the past. That wasn't fair.

Then, for some strange reason, Andrea flashed on the time she hid at the top of the stairs and eavesdropped on her parents arguing. All she remembered was what her mother said. "You check out whenever it suits you. I don't have that luxury, do I? Would you even notice if I left? Maybe when you ran out of groceries."

She walked Brigid back to her apartment, telling her more about the TV appearance and how everyone had dumped on her afterwards. They stood in the foyer just off the living room. Andrea needed to leave, to sit with this new knowledge, but she also didn't want to go.

She had come here to accuse Brigid, not to seek comfort, but that's what she wanted now.

"I can't do this anymore." Andrea slumped, as if her legs gave way, and Brigid grabbed her and pulled her into a hug. Andrea resisted at first—Brigid was not her mother and never would be. But then she let go and fell into Brigid's arms. Almost knocked her over.

"Steady there," said Brigid, into Andrea's ear. "We both miss Robert. We both miss Celeste."

"I talked with her every day," said Andrea. "My mom." She didn't want to cry, but here came the tears.

"Andrea, call me anytime. Come by anytime."

"Why didn't you tell me this before? On top of all that Lamar has done. It's too much."

She sounded so melodramatic. She decided she would say no to more TV. That would be better. Back to blessed anonymity.

"It wasn't my responsibility to tell you," said Brigid. "If your mother or father didn't tell you, why should I?"

25

Broken Branches After a Storm

Santa Fe, New Mexico
July 1, 2008

Tuesday afternoon, Lamar set Skip—and himself—free.

He was as resolute as with Janis. This was easier. This was business. There was no TV to unplug.

He moved the chairs further apart than usual, dispensed with small talk. "This will be our last session," he said.

When he shooed Skip out the door, after more than an hour of talking and an awkward, but heartfelt hug, Lamar said, "I'm proud of you." He stood holding the doorjamb until his heartbeat returned to normal, then he wrapped his arm around his shoulder and gave himself a pat on the back. He was proud of himself, too.

That pleasant feeling didn't last. He checked his messages, hoping for one from Diana. He had left a voicemail for her Sunday night saying he'd love to see her again.

Her message was apologetic, but unambiguous. No.

He called her. Immediately. Grabbed the hassock he hid

behind his desk, and stretched his legs onto its worn leather haunches.

She picked up.

"Hi, it's Lamar. I got your message. Do you want to hear my spiel about why we should get together again, or should I save it for never?"

She hesitated. He heard her shallow breaths in the receiver.

"I enjoyed meeting you," she said. "I had fun. But you want a date, and I want a mate. You split up with your wife, what, five days ago? A week? You've got danger signs sticking out your ears. Your child is grown. I don't have time to waste."

"Is that what this is about? Wanting to have a child?"

"I was clear about that in my profile."

He *had* noted that, but it hadn't come up in their conversation at the café. He had thought of asking, but hadn't.

"I understand," he said. "You don't want to squander your limited time. But I suppose wasting time is *exactly* what I need to do now, *want* to do now—it's just that I was hoping I could waste it with you."

She laughed. "Now that—"

A knock on the door.

"Can you hold a sec?" He muted himself, opened his office door. Skip again.

He waved Skip away, pointed to his phone.

"Please," Skip said. "I have one more—"

Lamar mouthed no and closed the door in Skip's face. He didn't slam it. He felt bad for Skip.

He unmuted the phone. "You still there?"

She was.

"You have to understand," she said. "I've been here before, with another nice man who wasn't ready, and I wish

I had that year back. You're a decent man, even—I hope you're not offended—gentle."

"Why would I be offended?"

"I don't know. Men are sometimes so concerned about being manly. I give you credit—you didn't give me grief for leaving a voicemail. I've had guys yell at me for that, call that 'breaking up,' because I'm not up for a second date. Sorry, but no is no. I have to go."

"You sure know how to turn a man down nice," he said.

"I'm going to hang up now," she said. And then she did.

He felt strangely exhilarated. Something happened there. He sold himself. It was like he said to his clients: The doing is what counts. Acting is its own reward.

He was discouraged too, but that beat despair. He'd been dreaming of meeting women for years, but hadn't acted. Diana kept him on his toes, so different than walking on eggshells with Janis. In turning Lamar down, in that five-minute phone conversation, Diana gave him more engagement than Janis had in months.

■ ■ ■

The next morning, Lamar drove to the airport to pick up his daughter. He was late.

He was never late. He had no excuse except that he left late, and you didn't need to be a psychologist to see what that was about.

Once he helped Sierra pile her bags in the car, and they left the airport, he got her talking about her new job, which she was clearly excited about. It felt good to see his daughter doing so well.

The plan was to bring her to his cabin in Madrid, then back to town to pick up takeout for dinner with Janis at the house on Coal Avenue. Sierra was going breakneck about how she'd have to rebuild this dysfunctional coalition and she looked up as the road ducked under the freeway heading north.

"Dad, *where* are we going?"

They passed a new subdivision full of beige stucco ranch homes, then suddenly, there was nothing but shrubs and sky.

"Madrid. My shotgun shack. We're on the Turquoise Trail."

"Madrid? Isn't that, like a ghost town? That's where they had that prison riot, right, where the inmates took guards hostage?"

"Madrid is south of the prison," he said. "You've been there. Artists and hippies. We got your chili ristras there."

"What is a shotgun shack anyway?"

"A shotgun shack, says Professor Rose, is a small house that has no walls inside, so if a bullet were fired through the front door, it would go right out the back without hitting a wall. I looked it up. It's actually a corruption of the word "shogon," which means God's house, and comes from Africa, then Haiti, then New Orleans, and I'm sure you wish you hadn't asked."

"You'll do anything to avoid this conversation, won't you?"

He started telling Sierra the story he'd been telling himself, about how he had to leave Janis to save his life.

"I care for your mother. I do. I take marriage seriously. But there's a difference between the unconditional love I have for you and what I feel for your mother, which is conditional love. I'm going to love you no matter what. I want you to love me too, but if you don't, well, I'm never going to stop loving you or being your father. It's not a choice I have to make. I can't imagine not loving you.

"But I can't live a healthy life married to your mother. I can't heal her. I can only heal myself. I apologize for not consulting with you, but this has nothing to do with you."

Sierra sighed. Loudly. "Except now that I'm here, it does."

"You're right," he said. "Of course. This changes things for you too."

As he delivered his truth, as close as he could, he watched her face. As much as he could while driving. She didn't give much away.

Half an hour later, he took his foot off the gas as the road took a sharp curve toward a cluster of brightly painted buildings. Madrid. His new home.

"There's the Mine Shaft Tavern where I met some folks a few weeks ago. It's pretty much the community center. I had coffee there this morning."

He turned off the highway up a spur road, pointed out the mailbox jungle, and then pulled into the driveway next to his weather-beaten house.

He pushed open the door. Wow, it was bright inside. Light poured in through the west-facing windows, and the splatter-painted walls looked spectacular. Still the fresh paint smell, but Sierra said she liked it.

He had transformed the cabin in three days. Still spartan, but clean and colorful. He had even hooked up the TV and DVD player.

"I love the walls," she said. "Especially the orange drips."

"Wild, huh? Well, my plan was spots, not drips, but Greta, my landlady, came by and said she preferred the drips. I had been wiping them, then I stopped. My plan was two colors, then I added the gold, the orange. I might have gone for more, but you were coming home and I wanted to be finished."

"That's a lot of work," she said. "Are you going to stay here? I mean, it's small. What if you change your mind? Did you have to sign a lease?"

He set out a plate of crackers and brie and poured her a glass of the orange-carrot juice she liked. He pulled a folded index card from his back pocket. "A list here so I don't forget anything."

He gave her a chance to ridicule him, but she didn't, so he checked his notes and continued.

"I've been eating lunch or dinner with your mother a couple times a week and I plan to continue with that. I'm paying the mortgage and the bills. We're not legally separated or divorced. There's a house cleaner in there once a week and I'll hire a gardener if we need to. I'll continue seeing clients in the basement office. You know, your mother is no longer seeing clients."

"But why did you move?" she asked. "You love the house, the garden. Mom doesn't care about it the way you do."

"I brought that up, said we should figure out who lives where, to which she said something like 'after all you've done to me, I'll be damned if you kick me out of my house too.' Actually those were her exact words. They're seared in my mind."

Sierra shrunk into her shoulders.

"I should have kept that to myself," Lamar said. "Sorry."

"What did you *do* to her?"

"I don't know. Called her on her shit? Withdrew? I know she's got an illness and I'm sure it's worse than I can imagine, but you can discipline yourself. Sixty percent of success is showing up—putting one foot in front of the other. She says I think she's lazy when in fact she's depressed. But you can be depressed and still suck it up and go through your paces. Other people do. She's on medication, for Christ's sake. Though she doesn't always take it."

"You married her for better or for worse," Sierra said. "Now you're bailing to have your midlife crisis. You better not go chasing young women now, you with your new earring and all that. I've been hit on by men your age. It creeps me out. You don't want to be that creep."

Lamar chose not to respond to that, though he thought of telling her about his one date, with Diana, who was forty-one, eight years younger than he was. Not in the creepy category. But Diana was history.

"Remember you used to complain I treated you like a child?" he said. "I'm not doing that now. You are a grownup who can make up her own mind."

"Grown up enough I don't need you to tell me that."

She folded her arms across her chest.

"You have to understand," she said. "I have an important job that is *already* stressing me out and it's going to take *everything* and then some. Mom is a black hole. She'll swallow me up. You *can't*."

"Mija, do you hear yourself? Do you hear what you're saying, the black hole? I was married to her, I get it. I was thinking of *myself*, not of you."

Sierra bit her lip, then reached for the crackers.

Lamar waited until she had calmed down, then spoke slowly and calmly. "From the earliest age, you rarely wanted my advice, so I learned to listen, encourage, and, mostly, keep my mouth shut. For you, the best recipe. You're an amazing young woman, and you've been making a positive mark on the world for many years. But I'm going to give a little speech here, and you need to listen.

"I'm not asking you to give up your life, only to carve out *some* space for us. I'm sure you're correct that who wins this election is extremely consequential, the direction of the country and all that. I get that. But your mother is important too. She's hurting and I can't help her. You don't have to *stay* with her. You don't have to *fix* her. Live your life. Win your election. But check in on her. Keep an eye and an ear on her. Say hello. See if she engages. Now and then she does. She still knows how to talk."

"I have a hard enough time talking with her on the phone," Sierra said, but her tone was respectful. Humble even. She heard him. He thought of adding that he could use a bit of attention as well, but he didn't.

They drove back to the city listening to a "Wait, Wait, Don't Tell Me" podcast, with a front row seat for a blazing pink and orange sunset. They picked up dinner at El Patio and drove to the house that Sierra had lived in since she was four.

At the front door, Lamar stepped back so Sierra could enter first.

"Mom, it's me," Sierra said, but there was no answer. Lamar held his breath.

Caro bounded toward them, her tail wagging furiously, and Sierra raised her knee to keep her from jumping on her. But Caro went to Lamar first, poking her head between his legs as he closed the door.

Lamar had walked into the house so many times with tightness in his throat and dread in his stomach and he told himself it was just one more false alarm. Yes, it felt more intense, but he'd spent the weekend painting in Madrid and this house felt less like home.

Sierra took the stairs two at a time, Caro at her heels. "Mom, I'm home," she shouted.

Then she screamed. Lamar raced up to the bedroom.

Janis lay on her back in the middle of the bed, an orange

pill bottle on her chest, and her arms splayed on the blanket like broken branches after a storm. Sierra shook her mother's shoulders.

"Mom, mom, *MOM!*"

26

Radio Free Berkeley

KRFB Radio Station
Berkeley, California
January 25, 2016

Wennie wheeled Kira up the ramp outside KRFB radio station, Radio Free Berkeley, a red stucco building off University Avenue. The past two days in Berkeley had been sunny, but it had drizzled overnight, and the temperature plummeted. The ramp was slippery and the chair lurched sideways. Kira started to howl in panic, but Wennie righted the chair and the top of the ramp was dry. Kira gulped the cold air greedily as they headed inside.

In the waiting room was a man wearing a pale blue pork-pie hat and a stud in one ear, who sprang to his feet to greet them. Lamar Rose looked pretty much like the photo she'd seen on the web—intelligent perhaps, or at least thoughtful, and able-bodied. But not tough. Soft, sensitive, sheltered. She would eat him alive.

They were in a wide hall with comfy couches and coffee tables along one wall and a small stage with two music stands near the wall, one higher than the other. They looked like cartoon characters. Behind an interior window, a woman with a gray ponytail sat behind a microphone digging through her purse. The music playing was somewhere between classical and jazz, with strings and horns and piano. A bright, sunny sound on this gray winter morning.

When Lamar Rose introduced himself, Kira said, "I know who you are."

"Don't believe everything you've read," he said. He added he was *surprised* to learn she was going to be on the show with him.

"The plan was for me to call in," Kira said, "but I convinced the host to invite me to the studio. I live in North Oakland, a few miles away. I'm looking forward to our *debate*."

She said that with quiet emphasis, and he blanched for a second before he rubbed his neck, and then pressed his hands on his knees, spreading out his fingers. Clearly some tic or calming ritual.

"I don't recall," he said, "signing up for a debate. But let the music play."

Kira's attempts to fire Wennie had failed, and now that she was representing this disability rights group with the ill-conceived name of Alive and Able, her life was even more entangled with Wennie's. At least she had pushed Wennie out of her bed.

Wennie had been taking her to meetings and trainings since October, then, in the new year, she *pretended* to "stumble across" a story about a euthanasia case in Chicago that was, she said, jumpstarting a conversation about end-of-life issues and disability rights.

"This man apparently killed his father," Wennie had told Kira, "and his sister accused him, in public, and then the Illinois Disability Coalition did this video that went viral and, well, now *you* have an opportunity to use your formidable skills."

"To do what?" she'd asked. "Drive to Illinois and run this guy over with our van? Your job is to help me with what *I* ask you to do, not chase down things *you* want to do."

Wennie hadn't backed down. "You said you wanted someone who would take *initiative*, not sit around to be micromanaged." Kira did not remember saying that.

But here she was at the radio station, after two more trainings, plus an intense phone session with a woman named Paula Merrill, who was working with Lamar's sister Andrea.

A minute before airtime, the show's host, Arun Dama, a bike helmet on his head, rushed into the waiting room, introduced himself, then ushered Kira and Lamar into the studio as the woman with the gray ponytail exited.

Now a newscast, coming from somewhere else, was broadcasting from the speakers.

Arun looked like an earnest graduate student, his dark curly hair disheveled, his backpack slung over one shoulder, only he wasn't *that* young. His beard was speckled with gray.

He did a thrice-weekly public affairs show, with call-ins, and he'd hosted a widely acclaimed show the previous summer about how California's new End of Life Options Act might impact the disabled community.

Kira sat across from Lamar, the host off to the side. After the introductions, Arun asked Lamar Rose an easy question about his organization, Dying By Choice.

Lamar took his hat off, and she could see that he was bald except for a rim of fuzz behind his ears. He placed his hat on his knees, rubbing his fingers around the edge of the brim.

"We are an educational nonprofit dedicated to encouraging and deepening conversations about death and dying. Within families, within communities, within our nation as a whole."

He was a lean man around fifty. No muscles to speak of in his arms, but he looked like he might be a runner. He spoke like someone who *imagined* he had empathy, but clearly he had no idea of how hard it was to be paralyzed. She had run marathons, bicycled centuries, skied black-diamond slopes. He *acted* as if he knew, but he didn't.

"While we support death-with-dignity laws," he continued, "like the medical-aid-in-dying law California passed last year and the one Oregon has had on the books since 1994, we do not *actively* lobby for legislation. Our focus is on dialogue. Getting conversations like this going. 'The most important conversation no one wants to have,' we call it. What kind of care do you want? How much medical intervention? We appreciate that you and your station have been covering these issues."

Kira waited until he paused, then jumped in before he could start another sentence. She was not going to let him get away with sounding reasonable.

"I don't care about you killing your father," she said, cutting off Arun as he opened his mouth. "It's your *promotion* of euthanasia, your *embrace* of the culture of death, your *insensitivity* to the potential consequences for the disabled and for others who live on the margins. *That's* the problem. Once we make it *easier* to end people's lives, it's a slippery slope and all of a sudden, we're pressuring disabled grandpa to die because it's too damn expensive or painful or uncomfortable to give him a good quality of life. Better to buy that Tesla you have your eye on."

Lamar put up his hand and answered immediately. This time, the host didn't even try to intervene. "Your concern is *totally* legitimate," he said. "You're *exactly* right." Then he stopped. She was ready to jump on his answer, but since he just agreed with her, she didn't know what to say.

"There are people," he continued, "and market forces, bean counters, who might see you and your disabled brethren as extravagant. That's a *real* problem that's built on a *real* lack of empathy and understanding of the disabled *by able-bodied people*. That insensitivity *does* exist. Those financial pressures *do* exist. I support *whatever* safeguards are necessary so that scary slippery-slope scenario you describe does not come to pass. It's possible, and necessary, to draw a clear line between what the individual and family want and what is *'convenient.'*"

"What if the family *wants* to stop caring for their old gimp of a father?" Kira countered. "What if the family *wants* the 'convenient' path?"

He gave the usual pablum answer about how the affected parties have to verbally affirm they want to end their lives.

"The aid-in-dying laws are limited in their scope," he said. "Even if it were legal in Illinois, which it isn't, my father would not have qualified because he was not of sound mind. He would not have been able to get a prescription. The laws are *purposely* restrictive *because* of the concerns you bring up."

"You don't get it," Kira said. "You pretend you care, but you don't. You're just out to hurt people like me."

Now she got the reaction she was hoping for. He clenched his fists, and twisted his fingers together.

Kira jumped in before he could respond. "Let me add this about Dr. Lamar Rose and his sister Andrea, who accused him of killing their father. The fact is that she was left out of important conversations. The fact is that he took *unilateral action* despite her objections. That is a telling demonstration of his lack of empathy. His not caring."

Now he was clearly agitated, practically shaking. He started to speak, then put up his hands in a time-out gesture, and pointed to Arun.

Objection! She almost said it out loud. Arun broke in before she could continue. "Kira Baylor, those are *strong* words. Can you be more specific?"

But now Lamar raised his hand and started speaking.

"May I?" he said. Fuming, but in control.

"Go ahead," said Arun.

There was a second of silence before Lamar started talking, in a low steely voice.

"As a psychologist, as a friend, partner, parent, I try my best, *always,* to avoid attributing negative intent to others." His fingers were twitching, but his voice was steady. She should have gone for the knockout when she had the chance. "Hardly anyone *intends* to hurt others. They may be insensitive. But people are rarely cruel on purpose. Except for divorces, things like that.

"I suggest that for us to have a *productive* dialogue, we *refrain* from assuming we know each others' intentions, what we care about. You can say that giving people more power to end their suffering is bad policy, a matter of grave concern for disabled people. You can accuse me of not thinking things through, of not having all the information necessary, of using faulty logic. But *do not* tell me"—now his voice slowed, dropped in pitch—"do not tell me I *intend* to hurt people like you. That I don't care. You *do not know* what I care about."

She hadn't seen that coming. "Point taken." She struck a

conciliatory tone. "You have good intentions. I'll stipulate that." She stared daggers at him, made sure he read her loud and clear. "Being well-intentioned, however, does not get you a free pass when you're ending someone's life."

"What I do as a psychologist," he said, "is talk to people who are dying about what they want. And, while we're clarifying, less than a quarter of my clients are facing death, *soon*. Clearly, we're all facing death, but *later*. Most of my therapy is about living, not dying. They are both important. They are *connected*."

"Let me remind our listeners about some key facts," Kira said. "The video camera at Edgewater shows you leaving from the loading dock at 2:30 in the morning the night your father died. Your browsing history shows you researching how to kill someone using nitrogen. The police have a record of talking to you at 3 in the morning, walking in a daze down the middle of the street, as if you were in shock."

He shook his head. "You're just repeating my sister's baseless allegations." He seemed to be back in control of his emotions. Saying he didn't care clearly pushed some button, but her recitation of the murder evidence didn't seem to faze him. "I love my sister," he said. "She's family. But she is consumed with grief and taking it out on me. Or that's what it appears. I should do what I just urged you to do. Not attribute intention. I don't know what she's feeling, but she's building a case out of cobwebs."

"I don't hear you denying those accusations."

"I deny them. My lawyer has instructed me not to say anything more than that."

They took a two-minute break for some announcements. Arun said they were doing great. "All I need to do is stay out of the way," he said.

Kira liked it too. This beat suing sad-ass restaurants any

day. Maybe there was a way to get paid for this. She would put Wennie on the case. Tell her to find paid gigs like this.

After the break, there were some listener call-ins, which were mostly supportive of her, but not really against Lamar, and she repeated the evidence again, two more times, knowing they might grab clips for their social media. He had to issue his lame denial, again.

The last time, however, he turned on the charm. "This has been so much the kind of stimulating conversation that my organization is trying to facilitate. Kira Baylor, *such a pleasure* meeting you, sparring with you. You make a compelling case for your cause, and I support all you've said about that."

27

I Forgot

University of New Mexico Hospital
Albuquerque, New Mexico
July 2, 2008

Lamar looked out the window at the university soccer fields, where students were playing under bright lights. He would not hold Janis' hand. He couldn't.

They had pumped Janis' stomach in the ER, given her activated charcoal through a tube, and strapped her to an IV with saline and electrolyte solution.

An hour and a half later, she was awake and animated, and had been moved to a room on the fourth floor.

Still shaken, Sierra sat by her bedside, holding her mother's hand. She had saved her mother's life. After Lamar had called 911, she had taken charge, shaking Janis, dragging her out of bed, directing Lamar to help walk her around. They were holding all her weight at first, and her toenails dragged on the floor, but then Janis woke up and took a couple of steps, just before the paramedics arrived.

Lamar was relieved Janis had failed to kill herself, but

furious that she had so obviously timed her cry for help for the day her daughter arrived back home. So Janis. So hostile.

The takeout from El Patio sat in white bags on the window ledge. What if they'd had a flat tire, or stayed longer in Madrid? He was hungry, but couldn't eat. Too much bile in his belly.

Was this about punishing Lamar for moving out? Why would she punish Sierra? He often wondered if there was more going on with Janis than depression because she always managed to muster enough steam to stick it to Lamar.

He was not going to let Janis derail his life.

She said it was an accident. That she didn't mean to take so many pills, that the drugs made her dopey and she took more without realizing. That was her story. She repeated it for the nurses, the doctor, even for the aide who brought her chicken soup and crackers.

She sipped the soup from her spoon, then put down the spoon and slurped from the bowl.

Sierra wanted to know why she took sleeping pills when she knew they were coming with dinner.

"I forgot," she said.

"You forgot," Lamar repeated, but he didn't turn from the window. Let the hospital shrink ask the questions.

Five days later, the psych ward released Janis to her daughter and her dog, and a promise from Lamar that he would visit her three times a week.

He was not moving back home.

28

I Don't Want to Know

Albuquerque, New Mexico
January 26, 2016

Lamar was so happy to see Julia, waiting for him at baggage claim, he started crying. He turned away before she saw him, pretending to tie his shoe. Tightened his laces on both shoes. Then headed toward her, his arms outstretched.

She wrapped him in a big hug first, then stepped back and gave him a mushy kiss.

"What's wrong?" She held him by his shoulders. The tears welled up again.

"Nothing, I'm just—" He pulled back, shook his head. "Thank you for picking me up. So much. It means a lot. There's my bag."

He wasn't in love with Julia, but she was so *nice* and *normal* and *warm*, and he felt overwhelmed with emotion. Maybe it was Julia's embrace, the weight of Andrea's accusations, the loss of his father, the killing of his father.

All of it.

He hadn't seen Julia since the memorial. He'd been

consumed with strategizing with Todd and then prepping for his speaking gig and radio interview. He was proud of how laser-focused and locked-in he'd been.

But on the plane home from Oakland, with no pressing deadlines, the grief and discombobulation settled in on his shoulders like a heavy coat. The depth of his agitation surprised him, but no, it didn't. He felt so alone, and what made it worse was how familiar it felt. He had fought so hard for so many years, and made so much progress, and now here he was back where he'd started. Just like before he left Janis.

Soon enough, they were in Julia's kitchen in North Valley, chopping vegetables. Julia was a fan of stir fry, and Lamar was content to be her sous chef. He cut onions, celery, peppers, chard, kale, spinach, tofu, and chicken. Her knives were sharp.

"The talk in San Francisco, at the Unitarian Universalists, went well," he said. "Supportive, attentive audience. Old lefty intellectuals with white hair and canes, all wanting to take control of their own death. After overthrowing the ruling class, that is. The radio gig this morning was much more challenging."

He told her about how relentless Kira Baylor had been, how he almost lost it. "I held my own, but man, I sweated. I also felt, like, wow, I'm on the radio debating issues that are important to me, I'm anxious, I'm alert, I'm terrified, and it was intense in a way that I, that I *liked*. But I also felt, I don't know, *exposed, raw*. Not the most comfortable feeling."

He kept his eyes on the kale, cutting the leaves into smaller pieces.

"That's small enough," she said. The kitchen smelled of garlic. No such thing as too much garlic, according to Julia.

"But this was only an experiment. The talk and the radio gig. Todd said let's try these two, then assess. I'd like to do more, but he's wary."

Julia had been there for him at the memorial. After she witnessed Andrea accuse him in the church, she had stayed by his side at the reception for a damn lot longer than he had any right to expect. She seemed to care about him. He needed to tell her the truth.

"You know I value honesty," he said, "how I feel it's best—"

Julia stepped away from the counter and started typing something into her phone, waiting for Lamar to finish warming up and get to the point. She didn't do that therapist thing, hanging on his every word.

"I smothered my father with a suicide bag," he said. "That's what the Australians call it."

"You *what?*" She stared at him with her sharp green eyes. Julia had a glorious smile and an expressive face. No smile now. Her eyes hardened.

Saying what he did out loud sounded so stark, so cold-hearted. As if killing his father hadn't cut him to his core.

She sat down at the table and waited until he sat down opposite her. "What in God's name were you thinking?"

"I gave it a great deal of thought. Many months. Including some strikingly lucid conversations with my father."

"*No,* I'm not talking about what you *did*. I'm talking about *telling me*. What am I supposed to *do* with this *information?* You told me at the church your sister's accusation was baseless, dismissed it as her messed-up way of grieving. By blaming someone. Now you're telling me that she was right."

"I guess I was expecting support, not cross-examination."

"I was under the impression that I *was* giving you support," she said, "for the death of your father, that is, not for killing him. You know you could have kept all this to yourself and I would have been fine with that."

"I thought—"

The smoke alarm shrieked. They both jumped from their chairs. The vegetables were burning. She turned the burner off, then climbed on a chair and yanked the battery out of the smoke detector. She almost pulled the alarm off the ceiling. Then she threw open the front door, and a cold breeze gusted through the kitchen. Cold, but nothing like the winds whipping off Lake Michigan in Chicago the night he ended his father's life. Nothing like the iciness he was feeling from Julia.

She sat back down, hugged her shoulders. "I need another drink."

"I could use one too."

She sliced a lime and mixed two more vodka tonics. Lamar closed his eyes and exhaled.

They sat drinking their vodkas in silence, then Julia got up and closed the front door. The burning smell had faded. The stir fry stayed in the pan. He wasn't hungry. She wasn't either.

"I didn't want to burden you," said Lamar, "with any of my *perseverating* before the act. I didn't want you to talk me out of it. It was not fair of me to dump this on you."

"I don't want to know," she said.

Lamar stayed the night, but Julia kept her distance. When he slid toward her, she pushed him away with her elbow. He lay awake for hours.

He had met Julia the old-fashioned way, in person. The previous summer, at a not-so-old-fashioned three-day silent walking meditation at the Albuquerque Zen Center.

The rules were no eye contact, but when he passed her, he noticed, out of the corner of his eye, her trim body and the graceful, exaggeratedly slow way she moved. When he looked up at her, she was looking at him. She had such an inviting face. He immediately looked down. The second day they passed again and their eye contact lasted a few seconds longer. The third day, Lamar lifted his eyebrows in greeting.

They introduced themselves when the meditation was over, and he asked her for coffee. They talked for hours, both of them giddy and animated, the deep serenity of the retreat mixing it up with their desperate longing for conversation.

He told her one of his favorite stories, about the young man who joined a monastery where there was no talking at all.

"There was one exception," Lamar said, "which was that every ten years, you met with the head monk and you were allowed two words. So after ten years of meditating and praying and working, this man goes for his meeting and says to the head monk, 'bed hard.' Then he goes back for ten more years of meditating and praying and working. At the twenty-year mark, he meets with the head monk and says, 'food cold.'

"Then, after another ten years, he goes to his meeting with the monk, and says, 'I quit.'

"To which the monk replies, 'Well, no wonder. You've been complaining ever since you got here.'"

She chuckled and gave him a wide grin. "Yeah, like you were flirting with me the whole three days."

"You were looking at me when I looked up."

"I don't mean to burst your bubble, buddy, but I was trying to keep my eyes unfocused in the distance and when you looked up, I couldn't help but focus on you."

In many respects, Julia was more like Lamar than any woman he'd ever met, and that similarity made for an easiness he had never experienced before. But he also found himself wishing she were more playful, less austere.

She never dolled herself up. She wore the same loose black pants every time they met, with black Rockport walking shoes, and a pressed white shirt untucked. And a scarf. She changed up the scarf. Sometimes they were bright red or orange, but mostly they were muted colors. He liked her scarves. They gave her a gypsy feel. "There are many moving parts to every day," she said. "I make my life simpler by wearing the same costume all the time. The whole fashion industry is a disservice to women."

Well, it didn't look like how she dressed was going to matter any more.

In the middle of the night, coming back from the bathroom, Julia said she couldn't sleep. She seemed agitated, angry, but she *had* slept. Lamar had watched her, heard her peaceful, rhythmic snoring. He hadn't slept at all.

"You know I have women friends I tell everything to," she said. "Not every day. Not *everything* everything, but important things. You want me to tell them *this?*" They both lay on their backs. Lamar was looking at her, but her eyes were on the gauzy gold canopy draped across the bedposts. He could smell the burned garlic from earlier in the evening.

"I fucked up," he said. "I understand now. Too late."

"You think an apology is going to make it go away? That I can unhear what you told me? You think we're supposed to share all our secrets? Do you really want to know about my two abortions, about how I cheated on my husband with one of his co-workers, about how I used my son as a pawn in my divorce? How much do you want to know about the man I was seeing two years ago, how often we had sex, what he would say to me in bed? I didn't *ask* to be your confessor and I don't know what the hell to do with this, this *confession*.

"What if some *cop* comes around and starts hectoring me with questions? I have to lie to protect you?

"I was feeling sorry for myself last summer, like I was never going to meet a decent man, like I was going to send Jesse off to college and there'd be this big gaping hole in my life. My face is sagging, I've got chicken wings on my arms, and it's been a long time since I turned a man's head."

Lamar decided the best thing was to not say anything, but to murmur "uh huh."

"Before I met you," she said, "I went two years without sex or romantic intimacy, *two years*. And then you came along, breaking all the rules at that silent meditation, and you're kind and generous and you listen without judging, and maybe we're not soulmates and maybe this was just a stop along the way, but now—"

She didn't finish her thought. After a few minutes of silence, she spoke in a softer tone.

"Now that we've established that you messed up this promising, happyish, almost innocent relationship we were easing into, and I had my little tantrum, and we can *never* go back to where we were, why don't we heat up that stir fry in the microwave? I'm famished."

In the chilly kitchen, she in her robe, he with his Chicago winter coat over his shoulders, he told her pretty much the true story of what he had done for his father, to his father. She didn't interrupt. She did ask him how he decided to do what he did.

"When my father asked the first time, and the second, and the third, I said no without hesitation. But it got me thinking—here I am, a volunteer for Dying By Choice, advocating for people to talk about death and my father gives it to me direct, with no frills. 'I can't stand to live like this. You need to help me.'

"And then he cocked his thumb. *Out of here.* Sign language that could not have been clearer.

"From my hospice work, my talks, and so on, I know my dad's request was not uncommon. That mercy-killing happens more than we know."

"I believe that," Julia said.

"But I was not prepared to be the one who did the deed. You know, the other day, I found myself talking with my father, because he was the only one I *could* talk with, except that now he's not here. Because of what I did. I'm sorry I burdened you with my truth-telling, but I wanted you to understand why."

Lamar shook his head. He was tearing up and he didn't want that.

She placed her hand on his. "You've been through the wringer, haven't you?"

Now he was actually crying. "I have," he said.

She pushed back her chair and came up behind Lamar and wrapped her arms around his chest. "It's OK to be sad," she said.

She let go. "This doesn't mean it's OK what you did."

"What I did or what I said?" he asked.

"Does it matter?" she said.

In the morning he reached for Julia, but she pushed his hand away.

29

PlayDate

Santa Fe University of Art and Design
July 13, 2008

Life was different now that Lamar lived in Madrid, but wasn't that the point? No dog to walk. No painful morning conversations with Janis. He hadn't stopped doing yoga and meditation, but it was no longer an everyday thing.

He was surprised how comfortable he felt there, with Jeff, with Greta, with Justine, who was the proprietress of Turquoise and Coffee, where he ate breakfast several days a week.

They felt like his people, though they were so different than his usual crowd. Well, there was the problem. There was no usual crowd.

At one time he had a circle of friends, back when Sierra was young, but he had let it wither, and now friends were few and far between. It was his own damn fault, he had to own that, but Janis' depression and her negative energy contributed. The friendships he and Janis made when Sierra was young, mostly with other parents, had been held together by the women, and when Janis withdrew, no one made the necessary effort to stay in touch.

Other friends didn't disappear so much as recede.

Or was it Lamar who receded? One of his longtime friends, Terry, lived in Peralta, but it had been a year since they had any contact. They used to share so much of themselves, and Lamar told him about Janis' depression for hours upon hours. The story never seemed to change, however, and they both got tired of hearing it.

Now he was mostly meandering over to Jeff's with a six-pack of IPA from the Blue Corn Brewery, or down the hill to the Mine Shaft Tavern. Jeff and his gang friends weren't the most scintillating of company, but they were welcoming and they didn't demand anything of him. They drank beer, smoked pot, watched sports on TV. Some talk. Not much. Now and then they told stories about their wild motorcycle gang adventures, but they didn't act wild in Jeff's living room. Jeff said they weren't your typical bikers because they were old and still alive and not in prison.

Daytimes weren't that different than before. Three days a week, he saw clients in the office below the kitchen in the house on Coal Avenue and had lunch with Janis. Tuesdays and Thursdays, he saw clients in Santa Fe.

Janis seemed to be doing better now that he wasn't around. For his own reasons, he had not moved back home after Janis' OD, but it looked like the new living arrangement was doing her some good as well. She even joined him for a couple of walks with Caro.

The biggest difference for Lamar was dating, or, more accurately, trying to date. Most of his overtures were ignored and even some of the women who responded to his emails hadn't graduated yet to meeting in person.

He had a perfectly pleasant walk with Jessica, and the

conversation flowed when they strolled side by side, but when they sat for coffee, it stalled. She was cute but too short. Under five feet. How shallow was that? He was quite attracted to Kim, a bright, serious, and painfully shy intellectual property lawyer from India, who hoped to turn her company, Zero One, into the next Yahoo or Google. She was tall, but he had to fill the silence with his own blather and he didn't like that.

No one captivated him like Diana.

Lamar kept searching the dating sites, writing his careful, thoughtful emails, but one Sunday night, he decided to mix it up and try this in-person dating event called PlayDate. It was a hybrid of speed dating and parlor games, if the web posting was to be believed. Were they really going to play charades?

He climbed the terracotta tiled steps, and stood in front of the rec center on the sleek new Santa Fe University of Art and Design campus, studying, inside the glass doors, a couple dozen men and women milling around, checking in at a folding table.

He was tempted to go back to his car. He had paid in advance, partly to save five dollars, mostly to commit himself to showing up. But so what if he forfeited twenty dollars?

Give this PlayDate an hour, he told himself. Then you can bail.

He marched in and gave a cheery hello to the woman at the door, who directed him to the sign-in table. How bad could this be?

He wore a pressed white guayabera shirt, untucked, and a loosely knotted bolo tie. An earring, too, but the smallest, most understated of the four he had. On his name tag, he wrote "Lamar" in blocky uppercase and underneath, half the size, "Madrid."

Behind the table was another set of doors into a larger room. He saw a woman with curly blond hair lowering a baby carrot into white dip. In slow motion. She looked like she was studying the grain of the carrot.

He ambled through the doors, slowly but purposefully, to the hors d'oeuvres table. The blonde was gone. The pile of carrots was still there. The dip smelled of dill.

Taped to the wall were personal ads. There was a sign encouraging everyone to write an ad so others could seek them out in the crowd. The top one was headlined "Devil in a Blue Dress."

"Devilish, but not an actual devil. Dress is blue, however, and so am I when the world is too much. Seeking a strong and happy partner, who wants to go on new adventures. Celia."

He would look for her.

"Yin seeks yang. Linear, organized control freak seeks creative soul I can crush into submission. Or maybe someone who can help me loosen up and enjoy life. Juana. In the black dress with the embroidered butterfly."

Lamar looked down at his carrot and pivoted about a quarter turn toward the rest of the room.

There were at least fifty people there now, equal men and women, mostly middle aged like he was. He saw an animated woman with thick black hair gesticulating with her arms and laughing, but many of the women seemed too much like Janis—gray, puffy, bland. Not that he was such a prize. They were no doubt judging him in the same shallow way. If they noticed him at all.

Empty blue chairs were clustered in the center of the room. Before he could steel himself to mingle, the blonde he had seen earlier approached the table, glancing first at the vegetables, then at Lamar.

"You're from Madrid." She pronounced it correctly, with the accent on "mad."

"For now. I've been there three weeks."

"Do you like it?"

"So far, I'm thrilled, though it's very much an experiment. I've become friends with some unlikely people, like guys in a motorcycle gang. You've been there?"

"To visit. To buy art. I'm Alison."

"I see," he said, nodding at her name tag. "I'm Lamar." He pointed to his.

Alison had a lovely smile, but her face was sharp, hawklike—with a long, thin nose and a pointed chin. She stood too close. He stepped back.

Before they could continue their conversation came a low-pitched tone from a panpipe, like the amplified coo of a morning dove. Then a stocky man with a walrus mustache spoke into a wireless mic.

"I'd like you to organize yourselves into two circles. Men on the outside, walking counterclockwise, facing in. Women on the inside, facing out, and you can guess what direction you'll be walking. Once you're in your circles, we'll start moving and each of you will meet all the people in the other circle. Only one rule: Smile and greet everyone warmly."

Lamar tried to make eye contact with all the women. He did with all but one, who was almost too dazzling to look at. As if her megawatt smile would turn him to stone.

His mouth kept working. "Hi, I'm Lamar. Lovely to meet you. Hi, I'm Lamar. Good to meet you." Maybe this was going to be OK. Everyone follows the rules, nobody gets hurt.

Oh shit! Three women down, there was Diana. He cringed at the memory of that desperate phone call, but he snapped himself back to the moment. To the woman in front of him. Now Diana. Smile and greet her warmly, where was the problem?

Diana tilted her head, smiled. "I didn't think I'd seen the last of you."

That almost sounded good. Then he was onto the next woman. The circles completed their rounds, and then came the charades. The first word was three syllables and sounded like "elevator."

Everyone got a turn. After each round—signaled by that low-pitched panpipe—they all shuffled themselves like a deck of cards to meet new people. That three-syllable word was creator, which didn't sound much like elevator, with its four staccato syllables, but someone guessed it, and that was what counted, right?

The games were hokey, but tightly structured, which kept Lamar engaged, but the breaks sent him to the bathroom, where he stood in front of the mirror and washed his hands multiple times.

Then came the five-minute dates, organized by colored dots on the name tags. Lamar had an orange dot, then a green, then a red. During the break the room had been rearranged—seven pairs of facing chairs in each corner. Each chair marked with colored dots.

Before they headed to their respective corners based on their dots, the host explained the rules regarding the cards they'd received at the registration table.

"If you haven't filled out your cards, you might want to do so now. Your name, your phone and/or email, plus something distinctive about you that might help a prospective date remember you. What you're wearing, your earrings, your beard. After a round of five-minute dates—seven each if my math is right—we replay those concentric circles, with each man meeting each woman, and *now* there are *two* rules. Rule one, you smile and thank the woman or man across from you for a lovely evening. If he or she is someone you'd like to date, you give them one of your cards. Rule two, if you receive a card, you smile and say thank you, whether you're interested or not.

"When you get home, if you got a card, or several, *you* decide who you want to contact. If you gave someone a card, you might wait for a call that never comes and maybe you'll feel rejected. But that is *not* going to happen here tonight. If you receive a card, you smile and say thank you. And you need not wait until the circles start to present a card."

Lamar's second "date" was Diana, who had not been in any of his charades pods. When she sat down, he told her, "I'm a month more single than when I met you."

"Well, I'm a month more weary so maybe we'll lap each other and meet up on the back side." She asked him about how his dating was going.

His first impulse was to give a glib answer, but he changed his mind. "I haven't met anyone who engaged me like you did. Honest truth. How about you?"

"I'm not showing up at the pool as often as I used to. But here I am tonight."

He got her talking about a recent balloon trip and then the panpipe sounded.

He started to give her a card, but he wanted to write something personal. He gave a card to his fourth date, Lala, a shy, dark woman from Lebanon, a nuclear engineer. Like Lamar's father. She smiled and said thank you. That wasn't so bad.

When it came time for the closing circles, Lamar extended his hand to each woman with an earnest enthusiasm. "Jenny, nice to meet you." "Alice, good to meet you."

Alison, the hawk-like blonde from the veggies table, handed him a card. He smiled and said thank you. He liked these rules.

When Diana arrived in front of him, he gave her the card with his note. She gave him a skeptical look, like, "I'm on to you," then, as he turned to greet the next woman, she reached back and handed him a card. "I like to break rules," she said.

I'd like to break some rules with you. He almost said that, but another woman was in front of him and then another, and then he was done.

30

Garth

Albuquerque, New Mexico
January 27, 2016

Lamar took a cab home from Julia's Saturday morning, then a long walk, but not long enough to unsnarl the barbed wire around his neck, not long enough to rewind the calamitous developments of the past night, let alone the past two weeks.

He could not have sabotaged his life more if he had set out to do it on purpose.

The morning was cool and crisp and sunny, though Lamar barely noticed.

Julia was as good as gone, not that he could blame her, and he was alone, again. Flying home, he had been so looking forward to telling Julia the truth about what he had done, about how he felt, about how determined he was to screw his courage to the sticking place and deal with this impossible situation as if it weren't impossible.

For most of Lamar's professional life, he saw a therapist once a week, or at least once a month. Except for those two times he was on the verge of momentous decisions—leaving his wife back in 2008, and now, fulfilling his duty to his father.

That was no accident. At those critical moments, he didn't want someone calm and measured talking him out of what he had to do.

Helping his father die was a crime and if a client had come to him with this problem, Lamar would have said no, you don't have to take on that responsibility.

Now that he was in such deep shit, now that he'd scared away Julia, he needed someone he could be honest with.

When he got back home, Lamar called his old therapist Garth, whose first words were, "I've been waiting for your call."

Garth invited him to come in that afternoon, and he gave Lamar a bear hug when he arrived. Garth was an old man now, semi-retired. More hair grew out of his nose and ears than on his head. His beard was full, but scraggly. Lamar felt a twinge of guilt that he had not come sooner.

"You haven't been seeing anyone for how long?" asked Garth.

"At least six months," said Lamar.

"Six months?" His tone was neutral, but Lamar knew what Garth was doing. He'd learned that trick himself.

"Closer to a year," Lamar said.

"You didn't want anyone questioning your decision," Garth said.

"I can count on you to cut to the chase. A little empathy wouldn't hurt. Especially at your rates."

Lamar was not surprised by Garth's gruffness, but he'd forgotten how little he sugarcoated his words. "Yes, you are correct. I did not want you, or anyone, to weaken my resolve to do what I needed to do."

"You think I would have told you what to do?" Garth asked.

"I was afraid you would."

"Hmmm."

Garth had started with his shoulders against the back of the chair, but once they were talking, he leaned in, his hands on his knees, his eyes locked on Lamar's, his ears perked. He was earning his money.

"Well, I did what I have been accused of doing," Lamar said.

"Excellent."

"What do you mean, *excellent?* My father is dead. I'm in trouble. I'm all alone."

Garth probably didn't need to hear the details, but Lamar needed to share them, so he did. Garth nodded and kept his neutral expression. When Lamar finished, Garth asked him what he wanted.

"What do I *want?* To turn back time. For my father to be alive and well. What does it matter what I want?"

"From me, then," said Garth. "What do you want from me?"

"How do I deal with all this?"

"But you already know," said Garth.

"This is why I waited so long to see you. You make *me* do all the work."

"I'm like the boss from hell."

"But *you* work for me," said Lamar. "I don't work for you."

"If you say so."

"Let me guess," said Lamar. "You want me to frame this as a *growth opportunity*, another *fucking growth opportunity*. To tell myself that some people never get a chance to evolve like this. That I have to grab onto this disaster as if I chose it myself."

"See, you *do* know."

31

Dustballs Under the Bed

Albuquerque, New Mexico
July 24, 2008

Lamar met Diana at a small, brightly lit sushi restaurant on Third Street. She came from work, dressed in black velvet pants and a long-sleeved white embroidered blouse. Her lipstick was too raspberry red for his taste, but he appreciated that she had dressed up for him.

He was in an effusive mood. A few days after PlayDate, he had called Diana and suggested dinner at Asia Pacific, a popular noodle fusion restaurant. On Thursday, a weeknight, but almost the weekend. She said yes to the date, but no to noodles. Not enough gluten-free options. How about sushi? She had played it cool—not enthusiastic, but not disinterested. As if he had talked her into something. OK, let's give this Lamar fellow another shot.

After they ordered, Diana told him she had a guy on the side, a friend that she slept with now and then. "It's not serious. He wants it to be, but I've been blunt about the boundaries. Maybe not fair to him, except this guy is sort of pathetic."

"And now you want to swap out pathetic guys?"

"No, if I thought you were—oh, I see. My friends say I don't know when someone is pulling my leg."

"I'm glad you think I'm kidding." She smiled, real and phony at the same time, then speared a chunk of tuna into her mouth. The raspberry lips had lost their gloss. He liked them better now.

"I still believe you're looking for a rebound fuck," she said. "Not that there's anything wrong with that."

Their conversation went all over the place and back again. Lamar was usually good about not interrupting, as a matter of principle, but Diana kept interrupting him and it was contagious, so he went with the flow. Diana mostly talked about work and her bees. She had six hives on the roof of her condo building. Their banter felt easy and comfortable and fun. Even more than the first time.

Lamar told her about his new friends in Madrid, like Win, the forger, who showed him how to pick a lock. At one point, Diana asked him about splitting up with his wife.

He had been on seven dates by now and he knew better than to talk about Janis' suicide attempt, but he had gotten comfortable telling the story about how he decided to leave.

"I wasted a lot of time making lists of pros and cons—*should I stay or should I go?*—as if the list was some sort of talisman. Then I decided *not* to decide. To sit with my two options, holding them in balance, and let the decision *come to me*. Almost immediately, it did. *Leave.*

"The other thing I did—whoever came up with this deserves a prize—is flip a coin. Seriously. Heads was leave, and when I got tails, I felt like *damn,* I wanted heads. The coin toss didn't *decide* for me, but *revealed* what I wanted."

They didn't order dessert, but he drank a second beer.

"I'd love to invite you to my place," he said, "but like I told you, I live in a rustic shack in the middle of nowhere. It's clean, though."

"Mine is nowhere close to clean," she said, "but we're not going to Madrid tonight, even if you lived in a mansion."

She smiled, then wiggled her finger, beckoning him to come closer.

He slid his chair toward her on the sleek bamboo floor.

She placed her hands on his shoulders, and moved in, nose to nose. "We are going to get you laid tonight. How does that sound?"

He played it cool. "You have anyone in mind? You know because, I'm sort of particular."

"Oh, you are?" she said.

"She's got to be *at least* as smart and pretty as you are."

"Good to know."

He caught a whiff of her perfume—what *was* that scent? Orange blossom? Jasmine? He loved how she smelled. Because of her food issues, he hadn't thought she would wear perfume.

"There's this Paradoxical Dreamer I'm intrigued by," he said. "She requires more in-depth study. Maybe we go to your place and do more *research*."

"You'll learn more about her than you ever want to know as soon as you walk in the door."

Diana's condo, an airy third-floor apartment, was as cluttered as advertised. Bright and colorful, too. Mexican rugs on the wall. Chili ristras hanging from a glass-beaded chandelier. Open kitchen cabinets with olive green bowls and cobalt blue plates.

He noted dust on the windowsills and every horizontal surface filled. She gestured to a stack of papers on the dining room table. "Somewhere in there is a clipping about how to tame your clutter. I. Am. Hopeless."

She gave him a tour, including the bathroom, where the shelves were crammed with plastic cartoon toys. Dolls, action figures, Barbie, Spiderman, Bart Simpson, Big Bird, Elmo, the Jack-in-the-Box guy with the styrofoam ball head. Amidst the toys were dozens, maybe hundreds of shampoo bottles from hotels.

"Believe it or not," she said, "I cleaned up, thinking I *might* invite you over."

It was hard to believe it had been worse than this. Not that he was a total neat freak. He certainly was willing to ignore dust for a good cause.

They had kissed for the first time before she unlocked the front door, but she wasn't acting romantic now.

"I wonder if we might find a glass of wine or something," he said. "I need to relax. This is new for me."

"I've got wine, beer, scotch, pot, valium, percocet, you name it."

"Scotch with ice would be wonderful," he said.

He nursed his drink as they talked on the couch. He touched her arm. She touched his knee. When he finally got the nerve to kiss her again, she fell into him. Onto him. They rolled around on the couch for a long while, then she suggested they go to her bedroom.

As she set a candle on top of a dresser, Lamar watched her from the doorway. He took a last gulp of his drink. Only ice left. Diana sat on the high bed, her bare feet dangling, and patted the comforter, beckoning him to sit next to her. He counted six pillows on the bed.

"Am I your first," she asked, "since—? No, I don't want to know."

"You are," he said, as he sat on the bed. "Remember, I only just left my wife. Like two minutes ago."

"You're funny."

He answered with a kiss. She pulled him closer. They both still had their clothes on, but not their shoes. She was a hungry kisser, but he was feeling disconnected.

He unbuttoned her blouse, but she stopped him after two buttons.

"I want to keep my shirt on."

She moved his hand to her waist.

"I have condoms," she said. "I can't count on men to have them."

"I didn't want to presume," he said. "I'll bring them next time."

"There's not going to be a next time, buddy boy. And in the unlikely event there is, I might want to start working on that baby."

He jerked away, withdrew his hand.

"I'm playing," she said. "Looks like I'm not the *only* one who can't take a joke. Please, continue."

She took off her pants and handed him a condom. He tried to tear the package with his hand, had to use his teeth. By the time he extracted it from the package, his erection had wilted.

"Out of practice, I guess." He turned away so she couldn't see his face.

"You are not home, my friend. I hear noises in your head. What's going on in there?" She knocked on his head.

He turned back toward Diana, kissed her again, and ran his hands softly over her stomach, by her belly button. Slow down, he told himself. Focus on her.

She pushed his hand away. "*Please*, it feels like you're doing this because you think you should, not because you want to."

Shit, shit, shit. He wanted to dig a deep hole and climb

in. He wished he were anywhere but here. Well, except maybe back with Janis.

He shook his head. No, he was going to turn this around. No sulking allowed.

He sat up. "Can I tell you a story?"

"I'd like that," she said.

He lay back down, and angled two pillows under his head so he was lying on his back with his head turned to Diana. She lay on her side, hugging her knees to her chest, facing him.

"I read this story in a magazine, by a woman named Nina Wise. Have you heard of her?"

"No."

"Anyway, she wrote this story called 'Luck Disguised as Ordinary Life,' about meeting Carlos Castaneda in L.A. The writer of this piece, Nina Wise, is a moderately successful performance artist, of some renown. With a following, but not much in the way of material goods. She's newly single, facing a midlife crisis. No steady income, no matching dishes, not even a couch to her name. She gets invited by a friend to this Carlos Castaneda talk, and she and her friend have tea with him. She's thrilled to meet him, though he's older and shorter than she expects, and his suit is wrinkled and his boots are dusty. He tells them a story—yes, this is a story-within-a-story. About how his muse told him to leave L.A., go to Tucson, and work as a cook. Which he did.

"When he got there, he went into the first greasy spoon he passed, and asked for a job. The owner asked, do you know eggs? He didn't, so he bought dozens of eggs, rented a room with a kitchen, and practiced cooking. Fried. Boiled. Poached. Scrambled. Over easy. He went back to the diner, said he knew eggs, got the job. He did well and the owner gave him more responsibility, like helping with hiring, and he hired a young woman as a waitress and they became friends. She was bright, a little overweight, a little sad, and they talked about all sorts of things. She told him she was a fan of Carlos Castaneda, and one day, she brought in a book by him and suggested he read it. Everyone there knew him as Joe. He brought the book back after a few days and said he wasn't much of a reader.

"One day this waitress got all agitated because she had heard that Carlos Castaneda was in town, was in Tucson, and she was sure that was him outside the restaurant in the backseat of a white limo, writing on a yellow pad. Obviously Joe knew the man in the limo was not Carlos Castaneda, but he encouraged the girl to say hello regardless. She was shy. It would be good for her to be more outgoing. She knocked on the window of the limo, but the man was rude to her and she ran back into the restaurant crying. Joe took her in his arms and comforted her.

"So now, Nina Wise, the storyteller pulls back and says, OK, here is this young woman, this waitress, who would give *anything* to be held and comforted by Carlos Castaneda and that is *exactly* what is happening. But she doesn't know it. And Nina Wise says to herself that she is like this waitress, not realizing that she already has what she longs for. A creative, avant-garde life that is anything but predictable, and that *is* the life she wants, much more than matching dishes. But she didn't realize that. Or rather, that's the point of the story, that now she does realize it."

Lamar stopped, took a sip of the melted ice from his glass on the bedside table.

"Now we jump from the story-within-the-story to me, who's having trouble realizing that my ordinary life is lucky too. I want to have an erection, but I don't. I want to be having a wild sex life, but I'm not. I want to feel strong and confident with you, but instead I feel weak. No, no, not weak. Vulnerable." He stopped himself before saying pathetic. "*But, but,* this is not the same old same old me from before. I'm on a new adventure, and that *is* what I want. I'm thrilled to be here with you. I just imagined the fun parts and not the times like now when I want to bury myself under this bed, despite all the dustballs you promised."

"I did not *promise* dustballs."

"What I'm trying to say, I guess, with this story, is that I'm lucky to be here with you right now, just the way it is."

"I like the story," she said. "*A lot.* Why don't you sleep here on the bed. With me. No need to crawl down there with the dust."

To his surprise, he slept soundly, and woke at dawn with an erection. Her clock said 5:40. Diana hummed as she slept, her back to him, her palm under her head. Through the top of the window, above the floral curtains, he could see wispy clouds suffused with pink.

They messed around when she woke up and this time she slipped the condom on and guided him into her.

He was so delirious he wept.

32

Hoppy Trails

First Congregational Church Auditorium
Berkeley, California
February 10, 2016
7:15 pm

Kira had never been on stage in front of so many people before, and she was excited. Nervous too. The front four rows were jammed with wheelchairs—there was a huge turnout from the disabled community. That *should* have made her feel more confident, but it also upped the ante. They would be on her side, but expecting her to deliver the goods.

Deliver she would.

Lamar Rose sat a few feet from her in a caramel-colored leather armchair, which looked luxurious, but that was good for her. An able-bodied white man in a comfy chair next to a disabled woman in a wheelchair, the victim of a hit-and-run driver, cut down in her prime.

This was their fourth debate, the first in front of a live audience, at the Berkeley Congregational Church, a couple miles north of her apartment.

The podcast of their first debate, on KRFB, three weeks earlier, had become a minor viral hit, with more than a dozen requests coming in from radio and TV shows wanting to book the two of them together. Their second and third debate were call-ins, which covered much of the same territory as on the radio, but they hadn't felt as exciting as being together in person.

Lamar had texted her that morning and suggested they meet for coffee. She was surprised, but agreed, and they had a pleasant, albeit testy conversation.

They agreed in advance that Lamar would go first. He stood after he was introduced.

"I want to start with a story," he said. "About two old married couples taking a walk after dinner. The two women are in the front, the men a few yards behind. One man says to the other. 'Yeah, we were at this restaurant in Oakland yesterday and the grilled fish was *amazing.*'

"The second man asks the name of the place.

"The first man slaps his palm on his forehead. 'Damn, another senior moment. Help me out here. What's that flower, you know, that flower with thorns?'

"'Rose?'

"'Yeah, Rose.' Then the man shouts to his wife. '*Rose,* what was the name of that restaurant we went to last night?'"

The audience laughed. Kira smiled despite herself.

Then he segued into something about how easy it was for him, as an able-bodied man, to forget how different life was if you had a disability. He was trying so hard to be sincere.

"I'm here tonight," he said, "to talk about death and what it can teach us about living, and how to make death a better experience for everyone.

"There's actually a simple way to do that, which is talking. Of course, it's not *that* simple. We can't *prevent* suffering or pain, no matter how well we plan, but we can *increase* the odds that dying can be a positive experience instead of a wrenching one."

She could see what he was doing, trying to portray himself as reasonable and thoughtful. Not a heartless killer.

As Lamar continued, Kira grew impatient. She clasped her fingers together so she wouldn't fidget.

"I'd also like to address the disabled community's apprehension about aid-in-dying laws like Oregon's and California's. I understand those concerns more than ever before because of recent conversations with my debate partner, Kira Baylor, a remarkable woman and formidable opponent."

Buttering her up, was he? Expecting her to play the same game?

"More often than not," he said, "those people who are quote 'terminal'—that is, expected to die within six months—*are* disabled. Or will *become* disabled.

"Pain and suffering are cited as the primary reasons for choosing medical aid in dying, but from the experience in Oregon, we've learned that loss of autonomy, inability to engage in activities, and not being able to control bodily functions were the most common reasons people gave for wanting to die. The feeling of being a burden, too. Those are disability issues *more* than pain issues.

"So the concerns of the disabled community are *impossible* to separate from any discussions about end of life."

Damn, Kira thought. He was preempting her talking points. Her plan had been to lead with that very point. She was going to have to recalibrate her argument.

He kept going in the same vein, highlighting the challenges faced by the disabled, not touching at all on his usual talk.

"I *pledge* to do my very best," he said, "to be *certain* that in conversations and legislation the very legitimate concerns disabled advocates bring to the table are *always* front and center and are addressed in a *kind and humane* manner."

Now the M.C., Arun Dama, the same man who hosted their first debate on the radio, introduced Kira. But Kira was not paying attention to what he was saying about her.

With his false praise and specious sensitivity, Lamar had thrown her off. If she stuck with her script, she would sound repetitive. But she couldn't come out guns blazing and attack him or she'd seem vindictive.

Instead, she keyed in on the established body of research showing how often doctors underestimate the quality of life of people with disabilities, and how deeply ingrained is the idea that people are better off dead than disabled. But she could hear how dry it sounded as she was saying it.

So she shifted gears. She was going to kick him in the chin.

"Lamar Rose gave a remarkable introduction," she said, "in which he demonstrated his intellectual understanding of the issues the disabled community faces.

"He said things a lot like I would have said them, and in fact, as I have said them. I saw some of the people in the front row nodding their heads as he spoke. He talked the talk. I commend him for that.

"The way Lamar Rose talks about these laws, and the sensitivity he shows to the plight of the disabled is admirable. We can't count on everyone to be as enlightened and empathetic as he is.

"But really, he has no idea. He can parrot our rhetoric. But he's standing here, on his own two feet, oblivious to the real problem, which is that his support of assisted suicide has gone beyond advocacy. He took his father's life into his own hands, and, almost as horrifying, he thinks that what he did was right.

"We have recently uncovered new evidence that belies Lamar Rose's protestations that he's innocent. We already know about the browsing history on his computer and his visits to a notorious assisted-suicide website from Australia, which promotes nitrogen gas as a painless way to kill someone.

"The recent autopsy results are consistent with the use of nitrogen gas, which leaves no trace.

"We also know about the police log the night of Robert Rose's murder, the report of a disoriented man walking in the middle of Winthrop Avenue at three in the morning, five blocks from the Edgewater Care facility his father lived in.

"We have seen the videotape from the loading dock at Edgewater showing a man matching his description, leaving fifteen minutes before the police log of the disoriented man.

"And yesterday we learned that two days before his father's death, Lamar Rose purchased a tank of nitrogen from Hoppy Trails, a home-brewing supply company in Evanston, less than five miles from where his father lived."

She paused to let the evidence sink in. She heard gasps from all corners of the auditorium.

Lamar shoulders seemed to clench, but she didn't have a good angle. He took a drink of water, clasped his hands in his lap.

The audience was waiting for her to continue. She warned herself not to look smug. This was not about her winning, she reminded herself, or about punishing Lamar Rose, but about making things better for the disabled community.

"It was a cold day. January 5th. You may have read about the 'polar vortex' in Chicago. It was one of those freezing days, and the brewing supply store had only a few customers. What made them remember Lamar Rose was that most customers talked about beer, with passion and reverence. Lamar Rose did not."

33

Drug Trade

Madrid, New Mexico
July 28, 2008

The night was hot and still and Lamar was startled when Jeff knocked on the door. He could tell it was Jeff because he said, "It's Jeff," as he knocked.

Lamar had been replaying his night, and morning, with Diana, trying to figure out how to convince her to see him again. "You got your rebound fuck," she told him as he left, "and I got my tuna sushi, and we had a lovely time. I wish you the best."

"It was more than that for me," he said. "I don't understand why you—"

"Stop," she said. "I like to think of myself as generous, but sometimes I'm not. OK?"

Lamar didn't have a comeback for that. "Well, you have no idea how grateful I am."

"Oh, I think I do."

Jeff took a step through the doorway, hesitated, and looked down at his scuffed boots. He had braided the bottom of his white beard.

"I brought you some beer." He handed Lamar a six-pack. "I want to ask something."

"You want to drink one of these?" asked Lamar.

Jeff nodded and followed him to the refrigerator. "You know I have back pain and migraines," he said. "I had a doc in Santa Fe, but he's gone. I need a scrip for Vicodin."

"I'm not a psychiatrist," Lamar said. "Not a medical doctor." He had heard this sob story before.

"Sometimes the pain is so intense I want to scream."

"I'm sorry to hear that, but I'm not—"

"You told me you could prescribe drugs," Jeff said, with a mix of irritation and whining. He twisted his beard braid between his thumb and forefinger.

Lamar didn't remember telling Jeff that, but he had had more than a few drunk conversations of late, so he couldn't be sure.

"You told me," Jeff said, "that New Mexico is one of two states where psychologists can prescribe drugs, and that you had to take mucho hours of extra training."

"I'm not a proponent of drugs," Lamar said. "I believe they're overprescribed."

"You like getting high."

"I meant as a clinician."

Lamar knew Jeff had been in prison in Texas, for dealing drugs. Or something like that. He knew Jeff collected disability benefits in his own name as well as at least one other person. And that his ersatz gang was involved in some scam with Santa Fe Park and Rec workers to siphon water from the park district and truck it to Madrid to irrigate their pot farm. Which was hidden in the hills outside town.

He did not know any of this with certainty. Jeff and his compadres talked a good game.

Jeff was no choirboy. That much he knew.

Lamar smiled to himself. He folded his arms across his chest, stood tall.

"I don't just give out prescriptions. They have to be part of an overall treatment plan."

There were plenty of docs who prescribed pain meds liberally, but Lamar prided himself on not being that kind of practitioner. He had always played by the rules, though he wasn't sure all that upright behavior had paid off for him.

He recalled a joke from the comics, where an old geezer tells a new friend that he doesn't drink or smoke or eat sweets or gamble or cavort with women and now he's about to celebrate his eightieth birthday. And the other guy asks, "how?"

Sure, Lamar had a moderately successful career as a psychologist, an impressive daughter, a house in a nice neighborhood in Albuquerque. And his health, knock wood, was as good as he could hope for.

But he had lost three clients over the summer. One moved. The others disappeared. He didn't *think* it was anything he had done.

And he missed Skip coming twice a week. Skip had paid top of his scale.

Maybe he was being too scrupulous.

"I have to adhere to an ethical code of conduct," Lamar said, "which means I can't give out drugs without justification. Another beer?"

Jeff stepped aside so Lamar could open the refrigerator. "I'm in pain," he said. "A lot of pain. Construction accidents, bike wrecks. It's in my medical history."

Lamar opened a beer for himself, and sat down at his kitchen table.

"I have a question for you," he said. "I've been enjoying getting high at your place. I'd like to get some pot for my-self, and, you know, contribute to your Olympics fund."

"How much do you want?"

"What's an ounce go for?"

"Bud is $400, shake $250."

He whistled. "You're kidding. I remember paying $50, something like that." In truth, Lamar had never bought pot before. He had never had his own supply.

"Not for the sticky shit we got. You want the bud—a quarter ounce for a hundred." Jeff sat down, elbows on the table. He locked eyes with Lamar. "Or, we barter."

Lamar exhaled. "Tell me more about this pain."

34

Poker Face

First Congregational Church Auditorium
Berkeley, California
February 10, 2016
7:50 pm

Lamar was in deep shit. He thought he had been in deep already, now it was so deep he didn't know how he could climb out.

At least he was practiced at holding a poker face. He pretended he didn't notice everyone looking at him. He gave no sign of the panic shivering through his entire body. He didn't even take a deep breath, just kept breathing like he had been before Kira buried him in shit.

He had paid cash for the nitrogen. He had been bundled up from the cold, but like Kira said, no one else was buying beer-making supplies in January. He hadn't thought to make conversation about beer. He didn't even know the difference between a lager and an ale.

More circumstantial evidence, but enough to land him in trouble. In prison.

Finally it was time for audience questions. A line of wheelchairs quickly formed behind the microphone.

"We're going to start the questions now," said Arun, "but first, is there anyone who'd like to deliver a long rambling speech that has nothing to do with the subject at hand and isn't a question at all?"

The audience laughed, and a couple people raised their hands. "We're going to skip that part," he said. "Questions only, no speeches. We will turn off the microphone if you start giving a speech."

The first question was for Lamar.

"Tell us, Lamar Rose, how you used nitrogen to kill your father."

"I did not kill my father and I can't say any more on the advice of my attorney." He wanted to stop there, not qualify his answer, but his response felt too short, too unfinished.

"But I will say this. My charming and formidable opponent is quick to make accusations, but she's not as pure as new fallen snow. We all have our contradictions and she is no exception. Before her accident, she was an attorney for an employment law firm, which represented employers and other defendants in disability cases. She was lead counsel for four ADA cases, and in each of them, her opponent was a woman in a wheelchair. Now she has *become* that woman and because she knows the ins and outs of the law, she has been able to, I'm using her words, 'make herself a terrible nuisance.'

"I wonder, Kira Baylor, how you reconcile your current incarnation with who you were before."

This was not how Lamar wanted to conduct himself. He attacked Kira on the radio for questioning his intentions and now here he was attacking hers. Todd had briefed him on Kira's past and suggested he bring it up, but Lamar said it wasn't relevant. He wanted to take the high road.

But his back was against the wall.

Arun attempted to intervene, but Kira spoke over him. "That's an interesting question," she said. She was trying so hard to respond calmly that it showed. "It is true my law firm defended suits brought by women like me, in wheelchairs, and I worked on many more cases than those four as lead counsel. Those were high stakes cases, clients with big pockets."

She continued addressing her past, but then took an unexpected turn.

"One of the things I have done *since* my accident, which has made me *unpopular* in some circles," and here she craned her neck forward, pushing herself taller with her elbows pressing on the arms of her wheelchair, "is sue businesses that don't meet the Americans with Disabilities Act, the ADA. Now I'm on the other side. I have actively sought out restaurants, strip mall parking lots, and other small businesses that are not complying with the law, and filing complaints. This is how the law is enforced—there are no ADA inspectors. I earn far, far less from this than I did when I was representing employers, often around a thousand dollars per case. What I find so interesting—sad, to be honest—is that I am more vilified for what I do now than for what I did before, defending employers charged with violating the ADA. These days, I hear words like shakedown, hustler, predatory, shameful. People say I'm not even interested in having the violations fixed, which is totally false.

"I am not ashamed of what I do, and I do not apologize for it. I cannot say the same about what I did before my accident. But we're not here to talk about ADA violations. We're here to talk about the efforts of Lamar Rose and his organization, Dying By Choice, to normalize assisted suicide, euthanasia, and mercy killing. The disabled community stands united in opposing such measures."

Lamar noted how smooth Kira was, defensive at first, acknowledging her duplicity, then pivoting deftly to, and owning up to what was arguably the more unpopular behavior.

Lamar had succeeded in changing the subject, but the next questioner took another stab at him and he had to sidestep again. Not as adeptly this time.

The third questioner, a trembling old woman in a wheelchair, came to his rescue.

"My name is Cheryl Touhy and my question is for Ms. Baylor. I've been disabled for sixty years since I had a skiing accident in college and I've lived a life full of dignity, thanks to my friends and family and the amazing disabled community here in Berkeley, the wonderful advocates and service providers. But my organs are failing me, my macular degeneration is taking away my sight, and even with strong medication, I am wracked with pain. I do not have a terminal illness, yet, but if I did, I might *want* to take advantage of California's medical-aid-in-dying law. Not all disabled people see this law as a danger. Some, like me, welcome the options it gives me. Ms. Baylor, why are you working to deny me these options?"

Kira looked like she was taken by surprise. Lamar wasn't expecting a question like that either. This time Kira was not as smooth. She repeated the same line about how interesting the question was, and then seemed to be at a loss for words.

But she regrouped. "I understand wanting options. In a perfect world, I too would support those options. But the danger that these laws will be used against the disabled community is too high.

"Groups like Dying By Choice, represented here tonight by my esteemed colleague Lamar Rose, are pursuing broad agendas, with a strategy of incrementalism, expanding the pool of people who might take advantage of assisted-suicide laws. People who are suffering, but not terminal. Suffering is not something to be taken lightly, but it *is* part of life, for the able-bodied as well as the disabled, and giving people an easy exit is dangerous in so many ways."

After the debate, Lamar caught up with Todd at a bar on Shattuck, west of the campus.

"So when the fuck," said Todd, "were you going to tell me you're getting into brewing beer?"

"I bought that tank of nitrogen in Evanston, that's true, but I never used it."

"So, your story is that you were *planning* on killing your father, and you purchased all the things you needed to do the deed, but you didn't do it, and then, he conveniently died that same night, of natural causes. The night the camera saw you leaving the loading dock, the night that you were stopped by the police walking in the middle of the street. I assume you have the receipt for the tank, so you can return it."

"I thought you were going to help me."

"I'm in your corner," said Todd. "But you're going to have to answer questions like these. The prosecutor will *not* be on your side."

"I'm done with my speaking tour, aren't I?"

"Look," said Todd, "My job is to help you, not—"

Lamar's phone buzzed. It was Diana Priest from Albuquerque. Diana, Paradoxical Dreamer. He hadn't thought about her in years. Well, no, that wasn't true. He thought of her often. She had made quite an impression.

"I need to take this," Lamar said, and moved to a quiet corner.

"Diana. I'm delighted to hear from you. You're still in my phone contacts."

"You're in mine too. Of course, if you recall, I never purge anything, so don't read too much into it." But she said it in a nice way.

"To what do I owe the pleasure?" he said.

"Funny you should ask, because earlier this evening, a man named Bryce called me, *out of the blue,* and asked about *you.* He appears to know all about our dating history, or at least our email correspondence. From eight years ago. Could you have, like, been hacked? I didn't tell him anything."

Lamar hesitated. "This is the first I've heard about this. You may be aware that, um—"

"Yes, I've been following you and your controversy closely—you're sort of famous now, at least here in Albuquerque—and this has *got* to be connected. You're causing quite a stir."

"That's a nice way to put it," he said. He looked across the bar toward Todd, and decided he'd better stop before he said too much. "Let's just say I'm in more trouble than I could have possibly imagined. How are *you?*"

"Remember how I wanted to have a child?" Diana said. "Well, she's six now."

"Six, wow. Congratulations."

For a second, he panicked. Could this be his child? He only had sex once with Diana and he used a condom, and it was eight years ago. It couldn't have been him.

"Anyway," she said. "I wanted to warn you that someone is digging into your past. My past too, but he's not interested in me. He's looking for dirt on you."

PART FOUR

When We Played Zoo

35

The Scene of the Crime

Schaumburg, Illinois
February 11, 2016

Andrea's sun room was overflowing with seedlings in egg cartons and black plastic nursery pots. The dining room table was covered with seedlings too, and she had hung two full-spectrum grow lights from the chandelier with fishing twine. She had five times more seedlings than her garden could hold, but she kept planting more because she had started too early. The starts from January would be ready to plant long before the ground thawed.

She knew Drew wasn't happy she'd taken over the dining room, but he didn't say anything. He preferred a house full of vegetable starts to Andrea going back on TV and attacking her brother.

Since her explosive interview with Alice Ketting, Andrea had been hiding out. She and Paula had talked every day when they first met, but now she wasn't returning Paula's calls, though she listened to one voicemail, where Paula explained about the brewing supply store evidence. But now it was all over the news. The evidence was piling up. She had some qualms about how she had gone after Lamar, but clearly she had not falsely accused him.

She wasn't sure what to think about the young lawyer in the wheelchair stepping into her place—debating Lamar on the radio, on television, and, the previous night, at a church in California.

While she was transplanting broccoli seedlings to larger pots, she heard a knock on her front door. She looked through her blinds and saw Paula stomping her feet on the porch to knock the snow off her boots. Paula had never been to the house before.

Her first instinct was to ignore her. But, while the polar vortex had moved on, it was still well below freezing. The least she could do was invite Paula inside, as long as she stood her ground, and didn't allow herself to get roped back into something she didn't want to do.

"What are you doing here?" Andrea said. "Come in out of the cold. How do you know where I live?"

Paula unwrapped her scarf. "You're not answering your phone, so I thought I'd better make a house call."

"You made it quite clear what you thought of my TV performance," Andrea said.

"I was overly hasty in my assessment," she said. "I had my ideas about how it should go and you had yours and it *was* great TV, and you attracted a lot of attention. For *us*. I did warn you it might get ugly."

"I didn't think the ugliness would come from you. Would you like some coffee?"

"I was stressed. I came on too strong. This is my first big campaign and I would love a cup of coffee. I'm here because we have new evidence I know you're going to want to hear."

"More than the Hoppy Trails?" asked Andrea. "You know I'm pro-choice. I looked you up—your main thing before this was all abortion."

"It's a long story," said Paula, "but I'm *passionate* about stopping euthanasia. It's personal. The hospice people— they killed my uncle. *I'm sure of it.* But let me get Bryce on Skype to explain what he found. I'm sorry if I was too harsh. I want things to be just so, and that's not the way the world works. Yes, it's more than the nitrogen purchase."

Andrea led Paula to her kitchen and the long table facing the backyard where she set up her laptop. Well, that had been quite the sincere apology, Andrea thought.

The investigator that Force for Life had contracted with was a youngish man with a red beard named Bryce, who was somewhere in age between Paula and Andrea. On the computer screen, he looked pale. The computer cameras were getting better, but without good lighting, most people looked worse than in person.

As they said their hellos, Paula fiddled with the angle, the volume, the brightness. Andrea handed Paula her coffee and sat down next to her.

"Here's what I've got," said Bryce, looking down at his notes. "First, not necessarily most important, we've logged in to your brother's email and we have all sorts of correspondence, mostly from the past. Including more than six months of emails with various women he met or attempted to meet on dating websites."

Andrea hesitated before she spoke. "I don't understand why his dating emails are relevant. That's personal stuff. Embarrassing even."

"*Exactly,*" Bryce said. "I would *never* want this kind of correspondence in someone else's hands. Anyway, as Paula told you, I'm in Albuquerque, where Lamar lives, and I've contacted several of the women he met in real life. Nothing to report yet. We're digging wherever we think we might find something useful. Everyone has secrets.

"Second, more significant, but murky. Yesterday I visited Madrid—that's pronounced *Mad*-rid, the locals instructed me—where Lamar lived after he left his wife in June 2008. He hosted a house party there during the presidential campaign, an Obama house party. His daughter worked on the campaign. After this party there was an altercation between Lamar and an outlaw motorcycle gang member named Jeff Greer, who has a long rap sheet. A physical fight over a rifle, and it led to Lamar leaving Madrid and moving back to Albuquerque. Reckless behavior. We have a phone video.

"Third, Lamar met a woman in Madrid named Greta Lang, his landlady, who had cancer, and they became friends, and, according to two sources, he helped her die. Per her request. In other words, his father was not the first person he killed, but the second."

Andrea felt a shudder in her shoulders. *Oh my God, he's done this before. I was right all along.*

She hesitated before she spoke. She could tell they were waiting for her to say something. Though she knew the investigator was digging into Lamar's past, she hadn't expected him to find anything. Now she would have to finish the job she started. Which is what she wanted, wasn't it?

"How do we know this?" she asked.

"Let me share one piece of this puzzle," said Bryce. "The county clerk shows that in 2008, Lamar inherited a house in Madrid from Greta Lang. That inheritance was contested by Mrs. Lang's daughters. I've identified the lawyer who wrote the will, but have not had a chance to speak with him.

"The daughters called for an investigation into her death,

but it didn't go anywhere. The law in New Mexico says that anyone who dies at home, with no witnesses, is reported to the medical examiner's office. Whether any action is taken depends on the circumstances. Nothing was done at the time. No autopsy. Lamar Rose reported the death, said he found her dead when he went to visit. He called the hospice people first. Of course, they weren't going to squeal on him.

"In light of what we know now, his actions have new significance, as does his involvement in hospice training and the Death Cafe he hosted in Santa Fe. This is where he started on the path to where he is today.

"I'll have more tomorrow, when you get here," Bryce said, "but I—"

"Get here?" asked Andrea. "Where? New Mexico?"

"Paula didn't tell you?"

Paula put her hand on Andrea's shoulder. Gently. "This has been a challenging time for Andrea, Bryce. That was me, thinking out loud. She has a lot going on here."

Then to Andrea: "I don't want you to feel like we're *manipulating* you for our own ends. *I'll* be there tomorrow. You don't need to be."

"You don't want me there?"

"I didn't want to commit you," said Paula. "I know you have reservations."

"You *really* think Lamar did this before? And why New Mexico?"

"Madrid is an awesome place to bring reporters," said Bryce. "It's like a western movie set here. An artist colony. Biker gangs at the tavern. All this hippie color in the middle of the desert."

"This seems tangential to our main objective," said Andrea. "Getting justice for what Lamar did to my father."

"It's the scene of the first crime," said Paula. "This will

strengthen our case. He's a repeat offender. A man with a shady past. A history of taking people's lives into his own hands."

"In case you're concerned, you won't run into Lamar here," Bryce added. "He's doing talks in California. But you know that already."

"I heard about Greta," Andrea said. "That she died, that her death was significant to Lamar. Though nothing like Janis'."

"Janis?" asked Paula.

"Lamar's wife," said Bryce. "Who OD'd."

"Right, of course," said Paula, who looked into the distance, and ran her fingers through her hair. "Andrea, do you think Lamar could have had *anything* to do with his wife's overdose?"

"I don't," Andrea answered, without hesitation.

But then.

"Well, I didn't. Now I don't know what to think."

36

No Is a Complete Sentence

Madrid, New Mexico
August 10, 2008

Jeff kicked open Lamar's front door.

No knock, no hello. Lamar hadn't seen him since he wrote a Vicodin prescription a week earlier.

"We need more scrips." Jeff put his hands on his hips and stared down Lamar.

Lamar waited him out. He could outwait anyone. He took deep breaths and counted to thirty under his breath.

A thunderstorm had hurtled through that afternoon, leaving behind the clean and husky smell of chamisa and sage. Nightfall was an hour away.

Then Lamar responded, calm as a desert tortoise. "No."

Just that afternoon, one of Lamar's clients had been talking about how he turned down a demand from his father with a one-word answer. No.

And then he added, "No is a complete sentence."

It was a sweet and satisfying moment. The client got that from me, Lamar told himself. When clients internalized what they learned in therapy and thought it was their own idea, *that* was the mother lode. *No is a complete sentence.*

Expecting more of an answer, Jeff got agitated, and repeated his demand. Louder. Lamar waited again. He used his stillness as a shield.

Finally, he responded calmly. "Not going to happen, my friend."

"You don't understand," said Jeff. "I'm not asking. You don't get to say no."

Lamar picked up a washcloth hanging on the sink faucet and wiped the counter.

"There are so many ways we can make your life suck," Jeff said.

"I'm not sure what you mean by 'make my life suck.'"

"Don't play games with me."

"Look, Jeff, I was wrong, *stupid*, to have given you those scrips in the first place. It's illegal and unethical."

"This is Madrid. No one cares. You traded for weed."

Lamar had felt uncomfortable after writing that first prescription, but he also experienced an exhilaration he did not expect. Breaking the rules to get high was a high in itself. He was in outlaw country, he told himself. Do as the outlaws do.

For Jeff's second prescription, Lamar made him come to his office in Santa Fe and sit in the patients' chair. Which he did. Lamar wasn't peddling painkillers any more than thousands of pharmas and practitioners did every day.

But once he heard Jeff was selling the drugs, or the prescriptions—he heard different stories from different people—he knew he had to stop. Two was two too many.

"I thought this was a tolerant place," said Lamar. "I'm not calling in your pot farm. Why can't you accept someone who plays by the rules?"

"We invited you over. We were friendly. *Mi casa es su casa*. We do favors for each other in Madrid."

"I'm all for favors. You have been a gracious host and I appreciate it, but that doesn't mean I have to sell you drugs."

Lamar was determined to get himself back to ethical ground zero, but he was also afraid Jeff was going to hurt him. Maybe not now, but soon enough.

Lamar had been threatened by raving clients off their meds, about to snap. But here was a real bad guy, someone who'd served time in prison, who had followed through on threats, if he was to be believed. Jeff glared at him with a menacing look, his eyes like slits, his hands balled into fists.

But he was an old man. His sharp edge had been dulled by age. Jeff bought the best helmets and covered himself in expensive leather. He didn't even ride much any more. He was a homebody, as soft as Lamar.

Jeff walked over to the kitchen bar and grabbed the glazed wine glass Lamar had been drinking from. He lifted it in a mock toast, then hurled it at the TV. The wine glass shattered into pieces. The monitor cracked. Red wine splashed on the wall.

"That glass was an *original*," said Lamar, "from Janie down on the highway. As if you care. Support your local artists and all that."

"You'll be sorry." He kicked a big shard, the curve of the glass, as he left. It skittered toward the door. He stomped it on the way out. Lamar pointed the remote at the TV. It still worked. But the crack was like a bolt of lightning across the screen. *Fucking asshole.*

Lamar wiped the wine from the wall and floor. He swept up, fuming, but relieved he hadn't given in. If the only price he paid for this transgression was a cracked monitor and a broken wine glass, he was getting off easy.

His heart was still racing even after he sat down. Of course, he had been reckless to write the prescriptions. Had he done so *because* it was reckless? Well, he had wanted the pot.

It had been beyond stupid. Shaking up his life was one thing, but dealing drugs, that was leaping off a cliff.

Leaving Janis and moving to Madrid had been the right thing to do, but perhaps he'd taken the rejection of his old life too far. He'd lost clients. He continued to navigate this new terrain without a therapist. He promised himself he would make some calls tomorrow.

But he didn't need to wait to get back to his yoga. It had been weeks since he had done a single pose. He unrolled his mat and did some planks, but he was too agitated. Jeff could have done a lot worse than throw a glass at the TV.

The evening was still young, and ordinarily he would have walked over to Jeff's or down to the Mine Shaft. But he didn't want to run into Jeff or one of his mates, so he walked over to Greta's with a bottle of wine.

He waited at least a minute after knocking before turning around. That was when she opened the door.

"Free for a glass of wine?" he said, holding up the bottle.

She was short of breath and look drained, but seemed pleased to see him.

"Did I wake you up? I should have called." He hadn't seen her with a walker before.

"Nonsense," she said, and welcomed him in. He had only been inside once, to drop off the rent money. Her house was three times the size of Lamar's but felt more crowded because of all the heavy, portentous furniture, like a ruby red overstuffed couch. Her windows were covered by thick floral drapes. It felt stuffy instead of clean and fresh. It was a beautiful night. He would have opened all the windows.

"Jeff threw a glass at my TV," he said. "Cracked the monitor. He's threatening me because I won't write prescriptions for him."

Lamar liked how he said that, with no play for pity. Greta poured two glasses and motioned Lamar to the couch. She sat across from him in a recliner. "Jeff has a temper. Acts like a spoiled child. What I really want to hear about is your dating."

He wasn't finished talking about Jeff.

"I won't be jealous," she said.

"Nothing to be jealous of," he said.

"You'd better get busy then."

He was not going to tell her about sleeping with Diana, though he knew she would be interested. There wasn't much else to report.

"Jeff broke my television."

"Buy another one. You have a job. You're certainly not going broke paying rent."

He started to say that he was also paying a mortgage for the house on Coal Avenue, but Greta didn't tolerate whining. So he told her about finally meeting the yoga teacher he had been so excited about. She was as attractive as her photos, but their conversation was stiff and labored.

"She could not even—" Then Greta started coughing. And it got worse.

"Greta, are you OK?"

She pulled her elbow up to her face and coughed into her arm. The cough was harsh and raspy. Violent. She had tears running down her cheek. He walked over to her and put his hand on her shoulder, but she waved him away.

"Just wine going down the wrong pipe."

He went to the kitchen to pour her some water.

"Look," Lamar said, as he handed her the glass. "I'm trained to pay attention to people, and it looks to me like something else might be going on. You don't have to tell me, but if you want to, you can."

"Nonsense. It's nothing. I'm fine."

37

Lamar Rose Has Killed Before

Albuquerque, New Mexico
February 11, 2016

Lamar flew to Albuquerque the morning after the debate in Berkeley. Paid $437 for a one-way ticket. He tried one of those last-minute deal sites, but didn't have the patience. He needed to get home.

That night, he met Diana for dinner at El Patio, a cozy Mexican restaurant near the UNM campus. Sierra's favorite.

Diana was prettier than he remembered. Hardly looked like she'd aged. Her hair still reddish, but more subdued, a rich rust brown. Still overdressed in her quirky way. Bundled up as if she were in Chicago. Her turquoise and orange earrings matched her heavy necklace.

They both ordered the same dish, the green chile chicken enchiladas. Hers was gluten free. She had dropped her daughter at a friend's.

"Just want to be sure you understand," Diana said. "You and me. We have no future together."

"You made that clear enough on the phone. 'Two hours

is plenty of time, because we're not going to have sex.' I'm not saying I gave that no thought—you're an attractive and charismatic woman, very much so, and you look lovely tonight, by the way—but I do have a *few other* things on my mind.

"You do."

"Tell me about your daughter."

In her early forties, Diana decided she couldn't wait any longer, and moved forward with the process of adopting a child as a single mother, which was possible, but not easy.

The enchiladas came, and Lamar dug in, but Diana didn't even pick up her fork. The smell in the restaurant was glorious, especially the roasting peppers.

"I got lucky and found a six-month-old girl from Haiti," said Diana, "whose mother had died. She was living with her aunt. Her name is Lovely, which I *love*. She's in first grade. It's been wonderful, wonderful, especially the past couple years. It was hard at first. She was so demanding. I have a village now. Other mothers. Other families. So many kids in my life now, it's better than I ever could have hoped. Except for the husband part. That hasn't happened. I'm not on the dating sites, but it appears, somehow, that my past, *our* past, is still out there."

Lamar said that she *had* been clear, eight years earlier, that she had wanted a child, but he hadn't grasped how *important* it was to her. Now he did. He told her she seemed so much happier, contented, than she had been. She beamed.

She continued to talk about her daughter, her work, her parents, and Lamar listened, as was his wont, until she seemed to realize she had been doing all the talking. She said she wanted to hear about him. Lamar had cleaned his plate. She hadn't touched her food.

"You know this thing, this accusation, mercy-killing my

father," said Lamar. "It's true. What my sister says happened. It happened."

He girded himself for the reaction he got from Julia. But Diana was not Julia.

Her eyes widened, then she dug into her enchilada.

"Aren't you going to say anything?" he asked. "About what I did?"

"I'm sure you gave it a lot of thought, except for your purchase at the beer store."

He rolled his eyes. "The nitrogen tank is going to kill me."

"You didn't expect all this uproar?"

"No. I told my girlfriend, just recently—my ex-girlfriend, it appears—and she got angry at me. For telling her the truth. Said I handed her a burden she didn't want. That she would rather I kept it to myself."

"I'm not your girlfriend."

"You keep reminding me of that."

"I want to hear the whole story. You and your father. What you did. I assume what I've read is not necessarily accurate."

"The full story would take too long."

"We still have an hour."

The next morning, Lamar was rolling out his yoga mat when Diana called.

"Me again." He was happy she called, but her hesitant voice gave him pause.

"I'm sending you a link," she said. "You have to look at it right away. I'll wait."

But as he opened his email, he heard her talking. "No, I

can't wait. The newspaper is saying you killed before. Here in New Mexico. In Madrid."

There it was, the email from Diana. He clicked on the link.

"*What? The Chicago Sun-Times?*" He had to sit down. "You there?"

"The front page," she said.

"That explains all the voicemails," he said. "There was—"

"You didn't talk to anyone, did—"

"No, no, Todd, my lawyer, read me the riot act—don't answer your phone, he said. Don't listen to the voicemails. Forward them all to him. But I thought the calls were about the nitrogen tank. *Oh shit!*"

He saw a photo slowly coming into focus, a dark, grainy shot that he hadn't seen before. But he knew immediately what it was—the loading dock at Edgewater. A man bundled up, hugging himself, arms folded across his chest, mittens on his shoulders, his face in shadow behind his hood.

Under the photo was the headline—"Lamar Rose Has Killed Before." It was about Greta. How he "helped" *her* die like he helped his father.

38

Sliver of Blue

Coal Avenue
Albuquerque, New Mexico
August 20, 2008

While slathering toast with egg salad, Janis told Lamar, "You should have left long ago."

Lamar hesitated, wary of a trap.

"I don't know why I'm telling you this," she continued, sitting down with her sandwich, "except I'm doing my hopey-changey thing, like Sarah Palin might say. What I enjoyed *most* about my depression, and I know *enjoy* is not the right word, but what I enjoyed *most* was how *me* being so depressed drove *you* crazy. I brought you down with me, and you stayed there with me. When you left, there was no one paying attention."

Lamar was surprised by her honesty, but not by what she said. It was what he had long suspected.

"I snapped out of it," she said, "Maybe it's my meds."

"Or maybe having your stomach pumped in the ER," said Lamar, throwing caution out the window.

"I know you think that was a hostile gesture," she said, seemingly not bothered by his reply. "Sierra says my OD was like taking a dump on the living room rug. Whatever, it was a midlife tantrum, for an audience of two—my husband and my daughter. *See, this is how bad things are. Now pay attention.* But it didn't work. You went off on your dating odyssey—I know what you're up to—and Sierra barely has time to walk the dog. She has no patience for my *'indulgent bullshit'*—that's what she calls it."

Janis had come a long way since her release from the hospital. From the moment she came home, she was all about rebuilding her practice, walking Caro every day, reading the newspaper front to back. While Lamar was splattering his cabin in Madrid, she went on her own painting binge, repainting the entire house on Coal Avenue by herself. In gold, yellow, and orange. Bright, sunny colors. That had to mean something.

She seemed more animated every time he saw her, and, in small, but real ways, reminded him of the woman he had fallen in love with long ago. That woman was still there, behind the gray hair and pale face and decades of passive aggressiveness. And now here she was, acknowledging her failings.

She had been a force of nature back then, with a gleam in her eye, and a sexy, cheeky attitude. Maybe it had been mania, maybe youth, maybe the times.

She had been adorable, giggly-cute, too, but it was so long ago he wondered if he had made up that part. She was *so far* from where she had been and looked so worn out, though better than when he left at the start of the summer. She had lost a little weight and she was almost stylish in her blue yoga pants and white blouse. In the past few weeks, she had even started wearing makeup again.

What if she were tall and pretty like Diana Priest? Would he have been so quick to leave?

But he hadn't been quick, had he?

Janis finished her sandwich. Licked her lips. The kitchen was cold, the air conditioner on high. Lamar studied the kitchen cabinets, not sure whether he liked the glossy gold doors.

"You remember my friend Amy," Janis said, "she does this thing on Yom Kippur, she apologizes to everyone she knows, in case she's hurt them. A clean slate. I apologize to you. I hurt you. I blamed you. That wasn't fair. I don't want to wait until Yom Kippur."

Lamar had followed through on what he promised the doc at the hospital—to eat lunch with Janis two or three days a week. He never imagined he would open himself up to Janis again, but now she was presenting a vulnerability he hadn't experienced in a long time.

For the moment, she did not appear to be wielding her pain as a weapon.

He was no fool when it came to reading people, but he had his blind spots.

Diana had said no to more dates, and Lamar had continued to pursue other women, but it was frustrating, and, as he bit into a tart apple at the kitchen table, he found himself wondering if he should give Janis another try. He knew better, but still....

What he did *not* want was to get back with her because he felt defeated. But he wasn't defeated. Not yet. Lost maybe. Frustrated. Ungrounded. But not defeated. This new, more reckless Lamar was a revelation, as imperfect and uncertain as a teenager getting behind the wheel.

But for the first time since forever, he asked himself if there might be a future with Janis. It was a small opening, like seeing a sliver of blue sky behind a mass of dark clouds, but an opening all the same.

He took the dishes to the sink. "I have a question." He waited for her to respond, but she didn't. "What I want to know is, did you feel like you had no choice? When you were so deep in depression. I'm asking sincerely. I've accused you of not wanting to get better."

"Oh, I wanted to, but the climb was so steep I couldn't do it. It didn't seem worth the effort. Then you left."

39

Turquoise and Coffee

Madrid, New Mexico
February 13, 2016
9:45 am

Lamar planned to go directly to Jeff's, but he stopped first at Turquoise and Coffee on the main highway. He wasn't exactly friends with Justine, the cafe proprietor, but she had come up to his cabin for the Obama house party back in 2008, and he remembered Greta saying that Justine knew everyone's business. She had been part of the first wave of hippie artists to resettle Madrid in the late 1970s. If there were rumors swirling around town about Lamar killing Greta, she would know.

She did.

Turquoise and Coffee was a combination cafe, gift shop, and bed and breakfast, with a couple of cottages behind the restaurant for guests. She also had a greenhouse full of vegetables for the restaurant.

He ordered a blackberry-filled turnover. The restaurant courtyard was full of flowers, especially bougainvillea, and many of the prickly pears were blooming. Justine sat across a red metal table from him with the morning sun on her back. It was chilly in the shade, so Lamar moved his chair into the sun.

Justine said everyone in town was keeping up with Lamar's troubles, even folks who didn't know him. He was the local celebrity. Justine had seen the headline blaming him for Greta's death online, but she didn't know how quickly that news had traveled. Plenty of people in Madrid got their news from gossip, she said, not from reading the internet.

Lamar walked with Justine back to the kitchen.

"Has anyone been around asking questions? I'm trying to figure out where this news came from, where things are going."

"A couple days ago," she said, "this young guy with a red beard asked about you. I didn't tell him anything. He said he *heard* you had something to do with Greta's death, that what you're accused of doing to your father you may have done to Greta."

"'*May have done?*'" Lamar was incredulous. "*Greta had cancer. She died.* That's what happens when people get cancer."

"He claimed you were part of this '*death cult*' in Santa Fe."

The death cult. Andrea's words.

The *Sun-Times* story used those words too, and referenced his training in hospice, his hosting of a Death Cafe, that one time. Those things were true, but they got the chronology wrong. That all came *after* Greta died.

"The story refers to 'multiple sources,' Lamar said. "Any idea who they might be?"

"In Madrid," said Justine, "you tell one person, and

soon everyone knows. Maybe those multiple sources are repeating the same story they heard.

"You haven't been around—you probably don't know that Greta's daughter Cat is here now. She may have said something. She's staying in Greta's old place. I don't pretend to know what happened between her and her mother, but she was majorly pissed Greta left you her cabin. But you know that. Have you met her?"

"No. I got letters from her lawyer."

"Of course, you should ask Jeff. I always assumed it was him who helped Greta die. Not that I have a problem with him—or whoever—if he did."

40

Madrid House Party

Madrid, New Mexico
August 28, 2008
6:30 pm

On the last Thursday of August, the evening of Barack Obama's acceptance speech at the Democratic National Convention in Denver, Lamar hosted a house party and more than two dozen people crowded into his shotgun shack.

It was like a party in a dorm room, without the young people.

Part of his daughter's job as director of the New Mexico Democracy Project was organizing house parties and she persuaded him to host one. She was hard to say no to. His was one of more than two hundred parties around the state, she told him.

During the weeks leading up to the party, Lamar had knocked on every door in town, invited everyone he met. Greta helped him recruit guests, supplied a dozen folding chairs, and took charge of the refreshments. Lamar insisted on reimbursing her, but she wouldn't take his money.

Jeff was the first to arrive, wheeling a keg of beer to the house in a wooden wagon, with a big box of red plastic cups, enough for every house party in the state.

Lamar had not invited Jeff because of his threats, and besides, he had said he wasn't into voting anyway. He didn't want his name in the system, he claimed, though that didn't seem to be a problem when he was cashing multiple social security checks.

But there he was, friendly at first, bantering with others, listening to the talking heads on the TV. But he was guzzling beer like he had to catch up with someone, and then he became surly and obnoxious, and left.

Shortly before Obama was scheduled to begin his speech, while Al Gore was holding forth on the big screen, Jeff barged in through the front door waving a black rifle that looked, for a second, like a toy.

It wasn't.

The room went silent. Though the sun was low in the sky, it was still hot and the crowded shack smelled like a locker room.

"That nigger is going to take away our guns," Jeff shouted, aiming his weapon at Lamar's cracked big-screen TV, which flashed a photo of Barack Obama and the time of his speech under it. Start time, five minutes.

Lamar acted calmer than he felt. "Excuse me, Jeff, you're not welcome in my home with that gun."

Jeff turned and aimed at Lamar, who stiffened. No one spoke, except Al Gore, who marched along with his introduction of Senator Obama, oblivious to the drama in Lamar's cabin.

Lamar put up his hands, "Outside, Jeff," said Lamar, as he walked out the front door, his arms up above his head, hoping Jeff would follow. He was trying to balance playing at this like it was a game, which he hoped it was, and treating it like a serious threat, which he hoped it wasn't. Behind his gruff, Jeff was generally harmless. But he *was* drunk.

"Let's keep everyone else out of this," he said over his shoulder. "Just you and me."

He heard footsteps behind him, but didn't know if Jeff was following him. Until he slowed down and felt the barrel poke him in the back. They passed through the clump of cars in Lamar's driveway, to the dusty walkway in front of the mailbox jungle. "What kind of gun is that, Jeff?" Lamar asked, slowing his pace again.

"M-16," he said, coming up next to Lamar. "Like in Iraq. Better than the AK-47."

"What makes it better?" Lamar knew Jeff had guns, but they had never talked about them.

As Jeff answered, he lowered his gun, and Lamar grabbed it, yanked it away, and tried to heave it into the patch of prickly pear in front of the mailboxes. But Jeff got a hand on it and pulled hard, dragging Lamar onto the gravel. Lamar didn't let go, and Jeff fell on top of him.

As he pushed his way out from under Jeff, Lamar saw party guests hiding behind the cars, watching them fight.

Jeff climbed off Lamar, picked up the rifle and trained it on Lamar. "You come to town," he said, "and start making up rules we're all supposed to follow. No guns? Says who?"

"It's my house," Lamar said, standing up, brushing pebbles off his arm. Jeff was not going to shoot him. Not in front of all his neighbors. "If you don't want to follow the rules for my house, you're not welcome."

Greta, who was moving slowly because of her bad leg, waddled through the parked cars. "Stop acting crazy, Jeff. Put that gun down."

"I'm not crazy." he said. He was still pointing the rifle at Lamar. "I'm pissed off because this *pussy* won't renew our scrips. Some bullshit about ethics. This is fucking *Madrid*." Then, to Greta, "Get away from me."

Greta walked in front of Jeff and pushed the muzzle of the gun down. Jeff didn't resist until she tried to take the gun from him. He wouldn't let go. Neither would she. He almost threw her to the ground before he loosened his grip.

Once Greta had the rifle, she turned it around, held it by the barrel, and swung it like a baseball bat at Jeff's knee. He grunted, but stood tall. She hadn't hit him that hard.

Then Greta's legs caved in under her and she collapsed, and everyone rushed to help her.

Jeff grabbed the rifle and slipped away.

41

Cat

Madrid, New Mexico
February 13, 2016
10:25 am

Lamar had met Cat's older sister Grace at Greta's memorial. Cat had not come.

The house looked different. It was no longer Greta's. The living room walls were the same deep maroon, the wood floors scuffed and scratched, the cobwebs stretching between the ceiling beams. But the heavy furniture, like Greta's floor-to-ceiling armoires, were gone, replaced by, well, mostly nothing. The big room was empty except for a blond wood side table and a leather chair.

Cat offered him coffee. He followed her to the kitchen, also spartan, but with two chairs. This house had been built at the same time as Lamar's but was longer and wider, with a kitchen, bedroom, and bathroom at the back. With walls and doors. Not all one room like his cabin.

"Who told you I killed your mother?" Lamar leaned against the tile counter as Cat poured the coffee.

"Lots of people," she said. "I don't remember."

"I heard," Lamar said, choosing his words carefully, "you were *unhappy* your mother left me the cabin."

"Nothing personal. Just my loving mother sticking it to me from the grave."

"You inherited *this* place, I assume. Or do I have that wrong?"

Lamar knew that story, but wanted to hear Cat's version.

"Another bullshit move. She left it to me *and* my sister. Knowing we hardly speak. Plus there was probate. I spent more on lawyers than this place is worth, never expecting I would live here." She shrugged her shoulders.

Then came an awkward silence. He wished Diana were with him. She had offered to accompany him to Madrid, but he thought it would be better if he went on his own. She had her work and her daughter. But she also had a disarming way of being blunt and friendly at the same time.

"Your mother had a lot of regrets," Lamar said, "about you and Grace."

"You mean like how she left us behind to move to Alaska with her asshole new husband?"

She snarled that sentence, her voice low and harsh. More hurt than angry, it seemed, and the heat was not directed at him. He had enough people attacking him already. He didn't need one more.

"I'm sure she told you," Cat continued, "about how her new husband wasn't keen on having two teenage girls demanding their mother's attention, and he made her choose. Him or us. She chose him. I'm sure she told you *that* story."

She sighed as if in relief, like she had been holding that enmity in for too long.

"No, she didn't," Lamar said. Well, she *had*, but not *that* version.

"I let that go," Cat said. "I thought I did."

"Letting go is hard." Lamar paused. They were still standing in the kitchen, clutching their cups. For a moment, he forgot about the trouble he was in.

"Did you do therapy with my mom?" she asked.

"No, I sat with her."

"What's the difference?"

"Well, in therapy, you're usually addressing a problem. Creating a new life. Excavating a deep wound. In hospice, it's just sitting. Being present. Not fixing anything. Making the moment as rich as it can be."

"It wasn't me who said you killed my mom. It was Jeff."

42

I Don't Want Everyone to Know

Madrid, New Mexico
August 28, 2008
7:30 pm

"No doctors." Greta was adamant.

Justine and Lamar walked Greta to her house, their arms under her shoulders, carrying most of her weight. Justine kept saying she should go to the emergency room.

"I felt like a girl when that adrenalin kicked in," Greta said, "whacking Jeff with that rifle, ready to conquer the world. I just ran out of gas. That's all. Thank you, though."

They settled her in her recliner and Justine wet a washcloth for Greta's forehead. After confronting Jeff, Greta had fallen on her side on hard-packed dirt, and then hit her head. She had a scratch on her ear, but no blood.

Justine had to head back to her restaurant. Lamar said he would stay with Greta.

They watched TV together, the end of Obama's speech and then the talking heads dissecting it. There was a black woman he didn't recognize saying she watched the speech with her 90-year old mother, and they both had tears streaming down their faces at the end.

During a commercial, Lamar muted the TV. "Would you like me to rub your feet?" he asked.

"You would do that?" she said.

"If you want."

He found baby oil in the bathroom and took off Greta's socks.

"You can't keep pretending nothing is wrong," Lamar said. "I asked Justine." He pressed with his thumb just below the ball of her foot. She moaned, or was it more like purring?

"Justine told you? She swore she wouldn't. Oh, that feels good."

"I did my therapist voodoo on her. Why won't you see a doctor?"

"I have lung cancer. I used to smoke. Foolish me. What else do I need to know?"

Greta grimaced. He had pressed too hard.

"Don't blame Justine," Lamar said. "She didn't tell me anything. Just to ask you."

Greta gave him a stern frown to let him know she wasn't happy he had tricked her. But he sensed she wasn't angry. "I don't want *everyone* to know," she said.

"You've been grilling me for details about my silly dates," said Lamar, "and here you are holding onto life-and-death news."

"I'm not doing chemo," she said.

Lamar waited. Kept rubbing, but not pressing as hard.

"I watched my second husband die and the chemo was as bad as the cancer. It doesn't have to be that way."

"You get to choose," Lamar said. "Sometimes people get pressured into treatment they don't want. Are you in pain?"

"I've been in pain for years. I'm a tough old bird. Drugs help."

Greta fell asleep in her recliner, and Lamar closed his eyes and tried to nap as well, but there was too much to sort through.

It had been quite a day. The house party, fighting over the rifle with Jeff, but none of that mattered now.

Greta was dying, and that made him *so sad.*

43

But There Are Always Questions

Madrid, New Mexico
February 13, 2016
10:50 am

Lamar walked from Cat's to Jeff's in two minutes, feeling a bit of trepidation as he approached. Jeff opened his door before Lamar knocked.

"I heard you were coming," he said.

Lamar barely recognized him. He looked frail and sick. His beard was no longer braided, it looked more like a dried paintbrush. Next to him was an oxygen tank. He'd lost weight.

"Hey, my friend," Lamar said. "You look like shit. What's going on?"

"Fuck you, too. I'm dying."

"I'm so sorry. Soon?" He meant it, too. On his walk to Jeff's, Lamar had taken some long deep breaths to keep his cool, so his anger wouldn't get the better of him, but now he felt sympathy toward Jeff instead.

"Not soon enough," Jeff said. "Emphysema. I've got

a year, maybe three."

"How's your back pain?"

"Better. I have pills. Medicare Part D. Come in."

Jeff had never been much of a housekeeper, but he used to throw things away. Not so much now. The kitchen table, the chairs, the counters were all piled with, well, everything. Beer bottles, records, boxes of cereal, dirty dishes, stacks of toilet paper, motorcycle parts in shrink wrap.

Lamar found the least cluttered chair, lifted a basket of towels and set it on the floor.

"You know I'm in trouble," he said.

"We're watching," said Jeff, as he wheeled his oxygen tank and collapsed into his recliner. "We're rooting for you. You're an outlaw now."

"You make it sound romantic," Lamar said. "It's not."

Jeff used the remote to lean back in the chair. Lamar waited.

"You know I've been accused of killing Greta. Cat says that came from you."

"Don't believe her," Jeff said. "She didn't even come for her mother's funeral."

"Then who?" Lamar asked. "Nothing goes on in this burg that you don't know about. You're like the mayor here."

"Oh, that would be a *bad* idea," said Jeff. "Cat's angry you got the cabin, right?"

Lamar nodded. Jeff reached for a plastic bowl on the side table. "I can't smoke pot anymore. This is candy from Colorado." He extended the bowl to Lamar. "One won't do much. A light buzz. It's legal. In Colorado."

Lamar shook his head no. Jeff placed one on his tongue, closed his eyes for a second.

"So did you talk to this investigator?" Lamar asked. "Young guy with a red beard?"

"I might have."

"And?"

"He asked a lot of questions. About you. About Greta. He knew you visited her. That was no secret."

"And you said?"

"He said a lot of people thought it was me," said Jeff. "Who killed Greta."

"And?"

Jeff didn't say anything.

Lamar tried not to show his exasperation. "I'm guessing the guy asked, could Lamar have killed her?"

"I didn't tell him squat."

"Justine told me," said Lamar, "there are also stories floating around about me writing painkiller scrips for you."

"He asked about that too."

"I covered my ass with the drugs," said Lamar. "Everything by the books. Filled out all the forms. Still doesn't look good."

"The guy said he heard you left town because we threatened you when you wouldn't give us more scrips."

"You did threaten me."

"We weren't going to kill you or anything."

"Glad to hear it."

Lamar turned to leave, then stopped. He hesitated, then went over to Jeff and gave him a hug. As best he could with Jeff tilted back in the recliner. Jeff stiffened, and then, after a few seconds, pulled away.

He unwrapped another candy. "You know we—my troop—we take care of each other. Someone wants to go, it's done. No questions."

Lamar gave himself a moment to compose a response, but Jeff spoke first.

"But there are always questions."

44

New Mexico–
It's Not New and It's Not Mexico

Madrid, New Mexico
February 14, 2016
8:30 am

When she climbed out of the rental car in Madrid, Andrea marveled at how dry and warm the air was. Chicago had been buried in snow when she left. She had been to New Mexico before, to visit Lamar, but never to Madrid.

Bryce, the investigator who dug up the new dirt on Lamar, was walking Andrea and Paula through the gravel lot in front of the Gypsy Plaza, where they would hold their media event.

The building behind them was salmon-colored stucco with turquoise and baby blue trim. Andrea was not a fan of bright and gaudy colors, but she had to admit this Gypsy Plaza was picturesque, almost enchanting.

"You can see what a cool backdrop we've got," Bryce said. "Like a movie set. They did actually shoot a movie here. Wild Hogs. About a biker gang."

Andrea had read up on Madrid while Paula drove them from Santa Fe. Thousands of people lived in the town back when coal mining was big, then it became a ghost town. In the 1960s, artists and hippies repopulated it, painting the wooden houses in bright colors.

"This is not an interview," said Paula. "Alice Ketting wanted an exclusive, wanted an interview. But we said no. It's more like press conference. You make your statement, answer a few questions. We got RSVPs from five other outlets."

Andrea was sticking to her script this time. No improvisation. She would be measured and calm. She would not attack Lamar. The evidence would do that for her.

Alice Ketting and her camera guy arrived, introduced themselves. Andrea had not met Alice Ketting in person before, only on a TV monitor in an empty studio. She wore black boots with a more feminine, but still strident, red print dress. A crowd was gathering in the lot. Didn't look like a lot happened here, so a TV shoot was a big deal. A white van with one of those corkscrew antennas pulled into the lot. It said KRQE News 13 on the side.

At two minutes after ten, with the cameras rolling, Paula introduced Andrea, who started by reviewing the evidence, going into detail about the brewing supply store, even though that was already all over the news.

"We are here to present damning *new* evidence this morning against Lamar Rose, my brother, who, I am convinced, killed our father Robert Rose in Chicago." Andrea's voice was measured and calm, the way Lamar talked. She was not unaware of the irony, but no one had to know.

"You may have heard the serious charge that my brother Lamar Rose also killed Madrid resident Greta Lang. That's why we're here. We have spoken with law enforcement in

Santa Fe County to pursue leads in that case now, and they are coordinating with the Cook County District Attorney's office in Illinois.

"The organization I work with, the Sanctity of Life, has hired an investigator named Bryce Canyon." It sounded weird when she said his name. He must have made it up.

"He has uncovered evidence about Lamar Rose during the time he lived here in Madrid in 2008, after he left his wife of twenty-seven years and rented a cabin on Grasshopper Lane, across the highway." Andrea remembered the day Lamar had called to tell her he had split up with Janis and was moving here, but Paula said not to mention that because it might humanize him.

"The first thing Lamar Rose did was pursue women he met on the internet. There's nothing illegal about that, but according to email threads obtained by our investigator, he wrote letters to more than *seventy* women, all based on a formula, and met more than twelve, probably more than that, but we only have the correspondence, not phone calls or in-person meetings. All this during July and August. We have uploaded the email threads to our website, so you can come to your own conclusions."

When Andrea looked up from her script, she noted that the crowd had more than doubled in size. There were three TV cameras behind Alice Ketting, and everyone gathered was holding up their phones to take photos or videos. The whole town was there, hanging on her every word. She reminded herself to look up more often.

Her lips were too dry. The air was so different here. She stopped for a drink of water, and she could feel everyone's eyes on her as she unscrewed the cap of the water bottle. For some reason she recalled what Lamar once said to her about New Mexico—it's not new and it's not Mexico.

"The second thing," she said, "possibly of more legal significance, was the assault in front of his cabin on August 28, 2008. According to witnesses, Lamar Rose attacked Jeff Greer after a party. Jeff and Lamar were wrestling on the ground, fighting over possession of a high-powered rifle.

"Third, which most *definitely* has legal ramifications, Lamar Rose was writing prescriptions for painkillers for members of the outlaw motorcycle gang who lived nearby."

Andrea continued with the prescription story, how the bikers demanded more, but Alice Ketting was waving her arm, shouting out a question. Andrea didn't want to talk over her, so she stopped. She wondered if any of the bikers who got drugs from Lamar were watching.

"How are your brother's dating emails," asked Alice Ketting, "relevant to the murder of your father? Those emails are not about your father, or are they?"

"They speak to Lamar's character," Andrea said, "his state of mind in 2008 when he left his wife and moved to Madrid. A lot happened that summer. He was fighting over guns, writing illegal prescriptions, and killing Greta Lang."

She didn't believe what she was saying. Andrea had pushed back about releasing the dating emails, but Paula convinced her that Lamar's love life, or lack thereof, was somehow fuel for this fire. Because his emails reeked of desperation, Paula said, and desperate men do desperate deeds.

But who Lamar wrote emails to and how many emails he wrote was his business. Who could blame the guy? After decades with Janis, he was starving. What right did Sanctity of Life have to post Lamar's personal emails?

On the other hand, if he *had* killed Greta Lang *and* their father, he was dangerous and he had to be stopped, however possible.

"I want to circle back to Greta Lang," Andrea said. "She had been Lamar Rose's landlord, and—"

Then came a screech and a gray Subaru wagon crunched into the gravel lot and stopped in front of a clump of prickly pear. The crowd parted. A tall woman with reddish brown hair climbed out of the driver's side, closest to Andrea, and, *oh God,* there was her brother Lamar popping out of the other side, his blue porkpie hat poking above the roof of the car.

He was supposed to be in California. How did *he* know about this? Did Paula and Bryce set this up?

Alice Ketting stepped away from Andrea. The camera turned, locked in on her brother, now in front of the Subaru.

"You're Lamar Rose," Alice Ketting said. "You've been accused of killing your father, and you've denied it. Now you're accused of killing Greta Lang. Did you kill *her?*"

45

Shipping Containers Stacked Three High

Madrid, New Mexico
September 12, 2008

One week, Greta was walking and laughing, the next, she only left her bed for the bathroom and grimaced in pain even on her powerful meds. One week, Lamar visited every few days. The next, every day. Before work and after.

She stopped getting dressed in the morning.

Since she was adamant about no treatment, Lamar persuaded her to contact the hospice program in Santa Fe and one morning, a nurse named Jamie came and explained how hospice worked.

"If you have cancer and you get chemo," Jamie said, sitting at the foot of Greta's bed, her hands pressed together as if praying, "you're sacrificing today for a better tomorrow. We make that deal for a lot of our life. Work at a job we don't like so we can retire and do what we like. Hospice is about living today. As if there won't be a tomorrow. We're not going to fix you, only make you feel better. How does that sound?"

Greta said that sounded good, but she was still afraid they would take her to the hospital. She hated hospitals.

Jamie repeated the explanation on her second and third visit, which Lamar found excessive. Then he saw how the repetition was no different than a yoga teacher walking students through postures they had done hundreds of times before. It was grounding, reassuring. Greta relaxed into it.

Greta also agreed to let Lamar spread the word, and now there were other visitors, almost every day, plus Jamie, who came twice a week. Greta said she was glad her cancer was no longer a secret, but she was sometimes overwhelmed by the visitors.

Once, when Jamie and Lamar visited at the same time, and Greta slept, Lamar asked Jamie about her work. She was petite and pretty and he liked the enthusiastic way she talked. She also had a wonderful, orange-blossom scent that was delightful. He realized, as they talked, that this kind of work, focusing on death and dying, might be his calling.

What if, Lamar wondered, he acted as a shepherd of sorts for Greta's final journey? He was already doing that, wasn't he? He had no experience with hospice, but neither had Jamie, at first.

She had fallen into it serendipitously, she said. A patient she'd become close to had a heart attack, and she began visiting her at home, sitting with her the way Lamar was sitting with Greta.

"It was hard," Jamie said, "seeing her deteriorate and not being able to do anything. But that was what made it so profound and powerful. I wasn't supposed to do anything except be with her. To witness. To listen. To honor. I wasn't being paid. I got some training at the hospice project in Santa Fe and that time with Dorothy was the most intimate relationship I've ever had, and that counts my husband of eighteen years. We have so much to learn about living from those who are dying."

"I get that," Lamar said. "I feel lucky to be here."

"Well, there you go."

One thing Lamar did try to fix was Greta's relationship with her daughters. She didn't want to let them know she was dying.

He couldn't let that go. Lamar's family was not as close as he would have liked, but they were still talking. They still gathered on holidays. His sister seemed to be angry at him half the time. His father was distant. And his mother was, well, loving but overbearing. One reason he lived two thousand miles away.

He tried speaking to Greta in weasel words, so it didn't sound like advice.

"Don't you wonder if *maybe* you might want to, I don't know, *reach out* and let them know? Your daughters. I'd be willing to contact them for you if that's what you decided, if that's what would be best for you and for them. Dying can be a time for reconciliation. What if there was even a tiny chance they might come?"

"They'll come after I'm gone, to spit on my grave. And to line up for their inheritance."

"That's so sad," he said, and didn't bring it up again.

At Jamie's urging, Lamar started hospice training in Santa Fe. He understood the don't-try-to-fix-them aspect of hospice, but somehow he thought it referred to medical treatment, not emotional issues like Greta refusing to contact her daughters.

At first, he felt unmoored, sitting with Greta, listening to her, but not doing anything. As a therapist, he knew how to listen, and not interrupt, not judge, not give advice. But he always took mental notes, if not actual written notes, so not doing anything was uncomfortable. It was especially hard seeing her decline.

He also learned, at the hospice training, to encourage Greta to get out of bed and into a chair in the living room, and help her if necessary. That made their conversations more reciprocal. Two friends talking, not a good samaritan visiting the bedside of a dying soul.

One night, Greta asked him to open a bottle of wine as they settled in their chairs in her living room.

"My daughters never cared for Russ," she said. "They said I abandoned them for him, but it wasn't like that.

"You wouldn't know it from how you see me here, but I was traditional—a housewife in the suburbs of San Antonio. I ironed my daughters' dresses. I never got high.

"But Russ swept me into his orbit. Took me to Alaska. I fished with him on one of those huge factory ships, where they processed frozen fish below deck, for McDonald's, you know, their fish sandwich. Awful, dirty, boring work. But visceral. The sun never went down in the summer. I was a foreman. We made tons of money. We drank. We screwed. Didn't sleep for days.

"Later, Russ ran a self-storage business in Anchorage, near the airport. Mostly I ran it. We bought shipping containers, piled them three high, built sturdy wooden ramps wide enough for trucks. I handled all the details, all the money. We had a bar on the bottom level and we served drinks on Friday nights. I was the bartender.

"The girls didn't want me to have another husband. They thought I was some party girl slut who left them to hook up with a con man. It was their father who fed them that poison, their father who treated me like crap, their father who ignored me while I raised them, then went crazy when I found someone better. The girls don't get along with each other either. The only thing they have in common is hating me.

"I buried two husbands. Three years apart. My ex, Warren, came first. We had a sort of reconciliation when he got sick. I brought him here to take care of him. In the cabin you're living in now. That's where he died."

"In my cabin?"

"I was there for him because there was no one else. Our daughters, his daughters, they had their own lives."

"His daughters never came at all?" Lamar asked.

"Once I brought him here to Madrid, no."

Lamar had more questions, but Greta wanted to go to bed.

Once she was under the covers, Lamar moved to the foot of the bed and rubbed her feet.

"Russ died here too," she said. "In this bed."

"Russ," said Lamar. "Husband number two."

"That's right, Russ. He had heart disease, not cancer, and no patience for pain." She motioned for Lamar to put a pillow under her legs.

"At the end," she said, "he made me promise to put him down. I fed him pills until he couldn't swallow any more."

For a second, Lamar couldn't swallow either. "I couldn't do that," he said.

"I'm not asking you."

46

Hurt People Hurt People

Coal Avenue
Albuquerque, New Mexico
February 14, 2016
7:55 am

Lamar was asleep when the phone rang.

"Sorry to wake you. It's Diana—"

He shook his head to clear out the cobwebs. "Good morning to you, too."

"No time for pleasantries. Your sister Andrea is hosting a press conference in Madrid this morning, and we—"

"*Andrea?* In *Madrid?* How do you—?"

"We have to be there by nine. Take a shower. Tell me your address. We're already late. Let's not get into how I know. I'm on lists."

She arrived in her gray Subaru seconds after he came out his front door.

She drove fast. Lamar grabbed his shoulder belt, then read again the printout she had handed him, which said Andrea would be presenting new evidence against him in the parking lot of the Gypsy Plaza. It was a place he knew well, a cluster of colorful shops across the highway from where he used to live. A strange spot for whatever this was, a press conference, or was it a guerrilla attack?

Diana caught him up on what she knew about Alice Ketting's Street Report show on the Freedom Channel, and then turned to him with mischief in her eyes.

"Now I want some answers," she said. "Like what the *bejesus* you did to your sister so she's—?"

She crossed over the centerline. *"Please,"* he said, "pay attention to the road. Why does everyone think I did something to her?" He threw up his hands in protest.

"I mean, yes," he said, "she was opposed to helping our father die. Wouldn't talk about it. But this goes beyond that. The way—"

"And before I forget," Diana said. "What kind of lame-ass lawyer let you speak in public like you have? He ought to be disbarred."

"One question at a time. Stop, don't get on the freeway here. Trust me on this. I've driven this a million times."

She swerved across the exit lane without slowing down. Lamar winced, but she didn't notice.

He took a breath to compose himself. "You may have heard the saying, 'Hurt people hurt people.'"

"No, but I see where you're going."

"Andrea is wounded and she's lashing out. She's jumped off a cliff and I don't know why. I'm not saying she's not in pain—she is, but I deal with hurt people all the time and most of them don't devote themselves to destroying others. Andrea's got issues, but she's not *broken*. What she *is* is a fucking drama queen who turns a bug bite into an emergency. Pardon my diplomacy."

"In other words," said Diana, "not your fault."

"That's not what I said." Lamar liked how quick-witted Diana was. And that she was a teaser more than a critic.

"So, Andrea and me," he continued, "we were best friends. As kids. We fought constantly, but that was because we played and talked and made believe with each other every day. We had our own language.

"I'm three years older, and I got to be twelve or so and I no longer wanted my little sister tagging along all the time. I'm sure I was mean about it and Andrea acted out, did this morose you-don't-care-about-me-anymore victim—"

"That doesn't explain—" Diana said.

"It's the best I can do," he responded. "Our mother swooped in to fill the void and she and Andrea became as connected as Siamese twins and Andrea took her death incredibly hard. Actually, Andrea blamed *me* for our mom dying too. Sort of. She blamed me for *her* not being there. I drained the battery of her phone, or so she claimed, and she overslept. All my fault. Our mother dying. Her cell phone dying. One and the same."

"Maybe she's not finished grieving for your mother," said Diana.

"When she went on and on, you know, about me draining her phone battery, I suppose I may have been dismissive. I mean, she was being ridiculous. But she took that as me dismissing her grief. It's just that Andrea's way is to endure more than to enjoy. Slow down on this curve."

As they approached Madrid, Lamar said, "Now what is it we're going to do when we get out of the car?"

"Oh, I'm sure you'll think of something," she said.

Lamar saw dozens of people standing in the gravel lot, many dozens, all facing Andrea, who was standing on a raised wooden walkway, next to a man with a red beard. The turquoise doors of the art gallery served as their stage set.

The car screeched to a stop in the gravel—for a second, Lamar feared Diana might plow into someone—but she veered to the left and her brakes held.

When Lamar leapt out of the car, he felt like he was in the movies. Everyone turned to face him. The camera too. A woman in a red dress elbowed her way through the crowd and shouted something at him. He couldn't hear her, but he recognized her. Alice Ketting. He'd watched her interview with Andrea far too many times.

He stepped onto a boulder, high enough he was facing Andrea, who looked lost in the sea of people and cameras.

"Andy," he said, loud enough so she could hear, but with a gentle tone, "we used to be so close, when we were kids. Do you remember?"

One second turned to two, then three. Cameras clicked.

"Remember when we played zoo, with our stuffed animals?"

Andrea remembered. He saw it in her eyes. She started to say something, but then she stopped.

Her eyes, big and brooding, looked the same as when she was a girl.

Alice Ketting was in front of him now and thrust the mic in his face, asking him about Greta Lang, and whether he killed her. The cameraman poked his long lens over Alice Ketting's shoulder.

"I did not. I knew her, of course. We all did." He gestured to the crowd, recognizing a few faces, including Justine and Cat. "I sat with her, as did others, as she went through the process of dying, but I had nothing to do with her death."

He thought of adding that he *had* contributed, in the sense that he had given her permission to let go, but he had said too much already. Todd was going to kill him for opening his mouth at all.

"And yet," Alice Ketting added, "we understand Greta Lang left you her cabin in her will, even though you'd only known her for a few months. The cabin her daughters believed was rightfully theirs."

He hesitated before answering, and decided that not answering was the best option. But it didn't matter because all of a sudden, a car alarm started blaring. Louder than any car alarm he'd ever heard. It sounded like horns from a train, over and over again. Alice Ketting tried to shout over it, but the alarm, which seemed to be coming from Diana's car, was too loud.

Suddenly, Lamar's daughter Sierra was in front of him—*where did she come from?* She gave him a quick hug, then led him by the arm across the road. He tried to protest, but she couldn't hear anything he said. There was Justine on his other side, pointing to the archway behind her cafe.

"Dad, we're doing an intervention," Sierra yelled into his ear. "You and Andrea have to agree to a truce."

They were across the road. The alarm continued to blare, but they were moving away from the sound. "Andrea's the one firing the shots," he said. "I can't—"

"You have to bend," Sierra said. "Give her something. You're a professional healer. You know that."

"I hope you're not expecting *me* to model gracious behavior after I've been accused of murder, *again.*"

"That is *exactly* what we are counting on. I believe the technical term is 'walk your talk.'"

Justine led them through the kitchen of the restaurant, then back outside through a maze of wooden arches and flagstone paths—Lamar had never been back here before. Didn't even know it was here.

"You want *me* to give in?" Lamar asked. "I recall just a week ago *you* complaining about how often your pal

Barack Obama compromises in advance, giving away his advantage."

"In politics, you want to win. In family, winning is losing."

"When did my daughter get to be so wise?"

"If I say I learned it from you, it will go to your head. Wait here. Don't move." Sierra tapped a message into her phone.

"How can I talk with Andrea?" Lamar asked. "I don't know what she said over there, to the TV people. Give me that paper. Is that what they were passing out? I have to catch up on what happened."

Under a bramble of bare branches with a few pink blossoms, he read the handout, willing himself not to hurry. Not to panic. No one was going anywhere. They could wait for him.

It was a strange sensation that he still wasn't used to, reading about himself in the news. In this case, a news release. Killing Greta, stalking women, dealing drugs, even fighting over that rifle with Jeff. He had forgotten all about that.

On the back of the handout was a copy of the story in the *Chicago Sun-Times*.

"Lamar Rose Has Killed Before"

His behavior that summer in Madrid was hardly a crime, except for the drugs, and even that was borderline. But he had been irresponsible, and it did not reflect well on him. He didn't like how much that summer looked like the clichéd midlife crisis, but he had to make changes.

The lurid headlines had it all wrong. Even if he had killed Greta, which he hadn't, no one understood how profound it had been to sit with her, witness her fierce dignity as she declined, and not try to fix anything.

Sitting with her had been the best gift he'd ever received. She had saved his life when he was going off the rails. Sometimes he felt like he had been selfish because he was doing it for himself as much as for her.

But that wasn't true. He had been acting with kindness. That's why it made him feel so grounded. Lamar believed in kindness, and killing his father, ending his suffering, hadn't that been the kindest thing he could have done?

It was time to make peace with his sister.

47

Intervention in the Courtyard

Madrid, New Mexico
February 14, 2016
9:14 am

Of course, Andrea remembered playing zoo. How could she forget?

But she wasn't going to say so on television. Paula had been adamant that she stick with her script and give only the answers she had practiced. It would be too easy for the cunning Alice Ketting to bait her into saying something she would regret.

This whole exercise was to highlight Lamar's bad judgment—she couldn't undo all she'd done by getting sentimental.

She tried to say no, she didn't remember, but she couldn't get the words out. So she said nothing.

Back when they had their own secret world, she used to wake up early every morning because she couldn't wait for their next adventure to begin.

She used to love her brother, but things changed. He changed.

Once Alice Ketting and the camera were focused on Lamar, and he started talking, Andrea didn't know what to do. She checked her phone to look busy.

What she didn't get was how Lamar could defuse explosive situations, like being accused of murder, and then ask her about playing zoo.

He'd been like that when they were kids—he would tease her to the point of tears, but when she taunted him, he ignored her.

All of a sudden, a car alarm started blaring, so loud she covered her ears. A moment later, a tug on her arm.

It was the tall woman who had driven Lamar into the parking lot. She shouted into Andrea's ear. "Come with me." Her grip was strong, her voice insistent.

"No." Andrea pulled away, but the woman wouldn't let go. "Who are you?"

They were about to cross the road. Andrea yanked herself free, but the woman grabbed her again and tightened her grip.

It was easier to follow her lead.

Andrea expected Paula to stop them, but the alarm was still blaring and the crowd scattered every which way to escape the noise. The woman slipped behind a maroon truck making a turn, then crossed the road into an outdoor restaurant on the other side.

"My name is Diana Priest," the woman said, "and I'm bringing you here to talk to your brother, in private. That's my car alarm. Deafening, huh?"

"I don't need to talk with Lamar."

Then Andrea's son Sully popped out from behind a pillar and opened his arms to give her a hug.

"Yes, you do," he said. Her first response was to stiffen up, but she melted into his arms.

"Hi Mom," he said. "We're from the government and we're here to help."

Her little boy. A grown man now. Still a goofball. But Sully was the only one grinning.

"Sullivan," she said sternly, "it's wonderful to see you, but you're here to make trouble for me."

"Seriously, Mom, we're doing an intervention. You know what that is?"

"Interventions are for addicts. How did you get here?"

"I flew here, just like you. Dad told me you were coming. Interventions are for whoever needs help. That's you and Uncle Lamar."

Sully guided her through a series of walkways, then sat her down at a round table, and massaged her shoulders. He hadn't done that for her since he was a kid. She could feel the pads of his thumbs, pressing into the tightness in her neck. It was a nice gesture, but she was too tense to relax. It was so quiet now that the car alarm had stopped.

"You're going to have to start acting like an adult in a few minutes," Sully said. "We are not tolerating this family feud. Do you understand?"

They were in the center of an eight-sided courtyard, sur-rounded by stucco walls and brick archways. Four flagstone pathways crossed in the middle, under the chair she was sitting in. Two of the eight exits dead-ended into garden beds, where tall green onion shoots poked out of the soil—in February! Two more went indoors.

That left four to escape through.

"Sierra is here too," said Sully. "She's getting Lamar. We're not going to let you go until you've made a truce."

■ ■ ■

Andrea held her breath as Lamar walked into the court-yard and sat down across the table from her. Sierra and Sully huddled under one of the arches, watching their parents. The woman who dragged her across the street sat on the edge of one of the garden beds tapping on her phone.

Lamar was waiting for Andrea to say something, but there was nothing she wanted to say.

They sat in silence for five minutes, maybe more. When she looked up, his eyes were on hers. She looked down again, at her hands folded on the table. She was hungry and thirsty.

She hadn't looked at him directly for some time. His face was more like their mother's, the deep-set pensive eyes, but he had the same lean build as their father.

Finally, he broke the silence. "How are you doing?"

How was she doing? Why did he have to ask such a loaded question?

He was *too* calm. He took all that meditation and Buddhism too far. To not caring at all.

Andrea had been determined to stay with her script for the press conference and she had practiced improvising for whatever traps Alice Ketting might spring. But she had not rehearsed talking to her brother.

He was going to wear her down with his damn patience.

"This is where you used to live?" she asked.

"Seven minutes from here, walking. I'll show you my cabin later. I've eaten a lot of breakfasts here in this café." He bent forward and began whispering. She had to lean in to hear.

"I know you've had a hard time of it and this hasn't been fair to you. Losing Dad. You thought you were doing the right thing accusing me, fighting for justice, fighting for our father, and this whole media and internet juggernaut got a hold of you, blew everything you said out of proportion."

What was he doing? Tricking her into talking?

"You had unfinished business with Dad," he said.

She bit her lip. He was going to take whatever she said and twist it. He was slicker than Alice Ketting, even more because he didn't look the part.

Of course, she had unfinished business with her father. Lamar kept stating the obvious as if it were some brilliant observation. He kept nodding his head, even though she wasn't saying anything.

"He wouldn't let me in," she finally said, and then her words came gushing out.

"I mean, he was *starting* to open up. Dad. He was *changing* as he declined. He wasn't as self-contained. But there wasn't enough time. Dad didn't know how to talk with me. He was old-fashioned when it came to women."

"I didn't have the easiest time talking with him either," Lamar said, "but because you and Mom were so close, had such a tight bond, we were thrown together, Dad and me. Outsiders in our own family. You must miss Mom so much."

"I miss her every day. I—" She stopped. Did she want to say this?

She did. Like it or not, they were having a conversation. What was the harm in that?

"Did I tell you about the last time I *traveled* with Mom?"

"Tell me," he said.

She must have shared this with him already, she must have. Maybe he hadn't been listening. "I had a tech expo in Las Vegas. I invited Mom, and we gambled and went to shows. We even got drunk together, which was a new thing. Mom didn't drink, but we were in Vegas. She propositioned the young waiter, well, flirted with him. Then she got sick and threw up. Not at the table, but later. She said we were never to speak of it again. Even with that, we had a gas. But when she got home, she said she was tired.

"Getting drunk didn't make her sick. She was *already* sick. She had night sweats. She never had them before. She kept that from me. But Brigid knew. Dad knew."

"You wanted so much to be there for Mom when she died," said Lamar. "I get that, but you know, she was in such bad shape, she hardly knew we were there."

"No, you don't get to fix that for me."

"I'm sorry," he said. "You're still grieving Mom, and now with Dad gone, you miss Mom even more.

"Oh, so you *can* apologize?"

"I can."

That *was* what was going on, wasn't it? She *was* still grieving Mom. But it was more complicated than that. Dad had closed himself off to her for so long and that had nothing to do with getting over Mom.

She wasn't going to say anything more.

"I have an idea," Lamar said. "I did not eat a proper breakfast this morning, and the food here is good. Let's ask the kids to get us sandwiches and coffee. It's on me, Mister Generous."

"I would like that."

Sierra took their sandwich orders and Sully stayed watching from his archway. Then Andrea started talking and couldn't stop.

About Brigid and her affair with their father. About Drew, how she promised him they would go to couples counseling. But mostly about her mother, their mother, and how she never had a relationship like that with anyone and never would.

Their sandwiches arrived and they ate and talked about nothing. The food, their kids growing into adults, how the sun had come out in Chicago and the ice and snow were starting to melt.

Lamar stood up, brushed the crumbs off his hands, and sat back down. "What do you *want?*" he asked. As if he really wanted to know. Another hard question.

"*You* know. For Dad to be alive. Mom, too. Short of that, justice."

"For me to be punished?" he said. "Locked up in prison?"

"Unless you can bring Dad back to life."

He sighed. "I was hoping you would say something different."

"Like what?" she asked.

"'I went too far attacking you. I know Dad kept asking you.' Something like that."

Lamar stood up, turned and looked at the kids, then put his hands on the table and leaned in closer to Andrea. "I did not volunteer," he said, raising his voice for the first time. "I did not whisper this idea into his ear. Dad didn't ask, he demanded. The duty of the son and all that."

"You could have said no."

"I did."

Andrea was tired of the fighting, relieved the kids had taken charge. But she couldn't just give in. If he served some time, not too much, but some, that would be justice. That *was* what she wanted, wasn't it?

"You're admitting it." It was a statement, not a question, but without anger. She was tired of being angry too.

"You've already accused me of admitting it to you."

"How did you do it?"

"Like you said." He sat down.

"The nitrogen."

"It was painless. He kept on breathing until he didn't. I was a wreck, but he was peaceful. I should have forced you to have the conversation. I should never have proceeded without your support."

"I wouldn't have agreed."

She had a hard time wrapping her head around this one. He was saying that what was wrong was acting unilaterally, *not the actual deed*. But she had been right to refuse to talk. Lamar and her father would have worn her down. Or she would have held them off, and then they would have done what they wanted anyway.

"That's what is so horrible about this," she said. "You convinced yourself you did the right thing."

"Andrea, we're all that's left. You and me. Haven't we lost enough? We can't afford to lose each other."

"It wasn't me who tore our family apart."

"Excuse me. You're shunning me. You're going on TV and accusing me of murder. You're maligning my character, making up lies about me. I'd say there's plenty of blame to throw around."

"You're guilty of murder. I'm guilty of demanding justice."

"You know I didn't kill Greta. You made that up out of whole cloth."

"I don't even know who Greta is. I just know you joined that death cult here in Madrid when you moved here."

"Are you enjoying this?" Lamar said. "This nasty bickering. I'm not."

Andrea knew that being defensive put her at a disadvantage, but she couldn't help it. She didn't get how Lamar could somehow not take attacks personally.

"I don't enjoy anything," she said.

"I'm sorry to hear that."

Lamar wasn't looking at her now. He was looking at his hands.

She drank the last of her coffee. "I've said some harsh things about you," she said.

"You're hurting."

"What do *you* want?" she said.

Lamar nodded his head the way he always did.

"What I want is for this reality show to go away. To go back to that life I thought was too bland. I could really go for a tall glass of that right now. And, *I really mean this,* I want us to be family again. We can make this better. It's more important than anything."

He was so smooth the way he talked. Could she trust him? She wanted to, but she wasn't going to be a fool.

"Our kids won't let us leave," he said, "until we come to an agreement."

"I had nothing to do with all those dating emails," she said. "I should have said no to that." That was as close to an apology as she could go. "Sully and Sierra—they're wonderful kids. Surely, we can agree on that. Is that enough?"

"It's a start."

She wanted to tell him she remembered playing zoo—her stuffed elephant from fifty years ago still sat on a shelf in her closet—but she couldn't get the words out.

PART FIVE

Bring a Toothbrush

48

Frantic Bird

Madrid, New Mexico
February 14, 2016
4:15 pm

That afternoon, still buzzing from the intervention in the courtyard, and home alone in a house too large, Lamar opened all the doors and windows, and in flew an orange-throated hummingbird that immediately wanted to escape. Flapping furiously, pecking at the bright, west-facing windows, backing away, attacking again.

Lamar swept at it with a broom, nudging it toward the door. Feeling as frantic as the bird.

When the bird finally flew out, Lamar's shirt was stained with sweat. A three-minute panic attack that felt like an hour.

That was pretty much how he felt *before* the bird flew into the house, rattled from the charges from Andrea's press conference and then the intense tete-a-tete with her in the courtyard behind Turquoise and Coffee. He was that trapped hummingbird *and* Lamar-with-the-broom all rolled into one, and then multiplied by itself.

Banging his beak against the window, trying to peck his way out of the mess he was in.

Except his troubles were happening in slow motion. And they wouldn't be over in three minutes.

It felt like the end of the world, but it wasn't. He was still standing.

At Gypsy Plaza, in front of TV cameras, Andrea accused him of being a serial mercy-killer, dealing drugs, and stalking women. At least he hadn't arrived in time to hear those charges in person.

And then, she dropped her dagger.

He had *something* to do with that. Maybe. He didn't attack her, he listened to her. But it wouldn't have happened without the kids.

Now, like Sierra said, he had to *give* Andrea something.

The day ended better than he had any right to expect, a detente with his sister, an agreement to talk again in a week.

Under the watchful eye of their children, he and Andrea had the longest, most heartfelt talk since *forever.*

Since back when they played zoo.

But everything else was overwhelming and grim. The accusations, the embarrassment, the hopelessness—they were just getting started.

The air in the house felt too thin. Could this have been what it was like for his father?

Robert Rose had not been a *bad* father, or an absent one. He'd been around, but he let Lamar's mother do the parenting. It wasn't even that he had been judgmental or that he rationed his praise. Though he had. That was his generation. He didn't want Lamar to be soft or weak.

Until he changed near the end, he had expressed his disapproval silently, with the downturn of his eyebrows, the purse of his lips. He didn't care for Lamar's decision to go to graduate school in psychology, but he never said so outright. Though he had once mocked Lamar for being *"too touchy-feely."* That had been mean.

His father was gone. Didn't matter that he wanted to be gone, he was gone as gone can be.

Andrea's investigator had dumped all of Lamar's dating emails onto the Sanctity of Life website. Fodder for bloggers and reporters to cherry pick for cheap mockery. Which they did. As if his dating correspondence was anyone's business but his own.

That evening, he made the mistake of searching for himself. It was weirdly addictive, and he knew it was poisonous. He read three blog posts ridiculing him, and then he forced himself to stop. There was one writer who seemed to have some sympathy for him, but it was still humiliating. Lamar didn't want pity any more than derision.

He never thought he would get caught. He had rehearsed. He had backup plans for his backup plans. He had been more concerned about having regrets. Whatever anyone thought of what he did, he had not been hasty. He had not been impulsive. He had weighed it every which way, and came down on the side of doing what his father wanted.

Shit, shit, *shit*, a basket full of shits. How was he going to show his face ever again out in the world? He was on the front page of the *Chicago Sun-Times*. Not something he ever imagined.

The prescriptions, well, they were only going to damage his *career*, not his entire life. As if he could ever see clients again without a disguise.

And what was that wrestling with the rifle all about? He remembered rolling around with Jeff in the driveway. It hurt like hell, all the gravel digging into his legs, his back, his forehead. His adrenalin shot sky high, but then Greta collapsed, and a whole new chapter started.

By then he was done with Jeff and his posse. They had been refreshing at first, but they *were* outlaws, and, though he may have fancied himself one that summer, he wasn't.

Why did people have to be so moralistic? Why was anyone even interested in him?

He wanted to get out of the house, but he didn't know where to go. Besides, Todd had warned him that reporters might be following him, even camping out on his lawn. No one there yet, but he closed the blinds in the living room just in case.

He wanted to talk to someone and he couldn't think of anyone to call. That was as bad as all the attacks and accusations. A distraught old man with no friends.

He thought of calling Diana, but he didn't want to wear out his welcome. They had had an intense day. She had to put her daughter to bed. She had work in the morning.

He could call Todd again, but Todd was his lawyer, not his friend, and he had already called Todd twice. Todd would be there in the morning. He had said the district attorney would be filing charges soon, now that the brewery evidence had dropped. What would Todd say? Do you have a passport? Have you ever been to Bolivia?

Sierra? Well, she had her own busy life, and he didn't want to burden her any more. She had driven him home and debriefed him on the twists of the day, though he couldn't remember how all the pieces fit together.

Sully had alerted Sierra about his mother heading to New Mexico, and floated the idea of an intervention, and apparently Sierra knew Diana from city politics, at least to say hello, and recruited her help. Diana setting off her car alarm was not part of the plan, but a stroke of improvisatory genius.

Lamar even considered calling his sister, but their tentative peace was too fragile.

Then, before he could talk himself out of it, he called Julia. He had only seen her once since the night he told her what he had done, and he hadn't said much, mostly just let her talk.

She was a night person. But he hung up after one ring.

If he wanted a sympathetic ear, he was calling the wrong person. If she wanted to call back, that was up to her.

He tried to sleep, but couldn't, so he climbed out of bed and retrieved a small box from the top shelf of his closet. His parents' papers, papers he had not finished exploring.

He was determined to stop reading the internet. By now, there would be more stories about him. It was hard to ignore your name in the news, but he had to. This would distract him.

After he put on his bathrobe and brought the box into the living room, he poured a tall glass of bubbly water.

He had skimmed through these papers before. Letters his father wrote to Los Alamos National Laboratory asking for raises. Rejection letters from scholarly journals. School papers of Lamar's and Andrea's. Itineraries for trips to Colombia, Peru, Venezuela.

He found a letter he had not seen before. Handwritten by his father in fountain pen, full of ink blots and determined crossouts.

My dearest Celeste,

I know you aren't going to be able to read this—you know I don't believe in that stuff—but I have to share this with you anyway. You live on in my heart and my head.

Everyone thinks I've moved on and recovered from your death and that I'm having a grand old time. Too grand, Andy says.

You would not be surprised that I am now coupled up with Brigid. We've always liked each other, and she's been lonely since she lost her husband, even more since she lost you.

I think you would approve. I would, if it was the other way around. Why not go for love as long as you can?

The kids are still taking your death hard, especially Andy. They have their own grief, so they can't fathom mine. At least Andy isn't urging me to get over it. She thinks I've moved on too quickly, that being friendly with Brigid is dishonoring your memory. I don't think you believe that. You were a people person. Lamar, to his credit, gives me space and doesn't tell me what to do, but he's worse off than me. Dealing with your loss as well as Janis', which he blames himself for. At least you didn't have to see him go through that.

Lamar was touched that his father understood how much he had been suffering. He had to put the letter down and take some deep breaths.

When he went back to the letter, it got repetitive and he skipped ahead. His father kept circling, as if he were waiting for the runway to clear.

His handwriting was large and regular, but there were more and more crossouts, and he had pressed hard with his pen so Lamar couldn't make out the words underneath. Lamar remembered how slow and methodical his father wrote, twisting the pen in his hand as he deliberated. He wrote full sentences in his head, then put them down on paper.

Lamar had never seen a letter from his father anything like this. The famously reserved and stoic engineer Robert Rose was writing as if it were a therapist-guided journal entry.

Then Lamar sat up with a start.

I keep writing this letter to you and then I burn it and start over. This is the sixth one. I keep writing new versions because I'm forgetting things and I'm afraid to tell you I'm failing.

It's little things, but they add up. It's my memory, but more than that. My rational self disappears. Like I've checked out, like I'm having a waking dream. You know how dreams make sense when you're dreaming, but then you wake up and you realize how ludicrous the logic is.

I'm keeping a log. I'm looking for patterns. Trying to use my brain, and reverse engineer the parallel universe I'm living in.

Brigid knows, and she's promised not to tell the kids. They'll figure it out soon enough. And take away my car. Brigid thinks it's only here and there, but it's every day, many times a day. I have a hard time even telling you and I know that you're gone.

Lamar had to put the letter aside, onto the table with the lamp. His tears were blurring his vision. His father *knew*. Of course he knew. He *saw* what was happening from the start, as it was happening.

The letter was not dated, but he clearly wrote it before they took away his car keys, before they moved him to assisted living.

Lamar was grateful for the crying, for his father, more than for himself. That's what he told himself. Either way, he felt cleansed, the way a rainstorm can refresh the dusty streets.

49

Coming Home

Coal Avenue
Albuquerque, New Mexico
October 2, 2008

It had been three weeks since Janis had dyed her hair orange, so Lamar was used to her bright and bold look.

Still, she surprised him, shocked him, on the night of the presidential debate, when she answered the door in an elegant gray and white shirt dress, with jewelry all over her body. Around her neck, in her ears, on her wrists, even on one ankle. She had that Santa Fe casual-chic, hip gallery open-house look, but how she dressed was the least of it.

She greeted him with a teasing twinkle, an exaggerated hello, nice to meet you. "Come in." She curtsied, guided him in with a flutter of her arm, abracadabra, here's the living room, as if showing it to him for the first time. Not the living room as much as her.

Her pumpkin orange hair, her bangles, her souciance. "Look at me," she was saying. Shouting, even. When was the last time Janis, leave-me-alone Janis, wanted attention like that?

More surprising was that he was knocking on her door in the first place. Knocking on the door to see the woman he left three months earlier. After only about ten years of deliberation.

Sierra had given him two tickets for the evening. "I want you and Mom to come," she said.

Not a question.

Sierra was going to be on a panel at the Kiva Auditorium, following the debate between Barack Obama and John McCain.

First the two presidential candidates would square off in a nationally televised debate, live from Albuquerque, and then, Sierra would join three other locals, including Governor Bill Richardson and Mayor Tomas Zamara, to discuss the debate and take questions from the audience. Heady company for young Sierra León.

Lamar had told Sierra he wouldn't miss it for the world, but would not *promise* to go with Janis. "I don't want to give her any ideas."

"What idea?" Sierra said. "That you're my parents. What are you going to do, *not sit together?*"

"I didn't say that, but that *is* what happens when people split up."

"For once you could think of yourself as my parents."

So Lamar and Janis were coming. Per their daughter's request.

But it looked like it might be more than that.

They were still standing in the living room. Janis complimented Lamar on his crisp white shirt and bolo tie and pinched the silver Hopi Kachina Dancer clasp between her thumb and forefinger to examine it more closely. As if she had never seen it before.

Here was Janis being playful, being someone else, which

is what drew him to her in the first place. In those few minutes since she invited him in, he saw the Janis he used to know. As if she had turned on a switch that had been painted stuck in the off position for years.

He felt like he was going on a first date. On the drive downtown, he asked her the same questions he had asked on some of his dates.

"What's the earliest thing you can remember?"

"Does it have to be the earliest?" she asked.

"It's an open-ended question," he said, "and you won't be graded."

"Aren't we always being graded?" she asked.

"Maybe so, but I'm an easy grader."

Expecting that traffic and parking at the convention center would be a challenge, Lamar avoided downtown, and parked on a residential street, almost a mile away. Janis made fun of him for that, and he was defensive for a second, and then he saw there was no intent to hurt.

They walked toward Kiva Auditorium, up empty streets before joining the swarms of people headed to the debate.

The weather was perfect. Shirtsleeve warm, slightly cooler after the baking sun-drenched day.

She was telling him how she lost her therapy practice. "If it sounds like I messed up, it's true. I had a severe bout of depression, but now I seem to have found the right cocktail to lead an almost normal life. Kicked my insufferable husband out and things are much better."

What he thought of saying: "Yeah, my life is better since I left my wife." What he said: "You seem like you're enjoying your new life."

"I have my moments."

Even though Lamar had been getting more comfortable with Janis during their regular lunches, he had not for a second imagined anything romantic or sexual happening. He had three condoms in a white cloth bag in his glove compartment. Not in his pocket.

He had gone on seven coffee dates or walks since his overnight with Diana, and the condoms had stayed in the glove compartment.

As they approached the venue, they ran into concrete barricades, streets closed to traffic, protesters chanting on opposite sides of the street. Police patrolled on horses, dogs sniffed at checkpoints, helicopters circled overhead.

Whether it was the electricity of the presidential campaign, the anticipation of his daughter on the panel after the debate, or walking next to this suddenly mysterious woman he'd been married to for twenty-seven years, Lamar was on hyper alert. Noticed everything as if seeing it for the first time, especially once they were inside. The gold-leaf sculptures embedded in the art deco ceiling, the way his tailbone sunk snugly into the gap between the chair back and seat cushion, his merino wool socks bunched under his toes in his right shoe.

It was almost too intense. This was what all that yoga and meditation that he had stopped doing was supposed to get you to. Laser focus on the moment. Experiencing all the senses.

The sound from the stage was crisp. Crackles in the silence, but most every word clear. The audience was rapt.

Except Lamar. Even in the most contentious moments between Obama and McCain, he was paying more attention to Janis, studying her out of the corner of his eye, than to the senators on the dais.

Dangling from her ear were two balls of turquoise the size of peas, and between them a shiny one-peso coin, bronze in the center with a silver steel ring on the outside. He'd given her those earrings as a present twenty-some years earlier, and he couldn't remember the last time she'd worn them.

This was not the way Lamar imagined his new life would unfold. The plan was to *break away* from Janis, not redefine his relationship with her. Even if he *were* coming home, which he wasn't, he would want to do so from a position of strength, with some triumphant sexual experiences under his belt instead of one sweet quickie with Diana.

What kept him from paying full attention to the debate was the preposterous question, *unimaginable* really, of whether he might have sex with Janis. How could he even be *considering* that?

He wasn't going to be stupid. He had to get a read on what this would mean to her. What was behind her flirting? For all he knew, this was not a game but a devious strategy. He was *not* getting back together with her. He was *not* moving back home.

Janis continued to treat Lamar as if she were just meeting him. She seemed charmed, but skeptical, as in I-like-what-I-see-but-I've-been-around-enough-to-expect-the-worst.

Who said this had to mean anything? If Lamar wanted to have sex with Janis and keep living in Madrid, he could.

But it was about more than sex. He saw a glimpse of the woman he fell in love with and maybe, just maybe, they could find their way back to the way they'd been.

Janis stood close while they waited in line at intermission for wine in plastic cups. No touching, but flashes of shy eye contact.

"Sierra has got to challenge McCain's voter fraud story," Janis said. "It's a made-up story but they keep repeating it. These people have no shame."

Janis forgot about their game, and gave herself over to fist-shaking. *Amazing.* She was animated and angry about something out there in the world and not inside her personal universe.

He listened more closely to the panel after the intermission. That was his amazing daughter up there, poised, beautiful, sharp as a gleaming knife blade resting on a whetstone. He watched her when the others were speaking and she listened with the intensity of a therapist. Taking in every word instead of rehearsing what she was going to say when it was her turn.

Sierra wore a navy blue business suit with a crisp white shirt. Hair tied back, black horn-rimmed glasses, her lips more purple than red. She was more concerned about looking serious than beautiful. Lamar had seen her in front of a room like this before but never with such a big audience, so many bright lights and television cameras. The panel was being broadcast live on KNME, the local public TV station.

"That's my daughter up there," Janis elbowed Lamar.

"Wait, who says *you* get Sierra?"

"I claimed her first."

After the panel, they nudged their way to the front to congratulate Sierra, who was smiling and shaking hands with audience members, basking in the attention she deserved.

After the debate, Lamar and Janis joined Sierra and her friends around three tables on the patio at the Blue Moon on Central, near the gas tanks at the entrance. They didn't say much—it was loud and there were too many young people unpacking the panel and debate.

At one point, Lamar whispered to Janis, "How about if I take you home?"

When he parked in front of the house on Coal Avenue, he didn't turn off the motor. They were talking about Sierra, as her parents now, not as two people on a date. Not that it wasn't a good conversation. Their daughter had been precocious from a young age, so they had attended their share of events where they saw her shine, but tonight was her *most* triumphant, and they were sharing deep feelings of pride. Not *your* daughter or *my* daughter, but *our* daughter. They were serious and earnest, in a happy kind of way, and Lamar didn't see the opening that had been there earlier. Janis was reminiscing about how driven Sierra had been to learn her multiplication tables that she made Janis quiz her with flash cards every day for a week until she had memorized everything up to twelve times twelve.

Lamar turned off the engine.

Janis stopped in mid-sentence, self-conscious, as if in the silence she could hear herself blathering on. Then she turned to Lamar with a small, shy smile, her lips closed. "Would you like to come in?" She pushed her hair behind her ears. Back to the date.

"I would love to."

He rushed around the back of the car, opened her door, and took her hand ceremoniously as she stepped up to the curb. Before he closed the door, he reached into the glove compartment, grabbed the bag with the condoms, and slipped it into his pocket.

Caro greeted them as they entered, wagging her tail furiously, nosing her head between Lamar's thighs.

"She is taken with you," Janis said. "As if you were a long-lost friend."

She gave him a tour of the living room, dining room, and kitchen. "You haven't shown me the upstairs," Lamar said. Gulp.

"Why would you want to see the upstairs?" A little challenge in her voice.

"In many houses," he said, "that's where the bedrooms are."

"Yes, we have three bedrooms upstairs." Just the facts, ma'am.

The difference between an opportunity and a trap might not be obvious until after the fact. The facts weren't always so obvious either.

"Come here," he said. She did. He put his hands on her shoulders and gazed directly at her face. She looked down, then met his eyes. He hadn't touched her all evening except when he helped her from the car. "You're lovely when you're witty, you know that?"

"What? All I said was how many bedrooms we have upstairs. I suppose now you want to see them."

"I do."

Janis had painted her bedroom walls a dusky olive green—if only all transformations were as easy as painting. He hadn't been in the room since her suicide attempt—he had set that boundary deliberately.

What was he doing? He wasn't coming back to his marriage, so what was this? A visit for old time's sake? A special occasion on the event of their daughter's appearance on the big stage of national politics? Was it as trite as wanting to get laid?

He washed his face in the bathroom and when he came back to the bedroom, the bedside lamp was off and the room was illuminated by three candles. Janis stood at the window, her back to him. She held herself erect, her shoulders and head high as if proud instead of morose.

"Do you have a garden out there?" As he walked toward her, she leaned languidly against the wall.

"I haven't had a man in my bedroom for a long time."

Her head was tilted, her lips slightly open in a small smile, her eyes locked on him. The candles put out a lot of light. She wanted him to touch her, to kiss her. She could not have been more obvious.

What surprised him most was how bold she was. She was leading the way. What if he turned her down? How would she handle that?

As far as he knew, Janis had not been searching for love on the internet or going on dates. He never thought of her as lonely, but she must have been. It had been masked by the depression.

He walked past her to close the bedroom door. Sierra and her boyfriend were staying down the hall and would be coming home later. Then he walked back to Janis and put his hands on her shoulders.

"I'm honored to be here." He leaned into her and she moved toward him to meet his lips.

He had slacked off on his yoga and meditation, but here was one of those perfect zen moments where everything felt new even though it wasn't. In the candlelight, he could only catch a glint of her orange hair. He could sense the color more than he could see it.

He undid the top button of Janis' shirt-dress, then stopped to look at her. She unbuttoned the next one. Lamar undid the rest. She slid under the sheet, then took off her dress and tossed it on the side table.

The night was still warm—fall was here but not fall temperatures. Lamar undressed and joined Janis in the bed.

He lay on his side, his jawbone on his fist, elbow on the pillow. "It feels good to be here with you." He took her hand. "This is new for me. It hasn't been long since I split up, but I know I'm not going back."

"Is that right?"

"I don't think she would have me anyway after what I did."

He kissed her then and reached down to touch her with his finger.

When they talked, it wasn't Lamar and Janis, but a man and a woman getting to know each other. Her body felt familiar, but everything else was strange and new. They went from kissing to talking back to kissing.

Janis delivered a few honeyed moans as he played with her. "You like that?" he asked.

"I do," she said.

He had the condom in the pocket of his pants, which he had folded and placed on the bedside table. He hesitated before reaching for it, not wanting to presume. But then it was time.

"I've got a condom," he said, sitting up.

"You better have a condom, buddy boy, or no trespassing, violators will be shot. I know what you've been up to. I'm not going to let you infect me with any of that internet VD."

Was that what she thought? "My worldly status is overstated, I'm sure." Humility always beat bragging. "Your imagination is wilder than my life."

She could have found him on the web. Even without a photo, it wouldn't have been hard.

"I never cheated on you," he said. "I mean, before I moved out."

He tore the condom package open on his first try.

Afterward, they lay side by side on their backs, touching at the shoulders and hips.

"Sierra asked me to take you to the debate, sit with you," Lamar said. "When she gave me the tickets."

"It's not easy for her that we're split up."

"No, it's not."

A pause.

"This doesn't mean we're getting back together." He didn't mean to say it so bluntly, but he didn't want to deceive.

"I don't want you back," she said. "I'm done with you. You go live your outlaw life."

In the morning, Lamar left early. He had three clients in Santa Fe, starting at nine, but he canceled them all after he stopped in Madrid to sit with Greta and found that she had died.

50

Hammered

Coal Avenue
Albuquerque, New Mexico
February 15, 2016
12:15 pm

Todd parked his suitcase by the door and marched into Lamar's living room. "When the *fuck* were you going to tell me about those prescriptions?"

Todd wasn't wearing his usual suit, but black jeans and a turquoise sweatshirt that said, "West Hollywood Pride."

"Listen," Lamar said, gesturing him to the couch. "When I talked with Andrea yesterday, this intervention I told you about, that the kids engineered, we reached, I don't know, some vague detente, an agreement to agree. The thing is, I have to *give* her something."

"*Give* her something? What do you mean?" Todd stood behind the couch, his arms across his chest.

"Like a confession," said Lamar.

"Stop. Don't say another word." Todd backpedaled to his briefcase, pulled out a fifth of whiskey.

"That's probably not a good idea," said Lamar. "It's barely afternoon."

"Exactly. Now get us glasses and ice."

Todd poured generous drinks. Lamar weighed the heavy-bottomed glass in his hand. Clinked the ice.

"Look," said Todd, now sprawled on the couch, "you ignored the advice of your counsel and you spoke out to the public, and surprise, surprise, you came across as reasonable and thoughtful. Good on you.

"But now you're allegedly a serial mercy-killer, a stalker of women, a drug pusher, and a scrappy fighter. We are fucked. You know that."

"Those prescriptions were eight years ago," Lamar said. "I did all the paperwork."

"Look, nothing from yesterday is going to amount to anything, legally, but they have turned you into a disreputable character. You made their job easy."

Lamar told Todd about the prescriptions, mostly the true story.

"When I heard Jeff was selling the prescriptions, I said 'no more.' That was when one of Jeff's cronies punctured my car tires. Two tires, and I had only one spare. Jeff dared me to call the police.

"It's true I moved home shortly thereafter, here, to this house, but not because of threats, like Andrea implied. But because of Janis, I thought we could work things out. You know the rest. I never expected any of this would matter eight years later."

Todd poured another drink and Lamar kept talking.

"As for the Greta accusation, I did find her dead, but—"

"Forgot to tell you," said Todd. 'Saw it on my phone after we landed. Man named Jeff Greer—I assume it's the Jeff who wanted the drugs—he's got a scraggly white beard."

Lamar nodded.

"He went on TV this morning claiming *he* killed Greta. Told the reporter that he and Greta set a date, it came, and he did what she asked."

Now things were making more sense.

"Jeff, yeah, he was a friend of sorts. When I found Greta dead, I remember being suspicious. The day before, I had promised Greta I'd get her an absentee ballot. She asked if her vote would count if she mailed it in and then she died. I asked Sierra, who said it would. But she was gone before the ballot came."

"The Sanctity of Life people are claiming this guy is lying to protect you," said Todd. "They have balls, that's for damn sure. It's like when the autopsy report came back with no clear cause of death, they seized on that as evidence that you used nitrogen. Because it left no trace. Is Jeff telling the truth? That's one accusation off the table."

"I only know it wasn't me. These accusations piling up—obviously I'm concerned—but what upsets me most are those dating emails out there for everyone to see, and, well, I couldn't sleep last night and I made the mistake of reading the internet, and there were, like, a dozen posts and comments ridiculing my boilerplate emails, the number of emails I sent. 'My pathetic obsession,' one wag wrote. I mean, I was trying to work the odds. I got one reply for every five or six I sent, so, sure, I cast my net widely. My clients, those I still have, are reading this shit."

Lamar drained his glass.

"I never thought anyone could die of humiliation," he said, "but obviously I was wrong."

"You have to stop reading this crap about yourself," Todd said. "These people are just projecting their hate and bullshit. You know, I got so much flak for letting you speak.

They said I was using you to sell DBC, and damn right I was. You sold me on that."

"You went along with it," said Lamar. "Pretended it was all my idea."

"Look, you've been a rockstar. Did I say we were fucked?"

"What do you mean, 'we'? You look happy enough."

"'We' sounds nicer, don't you think?" Todd said, pouring another glass. "Like I'm going down with you."

"Aren't we going to work today?" asked Lamar. "Legal strategy."

"I was a drunk back in the day," Todd said, "and I love drinking *so much* I will *never* become a drunk again. Because then I'd have to dry out. So I go to the limit, then I stop."

"Don't you think you're *at* that limit?"

"This is a special occasion, on account of us being fucked. Look, it's that trip to Hoppy Trails that's killing us. You. Everything else is hearsay. We'll look at strategy tomorrow. Or walk out with the white flag and our hands up."

"What would happen if we did that?" Lamar asked, suddenly sober.

"Do we need to talk about this now?"

"We do."

"Here's what I know," said Todd. "The Cook County D.A. says they're treating this like any other murder, but it's different and they know it.

"Until the nitrogen tank, they didn't have shit. That's why there were no charges. Now there's all this *drama* calling your character into question, the dating crap, the prescriptions, the Greta accusation, but it's mostly noise. For the court of public opinion, and in that court, we have already lost."

They had emptied the bottle when Andrea called.

She had not phoned Lamar since the morning of their father's death. They had a long way to go still, but the intervention in the courtyard had been a breakthrough. A start, anyway. He had to hand it to the kids.

He didn't know if he had turned her around or she did so on her own.

"Hello," he said, loud enough he surprised himself.

"Are you alright?" she said.

"Well, we are both drunk on our asses, my lawyer and me, in the middle of the afternoon, so yes, we're fine."

"I'm sorry" she said. "I tried to stop it. I tried."

51

Mariana at the Karaoke Lounge

Albuquerque, New Mexico
June 12, 2009

The Karaoke Lounge, on the west side of Albuquerque, had a restaurant in one room and the singing area next door. Apparently you could eat in the singing area, but Lamar chose to wait for Mariana in the quieter room, in a booth upholstered in red vinyl. He waited for an hour, longer than when they met for the first time.

He felt the thump of the bass vibrate through the floor, through his seat, but he couldn't tell what song was playing except when a waiter opened the door between the rooms. He caught a few bars of a gravelly voice singing an Elvis number.

He nursed a vodka gimlet, and when he finished that, a mineral water.

Mariana had been forty-five minutes late on their first date, at Birdbath, in Santa Fe. When she had arrived, out of breath, apologizing profusely, in black jeans, tight white t-shirt, and cowboy boots the color of coffee with cream,

Lamar could hardly believe she wasn't a fantasy.

He had been standing, ready to leave, but he sat down before she saw him.

He locked his eyes on her face, which was lovely in a lopsided way. Not like Picasso, with two eyes on one side of her face, but there was something off. Mainly, what was she doing on a date with him?

That first evening, she had smelled of jasmine. He wondered what she would smell like this time. If there would be a this time.

The bartender held up the vodka. Lamar nodded yes.

He thought about leaving, but where would he go? Home? That was the *last* place he wanted to be.

He had promised himself he would never live with Janis again. But there he was, back in the house on Coal Avenue.

Back in October, after his debate-night assignation with Janis, he had returned to living in Madrid.

When he ate lunch with Janis, there was more warmth, to be sure, but no more sleepovers. But then on Election Day, their daughter paired them up to knock on doors together, and then they were together at the convention center that night, watching President-Elect Obama on the big screen, delivering his victory speech in Chicago's Grant Park.

He and Janis were happy to be in the winner's ballroom, proud to see their daughter so victorious. Sierra was floating, and she kept taking photos of Janis and Lamar. She was clearly elated her mother and father were together.

He and Janis slept together that night, though they were too tired for any hanky panky. The next night, Lamar was back in Madrid.

But Greta was dead, Jeff and his gang inhospitable, and Madrid no longer felt like a friendly haven. Winter came early. Greta had warned him the cabin had no insulation, but it had only been an abstract concept until the temperatures dropped.

He moved back to Albuquerque, first into his old bedroom, and then, one night, back into Janis'.

"For the winter," he insisted. "I'm back to Madrid in the spring."

Janis said, "Let's see if you last that long."

They had a surprisingly good November, hosting Thanksgiving at home, inviting family on both sides. They had to borrow chairs. Andrea and his parents flew in from Illinois.

"We're going to give it another try," said Lamar as he carved the turkey. "Janis and me."

"Good for you," Andrea had said.

But by December, Janis had retreated to the depressed state she'd been in for years. Not all at once, but that effusive and mysterious Janis disappeared a little more each day.

Lamar refused to believe that he *caused* this change, but there seemed to be a correlation between *his* presence and *her* depression.

He should not have moved back home. It had been the path of least resistance, but not the right path. For him or for Janis.

Then, in the new year, Caro's legs started failing, and he had to put her down.

His dog's death left a hole in his heart.

It was a pathetic situation, two depressed people living under the same roof, in separate bedrooms, without even their dog for companionship.

By February, Lamar was staying at the Madrid cabin at least once a week, keeping warm in a down sleeping bag. Winter was short, he told himself. He would move back to

Madrid full time once it warmed up.

Then, in March, his mother got sick with leukemia, and, within a month, died of complications during chemotherapy.

His grieving for her was anything but simple, because he had to bring the family together. Andrea melted down, alternately hysterical or zombie-like, and their father retreated into himself.

At the same time, he knew he had to leave Janis. Again. He had given it a chance, but that chance was over. She put on a good show at the memorial, but wasn't there for Lamar.

He spent the spring as despondent as he'd ever been, though he saw a full load of clients and helped them with their problems. His work was the only way he made it through the days.

He knew he had to sit with his pain, and he did—half an hour here, an hour there. It was what he had to do.

But mostly he escaped—drinking, getting high, binge-watching movies.

He also took a second training at the Santa Fe Hospice Center, and began sitting with people who were dying. It was hard because he had to set aside his own suffering, and because most of the dying souls were not as colorful or spirited as Greta.

And then, he waded back into dating.

One email at a time. Keep it slow, he told himself. Like making love, finding love was maybe better at a leisurely pace.

One evening, a week after Mariana responded to his email, he poked his head into Janis' bedroom after dinner. "I'm leaving. Don't know when I'll be back."

"You always do what's best for you, don't you?" Janis said. Not exactly the seal of approval, but more than he needed to race from the house.

He learned a lot about Mariana on that first date. He was so enamored of her beauty he wasn't sure if she was actually interesting, but he listened intently and she basked in his attention. She was a therapist too, specializing in anorexic teen girls. When she was younger, she'd been manager for a rock band and she regaled him with her adventures on the road with them. He got in a few words now and then, which she quickly turned back to herself.

Looks weren't everything.

That night, before he climbed into his sleeping bag in Madrid, he got an email from Mariana that surprised him. She said she enjoyed meeting him and found him interesting, but was confused that he had left like the proverbial "bat out of hell."

He wrote back with the truth. "When it came time to say goodbye, I had an intense desire to kiss you because of how stunning you are, but I didn't get any indication you were interested in me. Thus the hasty exit." He also noted how colorful and spirited she was, and laid on the compliments pretty thick.

She responded immediately with a long apology, dozens of lines with no paragraph returns, about how she talked too much when she was nervous and how rare it was for a man to listen so thoughtfully and solicitously. "But I forgot that you might appreciate the same kind of amiable attention you gave me. There's no excuse for that."

An hour later came a second email. "P.S. In case it got lost in the details, I *am* interested in seeing you again."

How could he resist?

When Mariana finally arrived at the Karaoke Lounge, in a long gold wraparound dress and leopard-print high heels, she looked even hotter than on the first date.

She drank two martinis within the first twenty minutes, and could not stop talking about how bad the traffic had been. What made the situation more poignant was that she knew what a wreck she was. She told Lamar he was the first man she'd had a second date with.

"Even this level of intimacy," she said, "sitting across from you, I can't do without anxiety. And it's not like you're a matinee idol, so I don't know why I'm having such a panic attack. Sorry, that didn't come out right."

"Let's go next door and sing," he said.

They sang one song, and she was no better than he was. But they laughed and threw their arms around each other when they leaned in for the chorus.

Afterward, he walked her to her car, where she found a parking ticket tucked under her wiper blade. "The story of my life," she groaned. She had parked in a red zone. He spent the night in Madrid. He didn't want to go home.

The next afternoon, after a full day of clients in Santa Fe, he went back to Albuquerque.

The moment he opened the front door, he knew something was wrong. The stale smell. The quiet. He called Janis' name, then ran up the stairs, two at a time.

She was under the covers. Her forehead was cold. Her hands were cold. Everything was cold. Three orange pill bottles were lined up on the bedside table, tallest to shortest.

He called 911. Then went to the kitchen, poured himself a drink.

Not that anything could prepare him for the hardest conversation of his life.

He called his daughter. Janis' daughter. What if she didn't pick up?

She did.

"Mija, it's Dad."

52

Don't Stop Believing

Coal Avenue
Albuquerque, New Mexico
February 15, 2016
2:25 pm

The video of Lamar and Mariana singing "Don't Stop Believing," broadcast that morning on Chicago TV station WGN, already had ten thousand views on YouTube.

That included the two viewers in Lamar's living room, where Todd was stretched out on the rug, his back against the heavy hassock. Lamar sat on the couch, searching for where he could bury himself for the rest of his life.

"One more time," Todd said, pointing at the TV screen. "And tell me again what that sexy babe is doing with that old man?"

"Butchering the song, obviously," Lamar said. He was not as drunk as Todd. Watching the video had sobered him up, as if he had been dunked in ice water.

"I cannot watch this again." But he did.

Mariana was grinning, preening, laughing. She *looked*

like she was having fun. God, the singing was atrocious, but that was not the problem. If only.

The problem was that someone had dug deep into that treasure trove of Lamar's dating emails, and connected the dots between his second date with Mariana and the night his wife committed suicide, and decided that was something the public needed to know about.

The Chicago station had hired a stringer in Albuquerque, who tracked down the video of Lamar's duet with Mariana. Seven years later, the Karaoke Lounge still had it.

Todd made Lamar watch the WGN clip one more time from the beginning. Already, it had three thousand more views.

"Seven years ago," the reporter said, "on June 18, 2009, Albuquerque resident Janis León took a cocktail of sleeping pills and painkillers and overdosed. Her death was ruled a suicide.

"Her husband at the time was Dr. Lamar Rose, who was accused in January of killing his ailing father, Robert Rose, in Chicago's Edgewater Cares senior home. An alleged mercy killing. He has also been accused of mercy killing Greta Lang in the former ghost town of Madrid, New Mexico.

"In the summer of 2008, he separated from his wife Janis, lived in a cabin in Madrid, and corresponded with dozens of prospective dates over email, going out with ten or more. He moved back home with his wife in November of that year, but continued dating.

"The following June, he went out with Mariana Milano to a karaoke bar in Albuquerque, and did not return home until the next afternoon, when he discovered his wife had overdosed and died while he was gone.

"We have been unable to reach Dr. Rose or Mariana Milano for comment."

"Damn straight he has no comment," Todd brayed at the TV.

They cut to Paula Merrill, Andrea's handler, who tied it tightly in a knot. "Dr. Lamar Rose cheated on his wife the night she committed suicide. What kind of man does that?"

Lamar poured the last of the scotch into his glass. Only a few drops.

"I'm a miserable human being," he said. "This calls for another bottle. They're making it look like I fucked Mariana while Janis was home swallowing pills. I got a goodnight kiss, that's all, and it wasn't an invitation. It was a goodbye."

Lamar steadied himself on the arm of the couch on his way to the pantry. "Beauty didn't keep her demons away," he said. "Not that I'd expect you to understand."

"What," said Todd, "you think I never slept with a woman?"

"I never gave that much thought," said Lamar.

Todd reached for the bottle when Lamar returned. "I was a stud in college," he said. "Girls *and* boys, I jumped them all. Boys were easier, didn't need flowers or foreplay. So here's the question. Why would they stoop to this kind of gutter attack if they had real evidence? Whether or not you fucked this delectable babe—"

"I did not fuck her. If only." Lamar shrunk into himself. Like a huge weight was being lowered onto him. He couldn't bear it.

It had nothing to do with Mariana. He hardly remembered her.

"What if you did?" said Todd. "Is it such a bad thing that people think that? You didn't cause your wife to take her life. Own this shit." Todd laughed. "That's not Todd West speaking, but the esteemed esquire Johnny

Walker Red. A legal legend."

"You don't understand," said Lamar, "It wasn't leaving Janis that was so wrong. It was coming back to her. I should have known better."

Todd wasn't listening. He had drunk more scotch than Lamar. Didn't matter. Lamar needed to talk.

"I came back for my own selfish reasons." Lamar could hear how hoarse his voice was, as if he'd been screaming all day.

There had been so many deaths. Lamar tried to convince himself that loss was a gift of sorts. An entryway to feeling deeper, to understanding the losses of others. It didn't feel like a gift now.

"Janis *had* been getting better, and I fucked it up by coming back. Anyone recovering from deep depression can easily experience a relapse. I knew that, but I convinced myself I was giving *her* another chance. She reverted. I reverted. It's almost like I wanted to bring her back down."

"Doesn't mean you caused her death."

"No, but I'll never know, will I?"

Lamar had been ready to leave Janis again and she must have known that. She almost certainly timed her suicide so he wouldn't find until it was too late. She knew he wouldn't be coming home that night, that he'd stay in Madrid, or be chasing some woman. For Janis, it was a two-fer. She put herself out of her misery and stuck it to Lamar at the same time.

How could he possibly have deluded himself into thinking it was a good idea to come back to Janis, to move back home? That whole summer and fall in Madrid had been one episode after another of Lamar Rose Makes a Bad Decision.

None were worse than coming back to Janis.

What he had done to his father, well, he had done what his father had wanted. What Lamar had wanted hadn't mattered.

But returning to Janis, he did that for selfish reasons and he would have to live with that.

The karaoke video with Mariana was only going to make that harder.

Lamar had taken the hospice training after Greta died and somehow that lulled him into thinking that death was just a part of life. That death could be easy or good.

But Greta's death had been clean and uncomplicated and he had become close to her *because* she was dying. Greta *was* a gift.

Caro, his dog, was too. His grief over her was real—sharp and sad—but he had no regrets. There was no unfinished business. It was the natural order of things.

But not his mother. Not Janis. Not his father. Those losses made him poorer. Those losses beat him down. They didn't make sense.

He remembered Janis' cold body in her bed, the pill bottles lined up by height, but the memory that haunted him most was when they were lying next to each other after making love, the night after the debate, and Janis said to him, "I don't want you back. I'm done with you."

She could not have been clearer.

Todd was in a stupor, staring at his empty tumbler.

"Can I make a deal *before* there are charges?" Lamar asked. "And what about, like, house arrest? I wear a bracelet and stay home. Or community service. I can't go to prison. That's what I'm shitting myself over."

But if that were the case, why was he feeling peaceful? It was more than the whiskey. Would it be so horrible to pay a price? To serve time behind bars? He didn't want to, but he could. Maybe he should. What he did for his father was right, but it was also wrong.

Todd put down his glass and shook his head, like a dog

shaking off water. "I did some research," he said. "About six years ago, an eighty-six year-old man named George Sanders killed his wife with a revolver wrapped in a towel. She had asked him to. She had MS and gangrene. He was her caregiver and *his* health was deteriorating. He pled guilty to manslaughter and the judge gave him two years probation.

"Then there are other cases where they lock the killer up for years. So don't get your hopes up."

53

Don't Make Me Wait

Cook County Municipal Court
Chicago, Illinois
April 27, 2016
1:40 pm

The courtroom gallery was packed—reporters, rubber-neckers, family, and more. Andrea had seen TV crews on the front steps, when she was escorted in through a side door, but the judge didn't allow cameras inside. She made everyone leave their phones with the bailiff. No cameras meant no cameras.

Andrea had not been in a courtroom since she'd been a juror in a murder trial. Before Sully was born. They had convicted the defendant, who was sentenced to life in prison. Now and then, when she least expected it, she felt a pang of sorrow for the defendant, even though she had no doubt he had committed the crime.

The judge, a small Asian woman with thick glasses and thin lips, said they would not be using the witness stand. This was not a trial, but a sentencing hearing. Lamar and his lawyer had made a plea deal before charges were filed, so this was their first time in court.

The judge asked Lamar to stand.

"You said, in your written statement, that your father repeatedly asked you to help him end his life. Tell us about that."

In the row behind Lamar and Todd were Sully, Sierra, and Brigid, craning their necks to watch Lamar. Andrea sat in the first row next to Drew, but on the other side of the aisle. Down the row from her was Diana, the woman who had helped the kids engineer the intervention. She wasn't looking at Lamar, but at Andrea, who looked down once Diana caught her eye.

Andrea was set to speak after Lamar. She paid close attention to what Lamar was saying.

"I had a flight home to Albuquerque," said Lamar, "and I stopped to see my father on my way to the airport. When I started to leave, he grabbed my wrist, grabbed it tight.

"'You have to help me,' he said. 'I can't stand it.'

"During my visit, he had been crazy demented *most* of the time, but also, in spurts, lucid as ever.

"I tried to empathize. 'It must be horrible. I don't know how you manage.' I put on my jacket. I didn't want to be late for my flight.

"He said he *didn't* manage.

"'Dad,' I said, 'you have your mind right now. You're as sharp as ever.'

"'*Right now* is what I can't stand,' he said.

"My father had been a nuclear engineer. A man of the mind. When he was lucid, he knew what was happening to him, and that's what tortured him. That's what he called it. Torture."

Andrea had heard Lamar recount this conversation when

he came to her home in Schaumburg for the follow-up to the intervention. It was far more powerful in the crowded courtroom.

Now that he had admitted what he'd done, and apologized to her, she no longer felt the need to punish him. Why had she been so vindictive when her brother took it all in stride? She wondered if she were angry at him for *that*. Because he bent like a willow in the wind and she had a fit when her shoelaces came untied.

She wasn't going to tell Lamar this, but she wanted to be more like him. To notice how other people were feeling. To listen instead of judge. He had made a mess of his life, but she admired his courage, his patience, his kindness. The way he stood tall in front of the judge as if they were giving him an award instead of a prison sentence.

It would be nice if someday she could tell him that.

During their conversation in the courtyard, Lamar had asked if she was talking to anyone about all that was going on, like a therapist or a priest.

He had given her the number of a therapist in Santa Fe named Sara, a woman, he said, with so much compassion he didn't how she carried it all.

Andrea only saw her in person that once, and then had three more sessions over the phone. If she had known how helpful a therapist could be, she might have gone sooner. Sara would listen intently, then make a statement that seemed so blunt it might have felt like an attack, except she spoke with such kindness that it was hard not to like her and agree with her. Some conversations with Sara were still fresh in her mind.

"You thought this would make you feel better, but it didn't?" She phrased her statements as if they were questions.

"You were angry at your brother because your life was

not as fulfilling as you wanted it to be," Sara had said. "Someone had to pay for that."

"No," Andrea had responded. "That's not it."

But later, she thought, yes, there was a kernel of truth there.

The judge was off on some procedural tangent, then she asked Lamar to elaborate on the talk with his father.

"I tried to distract him," he said, "asking him if he was listening to the music I brought him. Sometimes we would play his CDs and sing along, like Louie Armstrong. What a Wonderful World. We both knew that song."

Andrea tried singing with her father once, but he didn't cooperate. She should have tried more than once. This was what her life had come to. One regret after another.

"He started talking crazy," Lamar continued, "about not being able to pee in the bathroom, about the soup being poisoned.

"I played along. I asked him questions.

"Finally, I asked him what I'd been afraid to ask him before. 'What do you want?'

"When I said that, he grabbed my wrist again and locked his eyes on mine, which was something he rarely did. All of a sudden, he seemed relaxed.

"'I want you to help me,' he said. 'I want you to help me die.'

"I didn't know what to say, so I said nothing. Then I said, as gently as I could, 'I can't, Dad.' That's what I said. 'I can't.'

"Then he said, 'You can't? Or you won't?'

"Then he got agitated again. That was not the first time Dad talked about wanting to die, but the first time he had been so direct. How does a supposedly compassionate person walk away from such anguish? Well, I had a plane to catch. That was my excuse.

"He asked every time I visited. I said no. I humored him, or distracted him, and sometimes that worked.

"One time, I didn't say no. I said I would think about it.

"He took that as a yes.

"'Thank God you've come to your senses,' he said. 'I'm ready whenever you are. Don't make me wait.'"

54

Change of Heart

Cook County Municipal Court
Chicago, Illinois
April 27, 2016
2:05 pm

"I helped my father die," Lamar said, "and that's against the law. I understand that. We are a nation of laws."

He could hardly believe how light and free he felt, standing there before the judge, even though he was about to be sentenced for his crime. He was telling the truth, *his* truth. He knew how treacherous lying was, but he had never known it this viscerally before.

The courtroom had only one window, a long slit near the ceiling, where he could see the pink blossoms of a crabapple tree. The sun was shining, even in the canyons of downtown, and Chicago seemed a much friendlier place now that winter was over.

The judge's eyes were hard to read behind her thick lenses, but she was attentive, her head bent forward, her fingers pressing against her chin.

"Helping my father die was also *wrong*," he said, "but not in the way you might be thinking. What was *wrong* is that I did it *unilaterally*, without consulting my sister, without consulting Brigid, without consulting anyone. I didn't even talk to a therapist or a friend. Only my father and me. We were like Butch Cassidy and the Sundance Kid, pulling off a caper. No one else knew."

His father had made it seem as if it had been their decision together, but Lamar had been a reluctant collaborator. His father had pulled rank. And Lamar had let him. How much suffering was too much? Didn't his father have some obligation to hold on for his daughter's sake? To give her more time to get to know him?

The secret plan he and his father had hatched had been exciting *because* it was secret. *Because* it was wrong. Lamar the outlaw.

"This went against everything I believe," Lamar said, "the principles and values I aspire to live by. I would be the first to say that we need to be honest and open and brave and talk about things like death and dying, even when it's uncomfortable, *especially* when it's uncomfortable.

"I didn't do that. I tried, but not hard enough. Andrea didn't want to talk about it, so I acted alone."

When Lamar sat down, he half-turned and took a quick glance around the courtroom. He didn't see a single empty seat. He caught Sierra's eye and she gave him a slight nod. Diana, in the row behind Sierra, gave him a thumbs up. Todd, next to him, gave him a gentle clap on his shoulder.

The judge asked Andrea to stand. Lamar and Andrea had discussed what they were going to say, but with his sister, you could never be sure.

"Before we get to your statement," the judge said, "I want you to confirm what Mr. Rose has stipulated to as part of his guilty plea. That your father, Robert Rose, did ask Lamar Rose, on one or more occasions, to help him die. Do you agree to that?"

"Yes, I agree," said Andrea. "I heard my father ask my brother, *in my presence,* on at least one occasion. My brother changed the subject. I know there were other times."

"This is an unusual situation," the judge said. "In most cases, the sentence is agreed upon in advance when the defendant pleads guilty, but this is an unusual case. Ordinarily, I have sentencing guidelines, but for this case, the guidelines are not helpful. I am cognizant of the precedent we may be setting here today and the possibility it will be reviewed and/or challenged. I aim to get this right even if it means being repetitive.

"I am going to ask you a series of questions about your feelings regarding the sentence. In January, you were ready to throw the book at your brother. Now you are asking for leniency. Why the change of heart?"

Lamar held his breath.

Andrea had tied her hair back and wore a gray pinstriped business suit that made her look trim, though also severe. She looked vulnerable, heartfelt standing there, pressing with her fingers on the table in front of her. He didn't know if she was consciously showing her hurt and grief or she just couldn't hide it.

"What my brother did was wrong as well as illegal," she said, "but it *was* what our father wanted. He is correct in saying that what he did that was *most* wrong was acting on his own. Not that I would have agreed, but I never got a chance to talk him out of it. He and our dad had their secret plan and they left me out. He says that he refused many times, but Dad wore him down. I believe him."

Lamar started feeling calmer. Andrea was following

through. She sounded sincere.

"Despite my attacks on Lamar, he did not attack me. He did not question my character. Even when he trapped me on Metra on my way home from work.

"Still, he needs to pay for his crime and spend at least *some* time in prison. He should not be set free.

"But he is not a danger to society, and being in prison would mean he would be taken away from his daughter and my niece Sierra, his sister—me, his nephew Sullivan, his family friend Brigid, and other family and friends. And his therapy clients. A severe sentence would only add a new wrong to the existing wrong. I urge you to give him the shortest sentence you can, though you can pile on the community service, like cleaning litter along the highway. I know he would conscientiously do that."

Later, when the hearing was over, and the spectators were filing out of the courtroom, Lamar found Diana, who gave him an embrace, and then a kiss. Their first kiss in eight years.

"I'm so grateful you came," he said. "We're having a small gathering at Brigid's this evening at Edgewater, where my dad lived, where both my parents lived. For family and friends. Would you like to come? I can show you around the building. The scene of the crime."

"I'd love that," she said. "Pick me up at my hotel. And bring your toothbrush."

Epilogue

The Sweet Moline

Foster Beach
Chicago, Illinois
April 27, 2016
9:15 pm

After the gathering at Edgewater, Lamar took Diana for a walk along the beach and onto Foster Pier.

As they walked toward the lighthouse at the end, Diana asked why was there water on one side and sand on the other.

"Not sure," he said. "Because the sand washes away on one side and piles up on the other?"

"That's obvious, but why?"

"Do you want me to make up a reason or admit I don't know?"

"I can't promise I'll wait for you," she said. They were standing at the end of the pier, looking out over the dark water.

Lamar took her hand. "For a woman who once said, 'I want a mate, not a date,' you build a lot of walls. Or is it about me?"

"I thought we were talking about the lake," she said. "You're going to prison—now you want to go steady? Or do you just want to have sex again?"

"You say that like it's a bad thing."

"No, it's not," she said, leaning in to kiss him. "I'm looking forward to tonight."

The next morning, Lamar left for Midway from Diana's hotel, while she slept in, and for breakfast, minutes before he boarded his flight, he ate a steamed hot dog. His father had told him that you did not use ketchup on hot dogs in Chicago. Who knew?

"Here's to Dad," he said, lifting his hot dog, not caring who was listening.

■ ■ ■

A week after his sentencing, with the whole-hearted support of Todd, Lamar set off on a whirlwind tour of speaking gigs and interviews for Dying By Choice. That included another debate with Kira, at Northwestern University, in Evanston, not far from the brewing supply store where he had purchased the incriminating tank of nitrogen.

Everything was easier because he could tell the truth. Now that he didn't have to deny what he did, he was able to express his regrets as well.

One night, he was accused of using his notoriety to tout his cause. "You're right," he said, "but I've been given an opportunity to get people talking about something they might not want to talk about, and I'm not apologizing for that."

Though he was dreading prison, he found that talking about it gave him an unexpected feeling of exultation. Even liberation, crazy as that sounded.

The judge had sentenced Lamar to two years. Todd said

he could be out in fifteen months. The community service would have to be worked out later, as part of Lamar's probation.

While the accolades from the speeches and interviews were gratifying, the best part of Lamar's month and half window before his reporting date was Diana.

He wondered why she was all of a sudden so loving now that he was headed to prison, but he was enjoying her enough he decided it didn't matter.

■ ■ ■

On the second day of June, Lamar and Sierra flew to Chicago and then, in a white rental SUV with Andrea and Sully and Brigid in the back, drove across Illinois to the East Moline Minimum Security Correctional Facility on the banks of the Mississippi River.

Sierra had won her city council seat in the May election and was in an ebullient mood, which made for a spirited road trip.

Lamar did all the driving, and relished the miles upon miles of corn and soybean fields, the green shoots barely poking out of the black soil. He turned himself in an hour ahead of schedule.

The prison was nicknamed "The Sweet Moline" because of its picturesque location on a wooded hilltop above the river. And because it was the only prison in the state that allowed inmates to move freely throughout the grounds.

Lamar had done his research, but there was so little information to be found. North Korea was an open book compared to the Illinois prison system.

■ ■ ■

As soon as Lamar settled into his cell, he started writing letters. Prisoners were not allowed internet access, so he wrote longhand or stood in line to send email through a prison-run kiosk.

After he purchased a tablet from the prison, with the email app on it, he could write his messages without waiting in line, but only to approved contacts. Every email he sent or received cost him twenty-five cents or more. Diana was a regular correspondent, and they sometimes went back and forth three or four times in a morning.

The longest, most soul-searching letters came from Kira, who had moved away from the end-of-life debate, and was now venturing out in the world on her own in a new motorized chair. "It's red like a wagon," she wrote, "and I have one of those black bulb bicycle horns."

Mostly prison was boring. He missed his phone. Even after a few weeks, when he left his cell, he patted his pockets to check for his phone.

He had more visits than he expected, especially for a man who, a few months earlier, felt as if he had no friends. But there were also long stretches when no one came.

Andrea visited more often than anyone. It took her three hours to drive from Schaumburg. He looked forward to her visits because she asked him questions and acted as if she were really interested in his answers. On one visit, he did almost all the talking. That had never happened before with Andrea.

When she asked about his fellow inmates, he said he kept to himself, and she challenged him on that.

"What about what you learned from Dad," she asked, "what you said at the memorial? To be curious."

"Befriending a bully as a kid is one thing. These men are criminals."

"No one will be meaner to you than I was," she said.

It was strange to hear that kind of encouragement from Andrea. She was really trying, that much was certain, and that counted for, well, everything.

■ ■ ■

Four months after Lamar went to prison, a man in Santa Barbara helped his ninety-year-old mother die and then turned himself in to the sheriff. Asked if the Lamar Rose case had influenced his decision, the man said yes.

Then it happened again. Another man, another mother, and again he turned himself in.

Diana served as his de facto news anchor—sending him news stories every few days. She had to paste them into the email because all links were blocked.

After Andrea encouraged him to reach out, Lamar made a few friends, but also ran into more trouble. One man knocked him over in the yard, and tripped him in the tool shed. When Lamar tried to engage, the man sneered and turned away.

No one in prison said a word about death. Most inmates were young, but there were hundreds of men Lamar's age or older, many serving life without parole, and they must have known they would die in prison.

Lamar was wary to broach the subject, but with the permission of the warden, he hosted a Death Cafe. Just coffee and conversation, but the topic de jour was death.

Nine inmates showed, and the conversation was awkward at first, but once one man opened up, others followed suit. Lamar had been to half a dozen Death Cafes on the outside, but none were as profound or moving as this one in The Sweet Moline.

One man stayed afterward, helped Lamar fold the chairs. He told Lamar that he didn't want to live anymore.

Lamar interrupted him. "No."

He was never going to help anyone die again.

■ ■ ■

One visit, as Andrea stood to leave, she stopped and licked her lips. "I've been meaning to tell you," she said. "You know I told you that when Dad asked me to help him, I wouldn't listen. That's not *exactly* true. I considered doing what he asked. I even did some research. Like you."

Lamar was flabbergasted, and his anger bubbled up. He wanted to lash out at Andrea, for keeping this from him, for attacking him, for sending him to prison. But he bit his tongue. He would be out in four months. He didn't want to say anything he would regret.

"Dad was relentless," he said. "I don't know how you said no to him."

"I never said no," she said. "I pretended not to hear."

"So why," he asked, "why wouldn't you talk with me? I tried to start that conversation."

"Dad made me feel special," she said. "I mean, I had the health care power of attorney, and he said it like 'you can make it all better between us.' It was the only time he acknowledged that maybe we could have had a better relationship than we did."

So much for being the chosen one.

■ ■ ■

Lamar's second summer at Sweet Moline was hot and wet, and one of his few pleasures was standing by the fence in the yard, looking out at the Mississippi, and watching massive rain-swollen thunderstorms sweep across the plains. Then came a month of sweltering days, the merciless sun baking the land.

One afternoon, he stayed out in the yard during a torrential downpour, his fingers gripping the slats of the fence.

Within minutes, he was as soaked as he was ever going to get. Like swimming with his clothes on.

He relaxed into the rain for a few moments—more than a few—and there was nowhere else in the universe he wanted to be.

The rain was bracing, but it released the heat absorbed in the soil and the blacktop. Clouds of steam rose to his waist.

He had left his wife and killed his father and paid a heavy price. His accounts were settled and now he was free, or he would be in a month. He didn't know what was going to happen next and he couldn't wait to find out.

He was even looking forward to picking up litter along the highway.

THE END

About the Author

John Byrne Barry is a writer, designer, actor, bike tour leader, and crossing guard. He is author of *Bones in the Wash: Politics is Tough. Family is Tougher*—a political thriller set during the 2008 presidential campaign in New Mexico, and *Wasted*, a "green noir" mystery set in the Berkeley recycling world.

He lives in Mill Valley, California, with his wife and family.

See more at *johnbyrnebarry.com*.

Acknowledgments

It took a village to write this book—I could not have completed it without help from many people.

I was fortunate to get insightful feedback from beta readers, including Roberta Maloy, Chris Hurwitz, John Cammidge, Becky Parker Geist, Sean Barry, Michael Barry, Stan Kaufman, Judy Reyes, Leslie March, Carol Butler, Gayle Lacks, Mary Frandina, Sofia Qureshi, Linda Hartman, Bernadette Zavala, Paul Davis, Pat Barry, Lawson Legate, Ed Weisbart, Billy Prendergast, Clare Willis, Roy Schachter, Rita George, Joel Blackwell, Kate Moore, Susan Keller, and Nanette Zavala.

I asked for honest feedback, and I got it, which was sometimes disheartening and overwhelming. But the book is immeasurably better because of it.

I could not have written the book without the support and feedback from two wonderful writing groups.

At the Mill Valley Library Writers Drop-in, we wrote for an hour and then for the second hour, we took turns reading out loud and sharing feedback. What a lovely community we created over the years. Thank you to Kate Moore, John Geoghegan, Gary Nelson, Barbara Elwell, Asma Eschen,

Jen Hart, Bill Mena, Miguel Balboa, Jane Pusch, Nora Frey, and Rachel Zemach.

I'm also grateful for Riviera Writers, where we submitted our chapters in advance and met in person to share feedback. Thank you to Susan Keller, Tommie Whitener, and Joel Blackwell.

I want to add a special shoutout to two writing group colleagues, who read the book more than once, and gave extremely valuable feedback—Kate Moore and Susan Keller.

To learn more about dying and end-of-life issues, I talked with many people who had more personal or professional experience than I did, including Dr. Dawn Gross, a UCSF palliative medicine physician; Phil Rountree, minister turned hospice counselor; Kate DeBartolo, director of the Conversation Project; Pat Berube, host of the Death Cafe in Fairfax; and many more. I am grateful for their generous contributions to my understanding.

One of the unexpected rewards of writing this book was talking with so many people in the end-of-life movement, who, perhaps not surprisingly, seemed to be happy, vibrant, and grateful people. In one way or another, they all affirmed that awareness and acceptance of our impending death can help us live a more fulfilling life.

I also thank my colleagues at Bay Area Independent Publishers Association (BAIPA) and the California Writers Club Marin for support, encouragement, and sharing their skills and wisdom.

The most special appreciation of all goes to my wife Nanette Zavala, my fiercest critic and staunchest advocate, without whom this book would not have been possible.

Resources

While this book is fiction, I learned a lot about the real end-of-life community along the way, and would like to share some valuable resources for readers who may want to learn more:

- The Conversation Project—dedicated to helping people talk about their wishes for end-of-life care.
  theconversationproject.org
- Death Cafe—where people drink tea, eat cake, and discuss death.
  deathcafe.com
- Reimagine End of Life—a community-wide exploration of death and celebration of life through creativity and conversation.
  letsreimagine.org
- Slow Medicine Facebook Group—explores shared, nonrushed medical decision-making, palliative care, and treatment focused on preserving function and maximizing comfort, especially for elders.
  facebook.com/groups/108731512508516/
- Katy Butler, *The Art of Dying Well: A Practical Guide to a Good End of Life*

- Atul Gawande, *Being Mortal: Medicine and What Matters in the End*
- Anna Quinlen, *One True Thing: A Novel*
- Larissa MacFarquhar, "The Comforting Fictions of Dementia Care," *The New Yorker,* October 1, 2018. *newyorker.com/magazine/2018/10/08/ the-comforting-fictions-of-dementia-care*

You can also find interviews and more on my website— *johnbyrnebarry.com/end-of-life.*

Dear Reader,

If you enjoyed *When I Killed My Father*, I would appreciate it so much if you recommend it to a friend and/or write a review. There are hundreds of thousands of books published every year and it's a huge challenge to get the word out.

You might enjoy my other novels. My first, *Bones in the Wash: Politics is Tough. Family is Tougher,* is set during the 2008 presidential campaign in New Mexico and overlaps with *When I Killed My Father.* (Sierra is one of the protagonists, and Lamar and Janis are secondary characters.) My second novel, *Wasted,* is a "green noir" mystery set in the Berkeley recycling world.

You can find out more at *johnbyrnebarry.com.*

I would also love to hear from you. You can reach me at *johnbyrnebarry@gmail.com.*

WASTED

Murder in the Recycle Berkeley Yard

In *Wasted*, a "green noir' mystery, investigative reporter Brian Hunter covers the "recycling wars" in Berkeley, finds the body of his friend Doug crushed in an aluminum bale, and hunts down the murderer, all while trying to win the heart of Barb, Doug's former lover, now a suspect in his murder.

But *Wasted* is not just another trashy mystery. Set in the gritty and malodorous world of garbage and recycling, the novel is rich with resonant themes of reinvention, transition, and discarding that which no longer serves us.

> 66
>
> A captivating mystery combining romance, recycling and politics. What more can you ask for!
>
> 99

johnbyrnebarry.com

www.ingramcontent.com/pod-product-compliance
Lightning Source LLC
Chambersburg PA
CBHW072204130726
47910CB00011B/1827